'I've found you a declared triumphantl
be a complete fool!
come to offer you a
ever have hoped to
problems into the b
ever get again, so tak

Kate drew breath t... ...her onslaught on her father, but was neatly forestalled by Master Hartwell, who suddenly stood up and spoke with such firmness and confidence that Kate, at least, was sufficiently impressed to pay him close attention, thinking half-consciously that he seemed merely quiet and pleasant, yet there was certainly more to him than at first appeared . . .

'By your leave, Master Cressy, Mistress Kate,' he said, 'or without it, if you insist, but this has gone far enough! I do not make my offer with any intention of buying a wife, or merely finding an honourable means of providing for a man who has suffered as a result of the dissolution of a monastery. Neither purchase nor charity enter into the matter. I make my offer to Mistress Kate because it's my wish to share my life here with her. All else is incidental and peripheral.'

'You know where my heart lies,' Kate said, looking at him earnestly and searchingly.

'Yes, and if I thought for one moment that there was hope in that direction, I'd not have spoken. I do not ask for your heart—not yet, at least . . .'

Dinah Dean was born in Northamptonshire, but she has lived for most of her life in the Home Counties. She was a teacher until 1979, when she decided to give more time to her writing, and since then has fitted it in 'around local history studies, reading and conversation, well-seasoned with trips abroad, preferably to Scandinavia and Russia.' She lives in Waltham Abbey in Essex which, in some respects, bears a strong resemblance to the fictional Woodham, which also featured in her earlier novels, *The Country Gentleman* and *The Country Cousins*. Her sequence of six novels set in Russia at the time of Napoleon are *Flight From the Eagle*, *The Eagle's Fate*, *The Wheel of Fortune*, *The Ice King*, *Tatya's Story* and *The River of Time*. She has also written two Masquerade Historical Romances under the pen-name Marjorie May.

THE
BRIAR ROSE
DINAH DEAN

MILLS & BOON LIMITED
15-16 BROOK'S MEWS
LONDON W1A 1DR

First published in Great Britain 1986
by Mills & Boon Limited

© Dinah Dean 1986

Australian copyright 1986
Philippine copyright 1987
This edition 1987

ISBN 0 263 75638 6

Set in Linotron Times 10 on 11 pt.
04-0187-66849

Typeset in Great Britain by
Associated Publishing Services
Made and printed in Great Britain by
Cox & Wyman Limited Reading

For Madge,
Joy and Sheena.

AUTHOR'S NOTE

This story is set in the fictional town of Woodham, but the history of the real town of Waltham Abbey has provided many of the events and characters mentioned in it. We know very little about most of the characters, apart from their names, but a few have made their mark in history ... Robert Fuller was the last Abbot of Waltham, which was the last monastic foundation to be dissolved (in 1540): Sir Richard Rich 'flourished like the green bay tree', but seems to have reformed somewhat in old age: Edmund Freke, the youngest canon, made good use of his Cambridge education, and became successively Bishop of Rochester, Norwich and Worcester: Sir William Cressy's house really was the venue of the meeting between Cranmer, Foxe and Gardiner which led to the English Reformation: Christopher Cressy was a pensioner of the dissolved Abbey, but Kate and John, Amyas Calton and Matthew Hartwell and their stories are figments of the author's imagination.

CHAPTER ONE

KATE CRESSY walked sedately down the steep path from the Grange house to the road, crossed the rough, rutted surface, and continued down a narrow track through the copse beyond. As soon as the trees hid her from the house, she gathered up her heavy skirts and ran until she was out of breath, then still hurried, alternately walking and running, across the fields to the cornmill stream, and along its bank towards the town.

In her anxiety not to be late, she had hurried through all her chores that morning, in constant fear that her father would find some reason to keep her at home in the afternoon, but he had been shut away all morning in the little room which he called his cabinet, apparently going through the rent-rolls and inventories of the Abbey lands, and seemed so preoccupied that he had merely grunted when she ventured to enter the room and ask if she might go into town.

She was little more than halfway to Woodham, with a quarter-mile at least still to go before she reached the town, when the bells began to ring out merrily from the more westerly of the two towers of the Abbey church, and she slackened her pace, thinking she was already too late, but then they stopped again. Realising that it had only been a preliminary warming-up for the ringers, and she might yet be in time, she began to run again until she reached the old stone bridge by the hay-barn, where she slowed to a more seemly walk, in case anyone should see her as she crossed the stream and made her way to her uncle's house by the cattle-market.

Sir William Cressy's house was as busy as a hive about to swarm, for it lay next to the building known as the King's House, and was expected to accommodate some of the overflow of slightly less important persons when King Henry took up residence for a few days of quiet religious discussion with the Abbot, or to indulge his passion for hunting in the near-by Forest.

Already the royal servants had swept and aired the King's House, strewn fresh rushes, hung the tapestries, replaced the window shutters with framed glass, made the beds, and set a simple supper of a mere twenty dishes to cook in the kitchen. Some of them were now standing about in the cobbled market-place, exchanging gossip with the townsfolk and waiting for the distant trumpet to signal that the King was crossing the causeway across the several streams and marshes of the river.

Kate slipped through the crowd unnoticed, and entered her uncle's house, which was of no great size, but gave an impression of comfortable living, with fine oak panelling and furniture, gleaming from frequent applications of beeswax, which mingled its sweet scent with that of fresh rushes and a few autumn roses in a bowl on one broad window-sill.

'Mistress Cecy is still above-stairs,' one of the maids said as she hurried past Kate with a pile of pewter dishes, so Kate went up Sir William's fine new staircase, with its carved balusters and a dog-gate at the bottom, and found her cousin Cecily still prinking before her real Venetian glass mirror in her little room at the back of the house.

'Oh, there you are, Kate!' Cecily exclaimed. 'I feared that Uncle Christopher wouldn't let you come at the last!'

'He hardly seemed interested,' Kate replied, kissing the soft cheek which Cecy offered her. 'I fear he's had some news of the surrender of the Abbey, for he's above his ears in parchments and rent-rolls! You're looking very pretty today, Coz!'

Cecy was indeed a sight to admire. She was very fair in hair and complexion, with large grey eyes, which today looked blue with the reflection from her gown of deep blue damask, worked in a pattern of leaves in silver thread. The wide square-cut neck was outlined with a broad band of silver braid sewn with sparkling coloured stones, and was low enough to show the swell of her breasts. A wide silver necklace encircled her slender neck, and the frame of her gabled head-dress was edged with the same silver braid as her gown, with more stones to decorate it. The lappets were turned up and pinned across the back, and her long golden hair fell from beneath them to her waist, proclaiming her maiden status in an old-fashioned but most becoming manner.

'. . . and very fine!' Kate added, eyeing the silver necklace and the glittering gems.

'Oh, they're not real!' Cecy admitted with a giggle. 'Father brought the stones home from London. They're all glass, but I think no one would know—except Sir Richard Rich, of course, for they say he knows the price of everything to a groat!'

Kate's smile faded, and she gave a little involuntary shiver, for she had an instinctive dislike for the Chancellor of the Court of Augmentations, whose

arrogant good looks covered, she believed, as mean
and scheming a mind as any in King Henry's court.

'You're looking pretty yourself!' Cecy said kindly,
sounding quite as if she meant it, but Kate knew
very well that it was only kindness. Her own gown
was a plain dark brown cloth, remade from one
that had belonged to her long-dead mother, and its
split skirt revealed a deep yellow velvet petticoat
which Cecy had discarded two years before. She
had no jewels, false or real, and her cap was of plain
linen, starched and spotless, but unornamented, as
was her hood, made from a left-over piece of her
gown, pinned to the cap and filled with her coiled-
up hair. With her unfashionable brown eyes and
hair and creamy skin, the reflection in Cecy's mirror
showed her a brown mouse, a country creature who
might have been an upper servant.

'I think a french hood might suit you better,'
Cecy said, pushing her down into the chair before
the mirror. 'They went out of style after Queen—
after the Bullen woman—was er . . ., but they've
come in again now, and I've one which would go
very well with your gown.' She whisked off Kate's
cap and hood and set to work with comb and pins,
tweaking a few of Kate's natural waves to lie a little
forward on her brow before replacing the cap and
fastening the pretty pearl-edged curved semicircle
well back on her head, so that the veil at the back
would hang straight down over her loose hair.

'It will fall off!' Kate protested.

'Nonsense! How can it? See, the ribbon ties under
your chin, and I pin it here and here, so! There, it's
perfectly secure! You may keep it, for I've two or
three more.' She brushed away Kate's thanks and
went on, 'Now, a silver chain for your neck, and a
brooch for your bodice, and there you are! Oh, and

there's the trumpet! Do you hear it? The King is across the river, and we must run!'

Far from doing anything so undignified, Cecy glided smoothly to the door. Kate gave a quick, startled look at her own reflection, which showed a much more handsome—even pretty—face framed by the unfamiliar head-dress, and hurried after her cousin, suddenly a-tingle with excitement and anticipation. Would he come? It was so long since she had seen him—more than six months. Would he remember her?

'They say that the King is to marry again,' Cecy remarked as they descended the stairs together. 'I thought he never would after he was so heartbroken over poor Queen Jane, but they say he's to wed a German lady—a Duchess of Cloves, or some such place—and it will be about Christmas—not much above two months! My father says he'll take us to London to see her come in.'

Kate was suitably impressed. London was less than twenty miles away, but she had been there only once, years ago, and Cecy had visited the city but twice, for all her knowledge of the latest Court gossip. Sir William, being a cousin to the Archbishop of Canterbury, was often in the City, and sometimes dined in the Great Hall at Whitehall, the King's new palace at Westminster.

He emerged from the back part of the house as they reached the bottom of the stairs, and gave his niece a distracted greeting, his mind obviously occupied with the impending arrival of the King and an unknown number of courtiers, servants and hangers-on. He was dressed in the latest style of embroidered, slashed and braided waistcoat, with a velvet doublet heavily collared and edged with

miniver. Not for Sir William a fur inferior to that
which his knighthood entitled him to wear!

He ushered the two young ladies before him, out
of the door and into the crowded square, where
there was now an air of hushed expectancy as the
townsfolk gathered behind the royal servants and
lined the way by which the King would come to his
house.

The bells began to ring again, this time in earnest,
and the grinding of wheels and the clop of hooves
became audible in the distance. Those people who
were near enough to the entrance to the cattle-
market to see down West Street to the causeway
began to stir with excitement and point, obviously
able to see the approaching cavalcade, and, at the
opposite corner of the square, the chanting of the
choir heralded the approach of the Abbot and those
of the canons who were at home and not out
working in their parishes.

Kate looked about her at the gay throng, for
even the poorest people seemed to have made an
effort to dress in their best, however old and
shabby, and there was an air of cheerfulness and
expectancy about them, for the coming of even a
small Court meant money in their pockets. She
wondered if this would be the last time that the
King would come to Woodham, for it was nearly
five months since Parliament had legalised the
surrender of the great monasteries, and everyone
knew that Woodham Abbey, along with all the
others, would soon cease to exist.

She wondered what would happen when the
kindly Abbot and the good Fathers were gone.
Would it all be pulled down? Would the townsfolk
at least be allowed to keep the nave of the church?
Presumably the land would be sold, or leased to

someone . . . not given, if Sir Richard Rich and
Master Secretary Thomas Crumwell had any say in
the matter!

So many changes! Why, even the square in which
she stood with this happy crowd had been affected
by them! It used, for some unknown reason, to be
called Romeland, but now, since the King's break
with Rome, people were afraid to use the name,
and called it the cattle-market, or market square,
which was confusing, for there was another market
square in the centre of the town, where goods other
than cattle were bought and sold.

It was apparent to Kate's observant nature that
even the attitude of the people had changed. The
old free-and-easy gossip had ceased to flow, and
there were no longer ribald comments about the
great men of the land. People were watchful,
distrustful of one another, and very careful about
what they said, for it was easy for a careless remark
to be counted treasonable these days. There was a
brooding uneasiness in the town, as the poorer
people wondered what would happen to them when
the Abbey was no more. They seemed cheerful
enough today, but their cheerfulness and the cheers
which were beginning on the far side of the square
seemed somehow more dutiful than spontaneous . . .
These gloomy thoughts and apprehensions suddenly
vanished from her mind as the first riders appeared
and clattered across the cobbles between the lines
of waiting people, and she stood on tiptoe, craning
to see if he was among them.

It was not a great procession—not above forty
gentlemen all told, and no ladies at all, for the King
had neither wife nor mistress at present. Kate's
anxious eyes recognised many of the faces. There
was the sour, piggy countenance of Master Crumwell,

little deep-set eyes darting about under the scholar's cap which he affected with his dark, plain clothing, no doubt suitable, in his estimation, for his post as Vicar-General. Sir Richard Rich rode at his elbow, nodding a smug acknowledgment of the cheers as if they were meant for him, although Kate knew that many here had known and loved Sir Thomas More, and would have booed the man who betrayed him to his death, if they had dared.

A dozen little girls were waiting near by with baskets of flowers to strew before the King, but one of them, overcome by excitement, dropped her basket. It rolled, spilling flowers, amid the hooves of the passing horses, but the child, heedless of danger, ran after it. Kate gave a cry of horror, expecting to see her trampled down, but one rider swung his horse across the path of those behind him, bent low to scoop the little girl up in the crook of his arm, then side-stepped across to deposit her, round-eyed and open-mouthed, in Kate's arms.

It was amazingly neatly done, saving the child, yet causing no more than a minor check in the advance of the cavalcade. Kate looked up approvingly at the rider as she took the child from him, and saw a well-set-up man, lean-faced and shrewd-looking, with a straight nose and firm mouth, and a pair of very dark brown eyes which looked candidly and curiously into hers without any of the veiled watchfulness of all the other men she had seen about the King. Even his dress, she observed as he rode on, was different. The fabrics were as rich in quality as any, but dark and plain. A thrush among the peacocks, she thought, remembering those bright, inquisitive eyes. 'And Master Crumwell and Sir Richard are crows,' she thought. 'Carrion crows!'

A sudden increase in the volume of cheering drew her attention back to the oncoming riders, and she turned to see the King enter the square. The child in her arms struggled to be put down, and ran with the others, grabbing handfuls of flowers from their baskets, and almost precipitating a rousing quarrel at the feet of the King's massive horse by trying to snatch her best friend's basket.

Somehow, the flowers were strewn, the King pausing with a benignity which had been rarely apparent in him for some years now, a look of something akin to amusement on his heavily-jowled face, and the slightest twitch of a smile on the petulant lips. He tossed a few small coins amid the flowers and rode on, leaving the children too awed to pick up the largesse, for they had never seen so huge a horse and rider in their lives—at least, not since the King's last visit, but that was six months ago, and they had probably forgotten.

Then, at last, Kate saw the face and form for which she had been so anxiously searching. He was there, among the dozen riders following the King. Sir Amyas Calton, tall, broad, and handsome, golden hair curling crisply about his jewelled cap, a fair beard framing a ruddy-cheeked, devil-may-care face, and his long limbs and broad shoulders most dazzlingly garbed in violet velvet and pink satin, slashed, embroidered with gold and pearls, massively furred at the collar with sable, shapely legs set off by purple nether-stocks, and rings flashing on every finger. He was laughing at some comment he had just made to his companions, but his quick eyes caught sight of Kate staring at him, expectant, fearful, the colour coming and going in her cheeks and her heart apparently lodged in her throat. He frowned for a moment, then smiled, a flash of even

white teeth between shapely red lips, and Kate
could breathe again. He had remembered her!

The Lord Robert, Abbot of Woodham, swept
forward in the quiet dignity of cope and mitre to
greet the King, using his inwardly-turned crozier as
a staff to support his gaunt frame. The perils and
shocks of the past few years had pressed heavily on
him and worn him down, yet his loyalty to the King
remained unquestioned, whatever it had cost him in
sleepless nights and agonised choices. The King
greeted him affably enough, condescended to say a
few kindly words to the nervous Prior as he
dismounted, clapped Kate's uncle heartily on the
shoulder in greeting, then disappeared into his own
house, most of his companions at his heels.

Amid the confusion of horses, dogs, servants and
gawping onlookers, the procession from the Abbey
turned itself about and retreated, the Abbot treading
stately in their midst, but with a droop about his
shoulders. Kate watched him go with pity and
sorrow, for he was a good and kindly man. Then
another man crossed her line of sight, and she
darted forward to touch his arm. It was Amyas. He
swung round, looking startled, then smiled down
into her face, and she forgot everything else in the
pleasure of seeing him again.

'So you've not forgotten me, sweet Kate!' he said
lightly. 'Have you missed me?'

'A little, from time to time,' she admitted,
conscious that her flushed cheeks and sparkling eyes
must be betraying a greater enthusiasm than her
words.

'I've been abroad—out of England. I went with
the embassy to Cleves, and have been to and fro
across Europe with messages. Not a moment to

myself all these months, or I'd have come to see you . . .'

Kate raised admiring eyes to his face, imagining him attracting all eyes at the Court of Cleves (wherever that might be!), but some small part of the deepest recess of her mind noted that his sapphire eyes had that same watchful, veiled look as all the rest of the King's Court—all but one member of it, that is . . .

'And is the King to marry the Duchess of Cleves?' she asked, pretending to be more interested in that than in him.

'Hush, sweetheart! It's all secret and undecided as yet!' He looked around him, and appeared to be genuinely alarmed that they might be overheard. 'Say you forgive me, Kate, and leave the King's business to the King?'

'I'll forgive you this time, but you're not to stay away again without writing!' Kate said firmly.

He laughed, and said, 'But I must go—there is the trumpet for supper! May I see you later—at sunset?'

'By the bridge,' she replied, turning away to hurry into her uncle's house, for the trumpet would be a signal for those who were to dine there as well, and she would be expected.

She found apparent chaos reigning inside the house. Personal servants of those lesser lights who were to lodge here were scrambling about in the vestibule and the screens passage, sorting out bundles of goods as the wagoners brought them in from the baggage-carts, and Sir William's servants were forced to edge their way through with loaded trays and salvers on their way from kitchen to hall. Kate dodged round a couple of valets arguing over a shirt which had escaped from a badly-tied bundle, and entered the hall in the wake of a stout serving-man with a massive dish of fish, neatly arranged in rows as if they had swum on to the dish in a shoal, ready-fried and decked with sprigs of tarragon and slices of lemon.

Many of the benches at the long tables in the body of the hall were already occupied, but the high table on the dais, and those immediately below it and above the salt were still unoccupied, so Kate hastened up the length of the hall and through the door at the back of the dais into the parlour, which was filled by a chattering throng of guests.

'Oh, thank goodness! I feared you'd gone home already!' Cecy exclaimed, emerging from the crowd and seizing her arm, as if to prevent her from disappearing. 'There are so few ladies, the King not having brought any, that you and I are to accompany Mother at the high table!'

'But I'm not dressed . . .!' Kate began.

'No one is! The King expects his supper immediately he arrives, and everyone else perforce must sit down as they are, dusty and travel-stained, and in no more finery than they choose to imperil on the road!' Cecy assured her. 'Come, now—Father is looking about to see that all are ready. Mother will go in with the Bishop, then me with Sir Richard, and you with . . .' But Kate could not hear what she said next, for she had darted forward to take her place in the line forming by the door into the hall, and Kate, following her, went in to supper with an elderly and very deaf gentleman dressed in a long gown which had gone out of fashion when the old King died, and, from the moth-eaten appearance of its fur tippet, probably dating from then as well.

As he was so deaf, Kate tried to converse with

him in as clear a voice as she could manage, speaking slowly, but not shouting, as she thought that might confuse him, but he barely bothered to reply, being obviously more interested in the food than her attempts at conversation, so she lapsed into silence, wondering if she would ever discover who he was, and looked about her with interest at the lively scene before her.

Sir William's hall was not large, and, as it had an upper floor above, it lacked height as well as length and breadth. Sixty-odd people at two long tables filled it rather too much for comfort, but the King's House next door was not much larger. Although the King's attendant gentlemen were comparatively few, this being a private visit, there were about twenty of them to be housed and fed by Sir William, together with their servants, the royal huntsmen, the senior grooms, the foresters and sundry other indispensables.

The clerics were lodged in the Abbot's house, and Kate wondered why the Bishop of Winchester had not chosen to join them. By leaning forward a little, she could just see past her aunt and catch a glimpse of his long-nosed, faintly melancholy profile, apparently absorbed in whatever Sir William was saying to him, but, like all the men of the King's entourage, looking watchfully about him as if he half-expected some sudden action against his interest or person. She wondered if perhaps the other clergy lodged at the Abbey were of the reforming party, to which Bishop Gardiner was opposed, as he was to Master Crumwell, who had ousted him as Secretary to the King. It was ironic to think that it was in this very house that he and Dr Foxe had first met Sir William's cousin, Thomas Cranmer, and introduced that obscure Cambridge scholar to the

King, which had led to all the changes that had confused and upset everyone since . . .

She breathed a thankful sigh that she did not have to go to Court and tread the tightrope of conforming to the ever-changing differences between right and wrong in religion, in opinions of other people, and in foreign affairs! It must be incredibly difficult, when yesterday's orthodoxy was today's heresy, apparently at the King's whim, and when a man high in the royal favour one day might be in the Tower, or executed, the next. No wonder they all looked so wary and apprehensive!

All but one, that is! At that moment she caught sight of the man who had plucked the child from under the horses' hooves. He was near the head of the table just before her, well above the salt, but she had not recognised him before because he had taken off his cap, and consequently looked a little different. His hair was dark, and curled a little about his ears and at the nape of his neck, but was vigorously brushed smooth otherwise. He was laughingly answering some sally from the man facing him across the table, but after that, he looked about him, half-smiling, alert, not with that secretive, wary manner apparent in everyone else, but with the lively curiosity and interest she had noticed before. She was amused to see that the front of his waistcoat was slashed in vertical rows to show the white shirt through the dark cloth, for all the world like a reverse of the speckled breast of the thrush to which she had likened him earlier.

As she smiled at the notion, he looked in her direction, clearly recognised her, and made her a slight bow, his dark eyes looking her straight in the face, as if to read her thoughts. She gave a little nervous nod in reply, and then looked away. At that moment, her neighbour managed to tip a platter of food off the table into his own lap, and the resulting confusion of servants and napkins quite put the dark-eyed man out of her mind.

The supper was lengthy and elaborate, as habitués of the Court would expect, and it was clear that Sir William had received some royal assistance in its provision, for there was a profusion of venison, game birds in variety, including very expensive quails, and, most significant of all, a roast swan arranged on a great charger with its wings and tail-feathers replaced and its carefully stuffed head and neck standing up grotesquely amid a garniture of green worts, the un-nicked bill proclaiming it the King's property. The interminable meat courses and their attendant subtleties of jelly, spun sugar and marchpane were eventually followed by dishes of russet apples and jargonelles from the Abbey's orchard, and little sour grapes from its vineyard on the slopes below the edge of the Forest, quinces which were not as ripe as they might have been, and a selection of conceits in the form of pastry and sugar castles, hedgepigs made of blancmanger with almond prickles, flummeries, and sugared flowers.

Kate, unused to such quantities of food, ate slowly and sparingly, and sipped but rarely at her goblet of wine, but the noise and fumes, and the rich sauces in which the meat was served, gave her a headache, and she wished it would all end soon so that she might slip away and compose herself ready for her meeting at sunset. She even began to fear that she might not get away in time, but common-sense told her that supper in the King's House would probably take even longer, and it was Amyas who was more likely to be late at the tryst.

Fortunately, the lack of space in the hall precluded

any sort of masque or other entertainment, and Sir
William had no musicians' gallery, for he had no
ear for music, and even complained that the Abbey's
music-master composed too many over-long and
intricate anthems for the singing-boys! Most of the
guests were anxious to see where they were to
sleep, and to arrive at the place in time to take the
best of what choice there might be, to shift their
travel-stained clothes and to chivvy their body-
servants about their baggage, so few lingered over
their walnuts and wine.

The dark-eyed man was one of the few who did
not hurry off, and presently Sir Richard Rich joined
him, descending from the dais with his usual self-
centred indifference to others, leaving poor Cecy
abandoned in the middle of what was meant to be
an interesting and amusing tale about a horse which
her father had once bought, which turned out to
have belonged to a travelling fair, and was given to
lying down and 'dying' when spurred to a gallop.
Kate noticed, but without much interest, that the
man listened to whatever Sir Richard was murmuring
to him with courtesy, but when he caught her own
eye over Rich's shoulder, he gave her a quick wink,
which she considered very presumptuous, so she did
not look at him again, and soon seized an
opportunity to make her excuses and slip away to
Cecy's room to wash her face and hands and tidy
herself.

She studied herself in Cecy's grand mirror, once
she was sure that the french hood was on straight
and its ribbon securely tied under her chin, for the
metal frame was quite heavy, and felt as if it was
slipping back on her head. It was already twilight in
the room, which had a small window, and there
were two lighted candles before the mirror. They

made her rather sad brown eyes look huge, and
imparted a flattering warmth to her complexion, but
she wished she had Cecy's blue eyes and golden
hair, and wondered, with a flutter of excitement, if
Amyas might possibly love her, despite her plainness.
After all, he had remembered her after almost six
months' absence, and it was now two years since
she had first met him. There had only been half a
dozen meetings in that time, so surely he must like
her more than a little to wish to resume their
relationship when they did manage to meet? If only
she could see him more often!

Beyond the closed door of Cecy's room, she
could hear the goings and comings of Sir William's
lodgers, seeking the beds which they had been
allocated—or, in most cases, a share of a bed!
Voices were upraised in argument, or in calls to
servants, and even the normally quiet tones of Dr
Gardiner suddenly rose in a carrying and decisive,
'Sir Richard may go to the Devil, sir, and the
sooner the better, in my opinion!'

Kate giggled, agreeing with the sentiment, but
wondering what could have stirred the cool, quiet
calmness of the Bishop to such an undiplomatic
speech. Presumably the Chancellor of the Court of
Augmentations had attempted to poach the episcopal
bed!

Fearful that Cecy might arrive at any moment
and delay her, she checked that the candles were
safe, and went out on to the narrow landing, for Sir
William had, for some unknown reason, decided to
have his upper rooms arranged round a narrow
space in the middle of the house, instead of opening
one from the next in the normal way. Kate thought
it a silly arrangement, as it robbed each room of
some much-needed space, and the dark landing was

too small for all these people to be able to move
about without much pushing and tripping over one
another. She supposed the privacy of a room which
was not a highway for the household must be
pleasant, but hardly necessary when every bed was
surrounded by thick curtains!

Dr Gardiner gave her a kindly if slightly absent-
minded blessing as she edged past him, which she
quickly acknowledged by bobbing a curtsy and
kissing his ring, and she managed to get halfway
down the stairs before she was momentarily trapped
against the balusters by two perspiring servants
with a leather-latticed bed-frame—presumably the
property of a guest who preferred his own bed!

Immediately in the wake of the bed-frame
followed a lithe figure which came face to face with
her as she tried to descend. It was the dark-eyed
man again.

'Is your little girl well?' he asked, smiling at her
in a friendly fashion. 'Not too frightened?'

'She is not my child!' Kate replied in a startled
voice.

The quick, lively gaze took in the long hair
flowing down her back, and the smile became
broader, as if she had just told him something
pleasant. 'My mistake—my apologies!' he said,
bowing with his hand on his heart. Considering that
they were now being jostled by four more sweating
serving-men with a large leather-bound close-stool,
it was quite a graceful movement.

'Let me see, now—you must be Sir William's
daughter?'

'His niece, sir,' Kate replied in an unencouraging
tone. 'If you will kindly let me pass . . .'

She had to admit that he tried to do so, moving
out from the baluster-rail to enable her to pass

between it and him, and it was hardly his fault that a large feather-bed was apparently making its own way up the stairs with a pair of arms clutched about its middle and two stout-calved legs invisible beneath it. It struck him forcibly in the back and propelled him sharply against her, so that she suddenly found herself held in a close embrace and tightly pressed between him and the carved rail, which caught her painfully in the ribs.

'Your pardon, Mistress Cressy!' he said, his lips so close to her ear that the perfectly normal exclamation somehow took on the intimacy of a murmured endearment. 'If I move a little upward, and you a little downward, perhaps we can contrive to pass one another . . .'

As the feather-bed was now wedged by their bodies, it seemed the only solution, but it involved an intimate movement of body against body, which Kate found strangely disturbing, and it was unfortunately prolonged when the brooch which Cecy had lent her caught in the slashing of his waistcoat, and they must stop, breast to breast, to untangle it. Kate could hardly wait to get free, and fled precipitately out of the house.

The sun was well behind the houses on the west side of the cattle-market, casting their long shadows across the cobbles and bathing the face of the inn on the east side with a lurid yellow light. Kate slowed to a sedate walk; she shook her skirts a little; ascertained that Cecy's brooch was securely pinned to her bodice, and made her way out of the market-place and along the cornmill stream towards the bridge by the hay-barn.

On the other side of the stream, the wall of the Abbey enclosure rose up from the water's edge, its stone glowing in the golden light, and its plain surface broken only by the gateway a couple of hundred yards above the mill. Here, a brick-parapeted bridge crossed the stream to the gateway with its two entrances, one a broad carriage-way and the other a small wicket. A man was leaning on the parapet, looking down into the water. For a moment she thought it was Amyas, waiting for her on the wrong bridge. The man looked up as she approached, then moved out to intercept her, and she saw, with a sense of foreboding, that it was Sir Richard Rich.

CHAPTER TWO

'GIVE YOU good evening, mistress,' he said in a silky tone that set Kate's teeth on edge. 'And where are we off to, all alone?'

'About my own affairs, sir,' Kate replied, more brusquely than was wise.

'And what might they be, I wonder?' Sir Richard enquired of the evening air. 'What can send a young lady hastening away from the town so soon after supper, with the King in residence, and like to stroll across to share a glass of wine with the Abbot? In what dark conspiracy might she be about to involve herself? What Romish spy to meet? What spells to weave to someone's ill by the light of the waning moon?'

Kate had sensed enough of the general air of suspicion about the King to take his meaning quickly enough, and to counter with, 'The King's movements are his own business, sir, as mine are my own, and the moon is waxing, not waning. By your leave, if you will stand aside from the path . . .'

Sir Richard remained where he was, blocking the path, and tapped a finger thoughtfully against his shapely lips. 'I know you, mistress. Cressy's daughter, or his niece—one or the other! Ah, yes—of course! An assignation with young Calton, I'll wager! Well, be wary of him, and enter no hay-barns at his urging, if you value your maidenhead! Or has he had it already?'

'You are impertinent, sir!' Kate exclaimed. 'Let me pass!'

'When you've paid toll,' he replied tauntingly. 'Come now—Calton will spare me one kiss, I'll be bound!'

'Possibly, but I will not!' Kate lowered her head and glowered at him under her lashes in a manner which might have warned a less conceited man that this was no compliant country girl.

Sir Richard, oblivious, made a grab at her, exclaiming, 'But I will it, and you shall conform!'

He had obviously calculated that Kate would start back, away from him, but instead, she took a step forward so that his grasping hands missed her shoulders. She put both hands on his chest and pushed with all her strength, then dodged past him, kicking his ankle for good measure, and darted away along the path. From behind her came a shout of alarm and a resounding splash, followed by a string of profanities most unsuited to the lips of the Chancellor of the Court of Augmentations, Speaker of the House of Commons, and Solicitor-General of England.

A couple of hundred yards further on, the course of the millstream bent eastwards, following the line of the enclosure wall, and Kate risked a look back. Sir Richard was still visible, but was retreating towards the town, wringing water from the skirts of his doublet as he went.

Kate hesitated, catching her lower lip between her teeth, and wondered if she had done something foolish. Rich was an ill man to cross, and she feared that he might be petty enough to take some spiteful revenge against her for making a fool of him. 'Well, it serves him right!' she told herself. 'He had no business behaving so to me, as if I were a town slut;

and he wasn't even sure if I'm me or Cecy! I'll wager my Uncle Cressy would be furious if he'd stopped Cecy like that, demanding a kiss. It's no way to behave to a gentlewoman!'

A little further on, the stream turned north again by a large clump of willows, and just beyond lay the bridge by which she had crossed it on her way to town. She was relieved to see a tall figure sitting on the parapet, swinging his legs and whistling softly. It was Amyas, his golden hair and beard shining in the last rays of the setting sun.

'Punctual to the minute!' he said, coming towards her with both hands held out to take hers and raise them in turn to his lips. 'May I kiss you now? You've no idea how I've ached for your kisses all these long months!'

Kate lifted her face, her lips parted in a smile of assent, and he gathered her into a close embrace, his mouth seeking hers hungrily in a long, lingering kiss which left her breathless, yet somehow unsatisfied. How could she doubt that he loved her when he could kiss her so, despite so long a time away from her, yet why did she feel this disappointment?

'If only we could always be together!' she sighed. 'I see you so seldom, and never for more than a little while.'

'I know, sweetheart, I know. It's hard for me, too, for all that I'm always busy about the King's business. Perhaps one day I'll be able to spend all my time with you, but it's not possible yet.'

'If . . .' Kate began, then stopped. She had meant to say, 'If we were married', but something prevented her, some inner pride which told her that it was unseemly for the woman to mention marriage first.

'If?' he echoed questioningly. 'Yes, love, if! If I were rich, and the eldest son, I could do as I please.

But I've to make my own way in the world, and for that I depend on the King's favour and my father's approval, and, believe me, both are hard to win, and need constant fostering to keep! I daren't be away from Court a day, save on the King's business, or someone will slip into my place and I'd be back at the beginning again. One day, sweetheart, there'll be time to dally with you by the river, but not yet!'

Kate stifled a sigh, and clung to him as he kissed her again. She longed to be his wife, to go with him on his journeys, help him in his struggle for position, if that was what he wanted. Riches she did not care about, as long as they had a sufficiency. She would wait, but her life at home was not of the sort to make the waiting any easier.

Amyas's kisses became more urgent and demanding, his hands more adventurous about her body, and she drew back a little, capturing them in her own and removing them from her breasts. 'Hush, now!' she whispered. 'We must talk. I shall have to go home in a few minutes, or Father will be angry! What will you do tomorrow?'

'The King means to go hawking along the water-meadows all day, I think. He'll attend Mass before we start out, of course, but he's bespoken hampers for dinner, so I expect we'll eat out in the fields. Can you come? Will your father let you join us?'

'I don't know,' Kate replied doubtfully. 'Will any other ladies be of the party? He'll not let me go otherwise.'

'Your aunt and cousin will be there, I believe, and some of the Colte ladies, I think. The King invited them, at least.'

'I'll ask, then, but Father may not give me leave . . .' She hesitated, then added anxiously, 'If I don't come, you'll know, won't you, that it's not because I don't want to?'

'I understand. If you don't come, I'll try to slip away as we return to Woodham and meet you . . . Kate, the hay-barn's near by. You won't . . .?'

'No, Amyas.' Kate shook her head all the more firmly because of the doubt cast on her virtue by Sir Richard Rich. 'I've little enough to offer a husband, and certainly not enough to compensate for the lack of a maidenhead!' She hoped he would tell her that she had no need to worry, for she was to marry him, but once again he failed to take the opportunity to mention the all-important word, and once again an ugly little doubt crept into her mind, to be dismissed angrily as a flaw in her love for him.

'Then let me walk you home—at least as far as the copse . . .'

To that Kate gladly assented, and they strolled together in the gathering dusk along the path by the stream, where sleepy ducks honked contentedly over a late supper of weed, and birds chattered their way to roost in the alders and willows on the banks. It was a magical hour, a time for talking lovers' nonsense, for laughing softly over shared jokes, for stopping to kiss and caress before they moved on. A hare ran across their path and stopped a few yards away, black in the moonlight, to sit up and stare at them, and Kate called to it warningly, 'Be off, Jack Hare, for the King hunts tomorrow with his cruel hawks!'

'Now you've spoiled the royal sport, and that's *lèse-majesté*!' Amyas said jestingly, then, suddenly serious, changed the subject abruptly, and asked, 'What will you do when the Abbey surrenders?'

Kate felt a cold touch of fear in her heart. 'When?' she said sharply. 'You said "when", not "if"?'

'You know the Act was passed last April. All the monasteries will be suppressed before long.'

'Yes, but the King has spoken of making Woodham a cathedral. He wrote out the plan in his own hand— my Uncle Cressy has seen it! Is it not to be so?'

'The Archbishop says not, for Woodham's too near to London. He favours Peterborough. The King named some twenty new cathedrals, but the Archbishop says there'll be but eight or nine in the end, for it costs more money to set up a new see than the King realised. St Bartholomew's is to surrender next month, and St Alban's by the end of the year, whether the Abbot agrees or not. The warrant is already signed for Woodham . . . I'm sorry, Kate, but it's best that you know, and I felt I should tell you.'

'How do you know?' Kate asked curiously.

'I—er—overheard Master Crumwell talking to Sir Richard about it.'

'Well, I suppose we've all known in our hearts that it must come in the end.' Kate clasped her hands together, and felt the coldness in her heart run out through her veins to every part of her body, and she shivered. 'When will it be?'

'In a few months—half a year, at most. The Augmentations men are few in number, and kept very busy. As I'm not in Sir Richard's confidence, I can't give you an exact date.'

'Sir Richard . . .' Kate thought bleakly that her thoughtless pushing of that gentleman into the millstream might prove even more foolish than she had earlier feared. 'Oh, but surely someone will buy the demesne land, and they'll still need a bailey. Won't they?' Her voice faltered, and she turned to Amyas for reassurance.

'There's some talk of Lord Dallance renting the Abbey for the building stone, to build himself a house on the site. I expect that's to ensure that the King may not have difficulty in pursuing his hunting in this part of the Forest, with the Abbey gone. His house here is far too small for any but the smallest party, and he'd rather the rest were entertained as guests at someone else's expense! Presumably Dallance will have the land as well. The Abbot won't resist, will he?'

'I think not,' Kate said sadly. 'After what happened at Reading and Glaston and some of the other houses which resisted . . . My lord Abbot is a realist—he'll see no sense in hanging at his own gate in a fruitless cause!'

'Then you've no cause to worry! All the Abbey's chief servants will get pensions and rewards. What's more, the money will be paid every year for the rest of their lives, not just until they are too old to work, as their stipends would have been.'

Kate took considerable comfort at that news, for she had no doubt that it was true if Amyas said so. He had several times confided little scraps of news to her before, and they had always proved true. So, at the worst, her father and she need not fear penury and starvation, and with that dreadful shadow dispelled, time enough to mourn the Abbey when the time of its demise arrived. Meanwhile, here was one of those all too rare occasions when she might have Amyas beside her, alone and unobserved, and the moments were too precious to waste any more of them.

Yet, all too soon, they came to an end. They stood in a close embrace, kissing and whispering, in the little copse near the Grange house, observed, had they but known it, by the Abbey's coney-master, Harry Warrener, who confided to his ferrets that it was pretty to see them together, all dappled by the moonlight through the branches, as fair a sight to see as buck and doe playing together in the meadow. The ferrets privately thought the latter a far prettier sight, but, naturally, did not say so!

'Until tomorrow!' Amyas said at last. 'I hope it may be all day; but if not, I'll be here in the copse at sunset, and I'll wait until you come.'

'But what if I cannot?'

'I'll wait an hour, at least.'

'Oh, bless you! How good and kind you are!' Kate exclaimed, giving him another kiss for reward, then she reluctantly left him, looking back again and again as she crossed the road, blew him one last kiss, then made her way up the steep slope to the Grange house.

Her thoughts were troubled again as she picked her way up the rough path which served as both farm-track and drive to the house. Her father's temper, never particularly good, had grown shorter and more uncertain these past two or three years. She knew that he misliked the changes in the Church, although, since the recent Pilgrimage of Grace and the wholesale accusations of treason and hangings that had followed it, he had learned to keep his thoughts on the subject to himself, expressing them only by aiming an occasional vicious kick at the wooden chest which contained, among other things, a copy of the detailed list of the Abbey's property made four years before, when the King's commissioners had valued all the religious houses in the land.

How would he react to the news that Woodham was to go the way of all those other monastic houses? Several times he had said confidently that the King's great affection for Woodham would save it, and certainly King Henry visited this abbey more often than any other. Only last week, he had said that a cathedral was not very different from a house of canons . . .

His jealousy of his brother seemed to have increased, too, as his temper worsened. Sir William was the younger by quite a few years, but he had gone out into the world and prospered, attending the Inner Temple to become a man of law, obtaining a post at Court, a seat in Parliament and a comfortable fortune in trade through his Parliamentary contacts. His knighthood had added the final lustre, while Christopher, Kate's father, had followed his father and grandfather in the office of bailey to the Abbey and had nothing but his stipend and a very old house to show for it, for whatever money came his way—and there was some, in the way of gifts and 'sweeteners'—was spent as soon as acquired, and not wisely, at that!

Kate reached the door of that same old house as she thought of it, and paused to touch the oak doorpost with a smile of affection, for she loved the building very dearly.

The main part of it was a stone-walled hall, built when the old Saxon college became an Augustinian abbey in the reign of the second Henry. Since then, various timber-framed accretions had grown on to it, and there were kitchens and sculleries, her father's cabinet, a housekeeper's room and a still-room in one wing, and two floors of living, sleeping and storage rooms in the other. It was old-fashioned, inconvenient, difficult to keep warm or clean, but it had been home for four generations of Cressys, and Kate knew that her only regret, if—when—ever she married Amyas, would be the leaving of it.

Her father was in the parlour, eating a belated supper on a tray in a very smoky atmosphere, and he greeted her with, 'This damned new-fangled chimney will be the death of me! Why Lord Robert should think he was doing me a favour by having it built, I'll never fathom! A week of mess and strangers about the place while it was built, and nothing but smoke ever since. How can a tube of bricks take off the smoke when the house is built against a hillside? Where the Devil have you been all this time?'

'It's green wood causing the smoke,' Kate pointed out after inspecting the fire. 'You must tell Martin to bring good dry logs, not the new-cut ones.'

'The lad's a simpleton!' her father growled.

This was no more than the literal truth, so Kate replied, 'He can't help it, and he manages well enough if he's told exactly what to do.'

'Argue, argue! That's all you ever do, just like your mother, God rest her! Always a back answer! I asked you where you've been.'

'To Uncle Cressy's. Cousin Cecy asked me to go, to see the King come in, and I was bidden to supper after.'

'Where did they seat you? Above the salt?' Master Cressy demanded sharply, ever on the look-out for a slight from his jumped-up brother.

'At the high table,' Kate replied, glad to be able to report the honour quite truthfully, but suppressing the information that there would otherwise have been a lady short on the dais.

'And who was there?'

'The Bishop of Winchester was the principal guest.'

'What, Gardiner? I suppose, then, that Crumwell was with the King, and Cranmer with the Abbot, or he'd have gone to one or the other. He mislikes both, and what they stand for.'

'Yet he keeps the King's trust, despite being opposed to his chief advisers!'

'Cranmer's a sensible man, apart from his Lutheran

ideas, and I fancy even Crumwell has to beware what he says to the King about Stephen Gardiner. There's advantage in a touch of Tudor blood, provided it's on the wrong side of the blanket!'

'Father!' Kate exclaimed in a low, warning tone.

'May a man not even think in the privacy of his own parlour these days, for fear the chimney's grown ears?' Master Cressy grumbled, kicking a smoking log. The result set him coughing and spluttering for a few minutes, and then he said, 'Did you see aught of Rich?'

'Sir Richard supped with Uncle Cressy,' Kate replied guardedly.

'My Lord Abbot sent word that he'll be bringing someone from the Court of Augmentations here in the morning. Pray God it's not Rich!' Master Cressy said, a wealth of dislike and contempt in the plain 'Rich'. 'I suppose your head's too full of your female fancies to know what that means?'

'I know what the Court of Augmentations is,' Kate replied warily. Sometimes her father was pleased if she showed a reasonable knowledge of the world, but at other times it angered him, it not being a female's place to know such things. This time, he merely looked enquiring, so she ventured to add, 'It looks after the property of dissolved monasteries.'

'Looks after!' Master Cressy echoed bitterly. 'Ay, looks after them very well—into Rich's pocket, and through the sticky fingers of the commissioners, until there's precious little left for the King, I'll be bound! The Abbey's to go, girl! Our Abbey, spite of all the fine talk of a cathedral. Surrendered! Dissolved!'

'When is it to be?' Kate asked wretchedly, the faint hope that Amyas might have been wrong disappearing.

'Oh, in the spring, when my lords the commissioners can spare some jumped-up lackey to come and accept the deed of surrender, and collect the keys and the seal! Four hundred years of prayer and praise, pretty near—five hundred, if you count the old college! All to be ended by a few names on a bit of parchment. It hardly bears thinking of! Well, tomorrow, whoever comes here will take account of the Grange and all the land in the valley between the river and the Forest. Every cow, sheep and pig, they'll count and write down, every ox and horse—every coney, weasel, squirrel and mouse, for all I know. You'd best be up early and see that the house is clean, girl, and a good dinner cooking for Lord Robert. I suppose we'd best sweeten the fellow he brings with him by feeding him well, too, so long as it's not Rich! I'll not waste good food on Rich.'

Kate agreed with him, although she thought best not to say so, and awaited the forthcoming visitation with some apprehension. If Sir Richard should condescend to honour the Abbey by visiting its Grange himself, she felt sure that he would be petty enough to take the opportunity to vent his spite on her in some way for this evening's discomfiture, and she could only pray that he would consider a mere Grange beneath his notice, and send an underling instead.

After a sleepless night spent worrying about that, and other uncertainties about the future, both for her father and for herself, she dreaded the Abbot's arrival, and it seemed an age before his richly caparisoned mule clopped slowly up the rise from the road, followed by a couple of grooms and a black horse carrying a man who was a trifle shorter and more slimly built than Sir Richard. Kate went out with her father to do honour to the Abbot with a lighter heart for having one of her fears removed, and saw, as horse and mule stopped before the door, that the rider of the black horse was that same dark-eyed man she had encountered the day before.

As her father kissed the Abbot's ring and received his blessing, she saw that Lord Robert looked suddenly older and more frail, and she felt a surge of pity for him, wondering what was to become of him when his Abbey was dissolved. He looked a sick man, but his hand was as firm as ever as she lifted it on her fingertips to kiss the amethyst, his touch on her brow as he made the sign of the Cross was unwavering, as was his murmuring voice as he pronounced his blessing.

'I bring you Master Matthew Hartwell of the Court of Augmentations, friend Christopher,' he said, gesturing towards the dark-eyed man, who had dismounted and was looking from Master Cressy to Kate and back again, as if noting points of resemblance between them.

Master Cressy gave Master Hartwell a frosty but polite greeting, and ushered both his guests indoors, leaving the grooms to take their mounts round to the stables. He chose to show them into the hall, which was chill on this autumn morning, with no fire lit on the open hearth, and no sun shining on the linen-covered windows yet, for it faced south-west. Kate sent a servant scurrying to the kitchen for mulled wine, then followed behind the men to the table on the dais, where they sat down. She hesitated a moment, then seated herself, uninvited, a little apart, so far as the table allowed. Her father scowled at her, but said nothing. Master Hartwell smiled, but the Abbot seemed to accept her presence as quite natural and proper.

'This is a fine hall for a farmhouse,' Master Hartwell observed. 'Why, you could divide it into two good-sized rooms, if you wished. Is it stone behind the panelling? It looked to be from outside.'

Master Cressy gave him a hard, inimical stare, and
Kate wondered how he had found time to notice that
the hall was stone-built in those brief moments
outside, for she had not seen him so much as glance
at the house.

'It is very old,' the Abbot said in his gentle voice,
which could be amazingly compelling and firm at
times, although he never raised it, except in intoning
the offices in church. 'As old as the canons' part of
the church and our domestic buildings. That is why
it's of stone, I suppose, for there must have been
enough left over from the Abbey buildings. It is the
only stone-built house for many miles about here.'

'The wings are timber-framed,' said Master Hartwell. 'I caught a glimpse of them as we came up
the—er—drive . . .' His slight hesitation betrayed the
fact that he had probably been about to say 'track'.

Master Cressy made no response to this, but stared
at his own hands lying clasped on the table before
him. He had given the Abbot his own great chair,
which had a back and arms, at the centre of the
table, and was sitting on a stool at his right hand,
with Master Hartwell at right-angles to him on his
other side, at the end of the table. Kate was at the
other, facing Master Hartwell.

'Friend Christopher,' the Abbot began after a
pause, in a reflective tone. 'The Abbey is to be
dissolved in the spring.'

'And will you surrender it?' Master Cressy asked,
harshly and over-loud.

'It seems best,' the Abbot replied, gazing into the
distance. 'It is God's will, expressed through the
King's command. I have long believed that the
monastic ideal is out of tune with these new times.
What served God for our forefathers may not be
equally suitable for their descendants, and there may

be better, newer, ways of doing God's work in the world. Many—nay, most—monasteries, even our own, have become weighed down with possessions—riches, even—and it hardly seems right that I, a priest, should be surrounded by the pomp and luxury of a prince when there are hungry and ragged folk at the very doors of my palace.'

'What will happen to you, and the good Fathers?' Kate faltered in a very subdued voice, half afraid to draw attention to herself in case Lord Robert or her father sent her away.

'No doubt the King's Grace will be pleased to grant us pensions, as he has done for all those who have surrendered their abbeys and priories. Father Thomas, I fear, is too old in religion to fend for himself in the world, so I shall keep him by me as my chaplain, perhaps, and Father Edmund is as yet only in deacon's orders, but the King has undertaken to send him to Cambridge to continue his education. For myself, I shall have a choice of rectories, and I think one of them, in the City, will suit me very well.'

'You'll be just a parish priest?' Master Cressy asked incredulously.

'Yes, plain Sir Robert! But not a poor priest, by any means! The King has already proved a generous master, and has promised more than Master Crumwell had allocated me, as a mark of his affection for Woodham. We have much for which to be grateful!'

Master Cressy's sniff sounded dangerously like the preliminary to some remarks which might not safely be uttered in the presence of an unknown quantity from the Court of Augmentations, but fortunately he was interrupted by the arrival of the mulled wine, which the guests welcomed appreciatively, Master Hartwell remarking that there was quite a nip in the

air this morning, and the spiders' webs had been an
amazingly pretty sight an hour or so ago, with the
dew on them.

'Spiders' webs!' Master Cressy muttered crossly
into his pewter mug. 'Has anything been decided yet
about the land?'

The Abbot looked at Master Hartwell, who replied,
'All the property of any dissolved house passes into
the care of the King, to be administered by the Court
of Augmentations. What becomes of any particular
part of it depends on His Grace. He may lease it, or
sell it, or even give it to someone—or keep it himself.'

'And what about the people who live and work on
it?' Master Cressy demanded, the raw note in his
voice betraying the fact that this, for him, was the
most important question.

'Those who hold from the Abbey as copyholders,
or other types of tenants,' Master Hartwell recited
rather than said, 'shall continue to hold as formerly,
subject to the King's will in the matter of rents or
services. As the land must be maintained in its
present use until the new owner or tenant is
determined, the Court will continue to employ the
day-labourers who so maintain it—namely, the
shepherds, field-workers, swine- and neat-herds, and
such other . . .'

'Yes, yes—that stands to reason!' Master Cressy
interrupted. 'But what about those who aren't tenants
or day-labourers?'

'The principal servants of the former foundation,'
Master Hartwell recited on, his eyes fixed on a small
mark in the wood of the table-top, 'will receive a
reward and pension according to their position and
seniority in the service of the former foundation, to
be determined by the Court of Augmentations in
consultation with the Vicar-General—Master

Crumwell, that is. For life,' he added as an afterthought.

There was an uneasy silence, and it was Kate who eventually broke it by asking the question that her father could not bring himself to voice.

'Does that include the bailey of the Grange?'

'Of course!' Master Hartwell looked at her with what appeared to be genuine surprise. 'Normally his name heads the list, either before or after the steward, depending on their relative importance in a particular case.'

'Are you a lawyer?' Master Cressy asked abruptly.

'Yes,' Master Hartwell replied with his ready smile. 'Of the Inner Temple, like your own brother, Sir William.'

He seemed to assume that this might be a recommendation to his noticeably wary and unfriendly host, but he was mistaken, for Master Cressy gave a more piercing and contemptuous sniff than before, and said, 'I might have known it! Well, you'll find naught amiss here. I've a copy of the survey the King's commissioners made for the *Valor Ecclesiasticus* in '35, and I've kept it up to date every month. Four score and eight sheep we have, and five score kine, two score and two bullocks, twenty-one pigs, six cart-horses, six yoke of oxen, six malt-horses . . .'

'Father,' Kate interrupted firmly, realising that he probably intended to go through the whole inventory in detail. 'Dinner is ready, and Dame Marjorie seeks permission to serve it.'

'And one mule,' Master Cressy finished—apparently. 'Eleven o'clock already, is it? Let it be brought, then! Unless my lord Abbot is to be permitted to keep his mule, that is,' he added. 'And that might be as well, for the animal will let no one else on his back, being as stubborn as any of his kind.'

'Thank you for the warning!' Master Hartwell said in a warm and friendly tone. 'I'd noted it as a remarkably fine beast, but I think I'll recommend that it be left with its present owner.'

'That would be a kindness. I'm very fond of my Roland,' the Abbot observed quietly, moving back a little to allow the servants to spread a spotless damask cloth on the table, supervised anxiously by Dame Marjorie, an elderly spinster lady who acted as housekeeper to Master Cressy as a means of earning her keep. She was extremely nervous, and given to clucking softly like an anxious hen, and her present concern was so intense that she sounded as if she were about to lay an egg.

The table was set with the best pewter plates, each with a good thick slice of wheaten trencher bread on it. The best pewter salt-cellar and spice-box were put before the Abbot's place, and covered earthenware dishes were brought with some ceremony, and unlidded to reveal a rich-smelling pottage with diced meat in it, all savoury with herbs and spices. Finally, a horn mug and a small jug of ale was set by each place.

'You do us great kindness to serve so fine a dish, sister Marjorie!' the Abbot exclaimed, his long, ascetic nose twitching at the warm fragrance rising from the generous helping which Master Cressy was spooning out for him. For all his great position, Lord Robert was a simple man at heart, and could still take much pleasure in a good, plain dinner, yet he was a sparing and abstemious man at table, and Kate knew very well that half the platterful before him would be left for the poor.

She realised, almost too late, that her father was not going to serve Master Hartwell—an omission which would certainly be recognised as an insult, so she seized a second dish of pottage from Martin, who was standing in a helpless and vacant fashion, waiting to be told what to do with it, and carried it along the back of the dais, reaching Master Hartwell's side just in time to serve him herself before he realised that his host was slighting him.

'You do me too much honour, Mistress Cressy!' he exclaimed, at which she gave him a suspicious sidelong glance, thinking he was mocking her, but he was looking at her with those bright, unguarded eyes filled with nothing but sincerity.

The Abbot said Grace when Kate had returned to her place and served herself, and then Master Cressy, scooping up a spoonful of his pottage and looking at it closely as if to see what was in it, asked his second most important question.

'And what about the house?'

CHAPTER THREE

THERE WAS a brief silence, during which Master Cressy waited with spoon poised, Kate, arrested in the midst of taking up her own spoon, sat quite still, and the Abbot sprinkled a minute quantity of ginger on his food. Master Hartwell tasted his pottage, nodded affably to Dame Marjorie with a friendly 'Quite delicious!', took another mouthful, tasted, swallowed, then regarded Master Cressy with interest, and enquired, 'The house, sir? Which house do you mean?'

'Why, this one, of course!' Master Cressy almost snarled at him.

'Ah, yes. It's about this house and its contents that I'm come to see you,' Master Hartwell said, tucking into his pottage between sentences, and, being a mannerly person, emptying his mouth before speaking, which made his reply a little slow in coming. 'It appears that there was an oversight in 1535, and this house was omitted from the *Valor*. I suppose the heavy rain washed it out of the commissioners' minds!'

The Abbot gave a gentle chuckle, remembering how Crumwell's agents had arrived like drowned rats at Woodham to take their inventory in that exceptionally wet summer, but neither of the Cressys present responded to the humorous reference.

'The *Valor* didn't include buildings,' Master Cressy

said flatly. 'It was concerned with income, not fixtures.'

'But the rent value of all property should have been included,' Master Hartwell pointed out, looking hopefully towards the covered dish nearest him. Kate hurried to help him to a few more spoonfuls of pottage, despite a scowl and a shake of the head from her father.

'Master Cressy does not pay rent,' the Abbot put in quietly. 'This house has always been provided for the use of our bailey. It was built for that purpose.'

'But is has a rent value, for all that,' Master Hartwell replied. 'Thank you, Mistress Cressy! This is truly excellent fare! In theory, at least, it could be let out to provide income, so it should have been valued. As it is, we are now valuing all the property of the Abbey in preparation for the surrender, so it is necessary that the contents be valued, as well as the building, so that the King and the Augmentations office may know what is to pass into their charge.'

'Contents?' exclaimed Master Cressy. 'What do you mean, contents? Are our few sticks of furniture to be taken from us for the King's use, for Heaven's sake?'

'I need to know what rooms the house has, and what furniture belongs to the house—to the Abbey, that is—and what to you personally,' Master Hartwell explained, sitting back from his plate and reaching for his cup of ale. 'There is no intention to deprive you of your own belongings.'

Kate noted that, as a good Christian, he had left his pottage-soaked trencher-bread for the poor, as had the Abbot and Kate herself, but her father had eaten his, possibly because he had been too

concerned in the conversation to notice what was
passing his lips.

'One of the chief concerns of the Court of
Augmentations,' Master Hartwell added, 'is to
ensure that everyone concerned is dealt with fairly.
There is a positive command upon us to see that no
injustice results from our decisions.'

Master Cressy looked doubtful, but he said, 'Well,
then! My daughter shall take you round the house.
Let him poke his nose into everything, as he will.
But take care that he writes down nothing that
belongs to me!' he admonished Kate. 'I'll not have
him reporting back to his master that Christopher
Cressy was uncooperative, but neither will I have
his Court taking what is rightfully mine. Take him
round now, and let's be done with it.'

Kate was nonplussed for a moment, for the
servants were removing the platters and dishes, and
Dame Marjorie and Martin were just bringing in
crusty bread and a fresh sheep's-milk cheese, but
before she could say anything, Master Cressy waved
it away, and the Dame turned about, nudging
Martin along with her, and went out again, clucking
in a loud and agitated fashion.

'If you will come this way, sir,' Kate said, bobbing
a curtsy to the Abbot, then leading Master Hartwell
through the door at the back of the dais into the
parlour. As soon as they were there, she waited
while he shut the door, then said quickly, 'I trust
you'll forgive my father, sir. He doesn't mean to be
rude, but he's very much overset by the news, and
anxious about the future. We fully expected that
the Abbey would be made a cathedral, and all go
on much as before.'

'In some places, men in a situation like to your
father's have set their dogs on me,' Master Hartwell

replied, looking about him with interest. He took a writing-tablet and pencil from the purse at his belt, and wrote a few words on it. 'Has he been bailey here very long?'

'All his life,' Kate said sadly. 'That is . . . His father and grandfather were baileys before him, and he helped in the work from his childhood.'

'And has he no son?'

He has—had—a son, sir, but he's a monk at St Alban's. Would it matter, though? Will there be a need for a bailey any more, with the Abbey gone?'

'That would depend on the new owner,' Master Hartwell replied non-committally. There was silence for a few moments as he continued to write on his tablet, and then he said suddenly, 'Oh, I'd best be honest with you! The truth is, the demesne here is likely to go to Lord Dallance, who has an estate near by, across the river—you probably know him— and he intends to run this and that together. He'll not need a bailey, or even all the land, for it's more than he requires. This house will be rented or sold, with some land to go with it. Your father will be asked if he wishes to rent or buy it—I'm not sure which, for it's not yet decided. It will all be made plain in the weeks before the surrender.'

'How much will the rent be?' Kate asked hesitantly, but already her spirits had sunk to a very low ebb, for she knew that her father had virtually no money. It was not that he had never had the opportunity to make any, but his spending had always seemed to match his income, which was, in any case, largely in kind—in produce from the Grange, rather than in coin.

'It would depend on how much land is allocated, but I'd say ten or fifteen pounds a year,' Master Hartwell replied, crossing the room to look closely at an old panel of tapestry which hung between the two small windows. 'What in here belongs to your father?'

'That chair,' Kate replied, pointing to Master Cressy's high-backed, elaborately-carved chair by the fireplace. 'The stools and the table. The chest— it belonged to my mother. Not the tapestry, or the cupboard.'

'Your mother is—er—no longer alive?'

'She died soon after I was born,' Kate said, thinking wretchedly that he might just as well have said ten or fifteen hundred pounds, for her father had no more than five or six in his possession, and was unlikely to get more if he had only whatever pension he was granted to live on.

'I'm sorry,' Master Hartwell said with rather more than conventional sympathy. 'What of the fire-irons?'

'They belong to us. Father had them made,' Kate replied promptly, for her father kept a list of all his possessions, with a note of where he had obtained them and what they cost, and had made Kate study it in case just such a situation as this should ever arise.

Master Hartwell's tablet was, in fact, a little book, and he seemed to have some brief method of noting items on it, for she noticed, as they went round the house, that he never used more than a page for a particular room. He made no comment on any of the furnishings, which were ugly and over-elaborate if they were Master Cressy's, and old and shabby if they belonged to the Abbey, but he did say several times, 'This house could be made very comfortable!' in a thoughtful manner, more to himself than to Kate.

Their arrival in the kitchen put Dame Marjorie

into a panic, but the combined efforts of Kate and Master Hartwell succeeded in soothing her and convincing her that her housekeeping methods were not to come under the scrutiny of the Court of Augmentations. She followed them round as Master Hartwell noted spits and cauldrons, cheese-presses and milk-pails.

The stairs to the upper floor were built, unusually, in the thickness of the wall of the screens passage, which was the outside wall of the old stone part of the building. Kate had often wondered where it had led originally, but now it served as access to the upper rooms of the wing which had been built on at the north-west side of the house. It came out on a small landing, just outside the door of Kate's own chamber. She hesitated before she opened the door, for, as it was at the front end of the range and did not provide a passage to any other room, she had grown used to considering it her own private place, and she was reluctant to admit a stranger, and a man, at that!

'This is my room,' she said, accepting the inevitable, and marched in ahead of Master Hartwell, who paused in the doorway, his eyes going first to the window, which was wide—almost the width of the room—and normally filled by an oiled linen screen. Kate had taken it down when she rose that morning, to take advantage of the fine day and air the room.

'You can see right across the valley!' he exclaimed, walking across to lean out of the opening. 'There's the town, and the Abbey church rising from it, like a hen amid her chicks . . . That must be Beetley, across there, I suppose,' pointing north-westwards, 'and see how the land rises, right away over there, on the skyline! It must be seven or eight miles away, at least. What a truly grand prospect! Yet you hide it behind a linen screen? You should have glass in the windows here—in every room which looks out from the house-front, for that matter. It's a sin to hide such a view!'

'Glass is expensive,' Kate said sharply, although she privately agreed with him, 'and my father does not approve of people wasting time looking out of windows.'

'And do you never look out, when he's not about?' Master Hartwell asked, looking at her in his thrushlike fashion.

Kate made no reply, thinking it none of his business, but she was secretly pleased that she had found someone else who thought the view worth looking at and was not afraid to say so. Then she reminded herself that he was an emissary of the Enemy, and said coldly, 'The bed is mine, and the little bookshelf and the chest.'

Master Hartwell nodded, writing busily. There was nothing else in the room but a small rickety table bearing a basin and ewer and a rushlight holder.

'And the books are yours?' he said, going to the shelf to look at them.

'Yes, all but the little psalter. Lord Robert lent me that.'

'You can read, then? Can you write as well?'

'Yes.' She hoped there was no detectable pride in her voice, but few females of her acquaintance could read and write at all, and none as well as she could.

'And you know Latin?' he asked, taking a volume down and looking into it.

Kate hesitated. She would dearly have liked to say that she did, but it would not be true, for she knew only enough to follow the services in church, and had no grounding at all in grammar. Before she could reply, however, he went on 'This is a copy of *Utopia*—More's *Utopia!*'

'His good-sister gave it me,' she said warily, wishing that he had not seen that particular book, for she feared that it might not be safe to have it, since its author had been executed for treason.

'His good-sister?' The dark eyes questioned her over the top of the small volume.

'Yes. His first wife's family live a few miles up the river, and often come to Woodham. Mistress Colte gave me the book when . . .' She stopped, afraid to say, 'When he was put to death,' and he did not ask her to complete the sentence, but turned his attention back to the volume and remarked, 'It has his name in it, written in the front. Is it his signature?'

'Yes.'

'Then you must treasure it and keep it safe!'

'I do.'

He put the book back without comment, and gave the rest a summary inspection, but they were nothing but a rag-tag of old chapbooks of no particular interest. 'Yes, keep it safe, and don't leave it where prying eyes or a thieving hand may come upon it!' he said, giving her one shrewd and meaning look before turning to leave the room.

Kate lingered for a moment, looking over her shoulder at the view from the window. The light over the water-meadows had a mellow, golden tinge in it, and the leaves on the trees were beginning to look more gold than green now. On the far side of the cornmill stream, she could see a group of people and, even as she watched, one notably tall and bulky rider flung up his arm in the graceful launching movement that sent a hawk winging after its prey.

She wondered which of those distant people, like figures in a tapestry, was Amyas, and marvelled that her heart could not tell her, even at half a mile. Her spirit rebelled to think that she might have been out there, riding with the hawkers, instead of being cooped up here with this objectionable, interfering creature from the Court of Augmentations poking his nose into her family's home and despising their possessions, and the prospect of a disagreeable time afterwards with her father, who would be filled with spleen and choler over the visitation.

'Mistress Cressy?' Master Hartwell's not unpleasant voice broke into her thoughts. 'Are you quite well?'

'Yes, of course,' she replied curtly, following him out of the room.

'I realise that this must be distressing for you,' he began, then paused, as if uncertain how to go on. It was dark on the landing, so Kate could not judge his purpose in starting on such a speech at all.

'No more distressing than the knowledge that I'm soon to lose my home,' she said coldly. 'And, since we cannot go against both King and Parliament, we needs must put up with it!'

'You don't think, then, that Master Cressy will ask to rent or buy the house?'

'The bailey of an abbey, even a rich and important abbey, has never been paid a great deal,' she replied, a distinctly hostile tone creeping into her voice, 'I doubt if my father ever had so much as ten pounds in coin in any one year.' She was painfully aware that her attempt to sound unfeeling belied her real emotions, for the realisation that, in a few short months, she would no longer live in this old house was slowly overwhelming her, and she feared that she would soon dissolve into helpless tears over it, and shame herself before this—this interloper!

She flung open the door of the first of the string of four interconnected rooms which formed the rest of the upper floor of this wing, and led the way into it, tersely indicating which of its contents belonged to her father, and so on through the rest of the range. Master Hartwell made no further attempt at conversation, but made his notes, and occasionally asked for clarification—did the hangings of the bed belong to the Cressys, or only the bed itself?—what of the linen in the presses, if the latter were the Abbey's property? Even Kate's natural prejudice against him could not prevent her from realising, however grudgingly, that he was being very careful to see that the Cressys did not lose anything which might possibly be theirs, and, in fact, had already saved them several items which she had overlooked. She was also forced to credit him with tact, for he made no comment on the ridiculously expensive and over-decorated furniture which her father had bought to replace some of the good old stuff he had inherited.

The tour of the house took the greater part of the afternoon, and left Kate depressed and tired, and she began to wonder how she and her father were to manage. Presumably they would find somewhere to live in the town, and since they would have to sell most of Master Cressy's grandiose furniture, they would have no plain, useful things left to their use. In any case, would they be able to live on whatever pension her father was given, and what would become of Dame Marjorie and the servants?

The stable wing was the last to be visited, and

Master Hartwell did not propose to go through it in detail. 'I suppose,' he said, 'that everything here belongs to the Abbey, being part of the stock and equipment of the Grange. Is there anything you can think of which belongs to you or your father? The horses, for instance?'

'No. The horses belong to the Abbey, although we have always had the use of them,' Kate replied sadly, fondling the soft nose of Jewel, the little mare which she had always thought of as her own. The animal seemed to sense that something was amiss, and had put her head out over the half-door to roll her eyes sidelong at Master Hartwell.

He rubbed the mare gently along the side of her head and behind her ear, looking soberly at Kate as he did so, but she was gazing into space, wondering if she dare lie, and claim Jewel as her own.

'This is your own mount?' he asked.

'I've always ridden her,' Kate replied scrupulously. 'My lord Abbot bought her when I was twelve, so that I might have a mount, for the other horses were all too big for me.'

'Ah—so she was bought for your use? Hm.' He made a note on his tablet, but said nothing more on the subject, only looked about him, noting the cobbled yard and the paddock beyond.

'If there is nothing of yours here, I can leave all this for when the clerks come to make the full inventory, after the surrender,' he said. 'I'm sure you'll be glad to have done with this sorry business. Shall we return to your father and my lord?'

Kate made some murmur of assent, and led the way back to the hall, which she had already said contained nothing of Master Cressy's save his carved chair, but Master Cressy and the Abbot had long left it for the privacy and comfort of the parlour, where Kate and Master Hartwell found them, sitting in a somewhat gloomy silence on either side of the fire, which was not smoking today.

'Well? Have you poked your nose into everything?' Master Cressy demanded aggressively.

Lord Robert shook his head deprecatingly at his bailey, and murmured, 'Master Hartwell has a duty to perform. Let us not hold him to blame for Parliament's decrees!' in the gentlest of tones, yet Master Cressy suddenly looked uneasy and a trifle shame-faced, and sent Kate to bespeak ale, saying a shade more agreeably that taking an inventory was thirsty work at the best of times.

Kate enlisted Martin to carry the jug and the best pewter mugs, but poured the ale herself and served it, knowing that poor Martin was quite likely to miss the mugs altogether, or drop them on the floor, but she gave him an encouraging smile as he went out, so that he would know that he had not done anything wrong, which was his great and abiding fear.

'Thank you, Mistress Cressy,' Master Hartwell said, taking the trouble to rise to his feet to accept his drink. 'You brew good ale here. Your health, and yours too, Master Cressy and my lord!'

There was a contemplative silence as the men savoured the ale, which was, indeed, good, and then the Abbot enquired, 'Did you settle the ownership of everything satisfactorily?'

Master Hartwell waited a moment for Kate to reply, although the question had been directed at him, but she said nothing, so he answered, 'I believe so, my lord, save for one item. The small chestnut mare, which I understand was bought by the Abbey for Mistress Cressy's use. Would that have been a gift to Mistress Cressy, would you say?'

The Abbot looked at him thoughtfully, and replied, 'It was purchased for her exclusive use, and I would interpret that to mean that it—or, rather, she—was intended as a gift, although no formal statement to that effect was made at the time. It was not, of course, foreseen that the question would ever arise. The same would, of course, apply to the harness. The saddle was especially made, I recollect, with an adjustable footboard to allow for growth, dear Kate being but—what?—twelve or so then.'

Master Hartwell's lips moved as he wrote something on his tablet, and Kate could have sworn that he had murmured, 'Kate'. She realised that he had not heard her Christian name mentioned before, but she could not imagine why he should find it necessary to repeat it to himself in that fashion. She was distracted, however, from any further thoughts by his next words, which were spoken aloud.

'So I have entered the mare and her harness as Mistress Cressy's property.'

'Oh!' Kate exclaimed, startled by the unexpected kindness of the gesture.

Her father, however, spoiled it by saying angrily, 'We don't ask for charity, young man!'

'Nor is it my place to offer charity!' Master Hartwell replied in a dry, but slightly acid, tone. 'I am here to make a fair and just settlement of the respective claims of the Court of Augmentations and of yourself and your daughter. It is clear to me that the property under discussion can fairly and reasonably be claimed by Mistress Cressy, and justice demands that I recognise her claim.'

'Thank you,' Kate said with quiet dignity. 'I appreciate your equitable dealing.' It sounded frostily formal, but her father's intervention and Master Hartwell's reply to it had made her too self-conscious to utter the spontaneous thanks which had been cut off by the interruption.

'And what questionable items have your equity and justice decided shall be your master's and not mine?' Master Cressy asked in a voice made all the more irritable by his set-down.

'Friend Christopher!' the Abbot said reproachfully. 'You will not accept charity, you say, but it behoves you to show it! Your distress is understandable, I allow, but no greater than that of all of us in our community, and we must all bow our heads to accept God's chastisement with good grace. Do not blame the man for the duties entailed in his office! Friend Matthew has shown himself a fair and disinterested agent in all his dealings with us, and we do not for one moment believe that he will do anything to deprive you of so much as a pin which can be made out to be your property with any truth or justice.'

This was an unusually long and outspoken reproof from Lord Robert, and Master Cressy was suitably chastened by it. He did not go so far as to apologise to Master Hartwell, but he refrained from attacking him again, and offered him more ale in a gruff and embarrassed fashion.

Master Hartwell accepted the peace-offering with good grace, and even gave Kate a mischievous, eye-twinkling glance as she filled his mug, to which she almost responded with a faint smile, but, somehow, her face seemed to have become stiff, and would not relax.

'I shall make out a proper inventory from my notes when I return to Westminster,' he said to Master Cressy. 'You shall have a fair copy in due

course, so that you may go through it and raise any
questions which may arise, and it will also serve as
your authority to remove anything on it from the
house. There is no intention by the Court to cheat
you of anything, nor, I must add, to allow the King
to suffer any loss of his entitlements! However, I
promise that you'll not find us unreasonable.'

Master Cressy murmured something which included the words 'greedy' and 'grasping' in association
with 'Rich', but added more coherently that Master
Hartwell seemed a well-enough soul, and my lord
Robert was known to be an excellent judge of
character, which was as far as his feelings or his
nature allowed him to go towards a more friendly
response.

'Time draws on apace,' the Abbot remarked, no
doubt thinking it best to remove Master Hartwell
before Master Cressy recovered his bad temper,
'and we must return to the Abbey for Vespers
before the King comes to supper. Friend Christopher, daughter Kate—thank you for your hospitali-
ty . . .' He rose to his feet and stood, a tall imposing
figure, although Kate could see that he straightened
his back with an effort. She sank to her knees, her
father creaking down beside her, to receive a
blessing and kiss the Abbot's ring, and then there
was a flurry as a message was sent for the horse and
mule to be brought round, and Lord Robert passed
slowly to the front door, keeping up a flow
of sociable conversation to prevent any further
unfortunate remarks from his host, and so brought
Master Hartwell safely to his horse. They bade a
final farewell, the Abbot blessed the house, and
mounted his mule, which looked monumentally
displeased at the interruption to its afternoon
repose. Lord Robert spoke firmly to it in Latin, and

it consented to depart. Master Hartwell rode correctly half a length behind, and the grooms brought up the rear.

'What did he say, then?' Master Cressy demanded before they were properly out of earshot.

'About what?' Kate asked nervously, wondering how soon she would be able to slip away to meet Amyas.

'About the house, of course! What do you think I mean? God protect me from an idiot daughter! Heaven knows, you're little enough use, girl, without you act the witless ninny! What did he say about the house?'

'That you'd be given an opportunity to rent or buy it, if you wished,' Kate replied tonelessly, refusing to be angered or upset by her father's ill-temper.

Master Cressy snorted, not even bothering to point out that he already knew that, and he had no money to do either.

'He also said,' Kate continued, dredging her mind for something more pleasing, 'that the new owner of the demesne—whoever he may be—will probably wish to continue to employ all those who work about the Grange, and he may also want a bailey . . .'

'And did he say who is like to get the grant?'

'Well . . .' Kate hesitated. 'It's not settled yet, of course, and I think not to be noised abroad, but he thought it might be Lord Dallance.'

'Then there's an end of it!' Master Cressy sounded more angry than depressed or resigned. 'His land marches with the demesne on the far side of the river, and he'll run both together with his own bailey, I don't doubt. God knows what's to become of me, or of you, for that matter! My God! What have I done, to be robbed of my wife, of my only son, of my home and my work, and be left with nothing but a useless daughter who cannot even catch herself a rich husband to solve my problems and ensure me a little comfort and security in my dotage! Give your mind to your duty, girl, and do something about it, for you've cost me enough, and it's time you began to repay something for all I've given you!'

Kate, taken aback at this sudden attack, was too astonished to make any reply, and by the time she had recovered her wits and lost her temper enough to make a reply which would have been far from dutiful or meek, Master Cressy had stumped away round to the back of the house, where, no doubt, he would work off his ire on whichever of the labourers he found there, and she was left seething.

As if it were her fault that her mother had died when she was little! It was not her birth which had killed Mary Cressy, but the sweating-sickness, and neither was it her fault that John had felt the call to enter Religion instead of following his father as bailey. As for catching a rich husband—well, Cecy might do that, with her blue eyes and ethereal blonde beauty, but dark-haired females were not in fashion and no one had ever called Kate a beauty— save Amyas—blessed, dearest Amyas! If only Amyas would propose marriage! If only some great stroke of luck would put him firmly into the King's favour, and earn him a sure place at Court, with a sufficiency to give him independence from his father! How long must she wait to be his wife?

A cold, frightening finger of doubt touched her mind, and she thought that the time might, in fact, never come. The doubt had already touched her, whenever the weeks slipped by with no word from

Amyas, and always, before, she had been able to dismiss it, confident that all must come right. Not this time, however! This time, it would not be brushed aside, but sat there, like a cold, clammy toad, in the back of her mind, exuding its poison of fear and uncertainty.

She stood for some time before the door of the house, staring unseeingly down the hill towards the copse, and, gradually, her confused mind calmed down, and she saw, beyond the trees and across the water-meadows, the hawking party, still casting, and the light breeze carried the faint, clear sound of the bells tinkling on the hoods of those hawks which were at rest.

After watching for a few minutes, she raised her eyes to the sun, which was still some way above the horizon, and she longed for sunset to come, so that she might run down to the copse to meet Amyas.

But first there was supper to be endured, and the sour company of her father . . .

CHAPTER FOUR

MASTER Cressy talked incessantly through supper in a low, complaining monotone, mainly about the problem of knowing what to do during the next few months. Normally, the winter wheat would be sown, the labourers re-employed at the hiring-fair in October, or new ones taken on, and the surplus beasts sold at the cattle-market around Michaelmas, but, if the Abbey was to be dissolved in the spring, were these normal activities to be continued or not?

'What did my lord Robert say, Father?' Kate ventured during a brief pause for the intake of roast pork and cabbage.

'That I must do as I think fit!' Master Cressy snorted, and spat out a piece of crackling with which his poor remaining teeth were unable to cope. 'And, ten to one, whatever I do will be wrong for my lords commissioners!'

'I should think it would be best to carry on as normal,' Kate said pensively and a little heedlessly, for her mind kept sliding away to wonder if Amyas was waiting yet for her in the coppice.

'You should think! Humph! What opinion have you worth the giving on such a matter? Tend your own business, girl, and leave me to mind mine! The cloth put on this table for dinner was darned, and monstrously badly, at that! You disgrace me before my lord with badly-mended linen, not to mention

Rich's creature from the damned Augmentations, and you venture to advise me what to do about the demesne land! And what was that gewgaw on your bosom last night? Some piece of St Audrey work from your sweetheart that you flaunt in a respectable household?'

'It was a brooch lent me by Cousin Cecy, since I had none of my own,' Kate replied tartly, regretfully feeling herself becoming shrewish in response to his ill-temper. 'Which reminds me that I must return it to her in the morning, for I should not have brought it away with me.'

'Why did you, then? To make an excuse to go hanging about the handsome young gallants at the King's House, I shouldn't wonder! To think that a daughter of mine should lower herself to peacock before the lewd eyes of these Court gallants in borrowed, shoddy finery!'

Kate knew that any attempt at explanation or protest would only make matters worse, so she took refuge, as usual, in stony silence. Master Cressy went on sneering and fulminating for a time, then, having vented most of his spleen, pushed the remains of his supper away and went off to his cabinet, as he usually did in the evening. Kate often wondered what he found to do there, but never ventured to ask, being thankful for the few hours' respite which his absence gave.

She finished her own meal with good appetite, rinsed her mouth and fingers and wiped them with her linen napkin, and then went quietly out of the house to meet her lover.

The sun was setting in a blaze of crimson glory, and a light mist lay in golden swathes across the water-meadows. At some time in the past, the woodmen had brought a sizeable log to the lower edge of the little wood, and adzed the upper side of it to make a seat where they could sit to eat their bevers looking across the valley. Kate expected to see Amyas there, but she was surprised to see two figures silhouetted against the sunset, and paused for a moment, her russet gown making her almost invisible among the many narrow trunks of the hazel coppice, not wishing anyone from the town to know that she stole out of the house in the evening to meet her lover like any common serving-wench.

The two figures had their heads together over something, and were talking in low voices, so Kate crept a little nearer, and found that the other man was no stranger, and had even more right to be here than she had herself, for his low, slow countryman's voice was saying, 'Yes, she'm a good li'l jill, being half polecat, and has three or five young 'uns every time, and raises them just as good as a Christian mother. Mind you, her husband's me old hob Rusty, and he'm the best fitchet for miles! Breeding tells, and the young 'uns fetch a good price.' It was Harry Warrener, discoursing on his favourite subject, his beloved ferrets.

'Good evening to you, Master Warrener!' Kate said quietly, paying him the courtesy due to a master of his craft.

'And give you good e'en, Mistress Cressy,' he replied, rising in an unhurried fashion and holding out a double handful of russet fur, black beady eyes and wicked little teeth. 'Diamond bids you good e'en too, and 'll bring you some plump coneys in the morning.'

'Thank you, Diamond,' Kate said politely, stroking the little wedge-shaped head with one cautious finger. Diamond was known to be a little snappish and liable, in the early evening, to mistake anything which moved for a rabbit.

'Well, now,' he said easily, stowing Diamond away in some inner recess of his clothing. 'No doubt yer young gentle has more interesting things to talk on than fitchets—more interesting to you, that is! I'll be off about my coneys, then, and I'll not forget a dozen good 'uns for Dame Marjorie, come morning. God and all his saints forfend you!' And, with a benevolent gesture worthy of the Abbot himself, he faded away among the shadows of the coppice-poles.

'What a strange fellow!' Amyas remarked in a condescending tone. 'He talks about those little furry vermin as if they were his children. Well, Kate love, could you not get away from your old tyrant today?'

Kate melted into his arms, and they kissed with all the more fervour for not having been able to spend the day together as they had hoped.

'My lord Abbot came to dinner,' she said eventually, 'and brought a man from the Court of Augmentations to make an inventory of our chattels, so I had to stay.'

'The Abbot brought a clerk to dine with you?' Amyas exclaimed incredulously. 'What was he thinking of? Did you send him to the kitchen?'

'Oh, he was no clerk but a gentleman! He said he wished to be sure that no mistake was made about the ownership of anything.'

'To be sure!' Amyas's voice took on a note of sarcasm which Kate found oddly jarring. 'Rich's men lose no opportunity to make sure that everything possible accrues to their charge, and God knows what of it will ever pass to the King! I've no doubt your visitor made a note of the things he wants for himself, and so the process goes on, clerk by clerk, up the scale to Rich himself, and Crumwell above him. You know, when he— Crumwell, I mean—saw the inventory of Launde Priory, he wrote *This for me* in the margin, and now his son Geoffrey has it in his behalf!'

'I don't believe the gentleman who came today was at all like that,' Kate said, moved, for some reason not clear to her, to defend the absent Master Hartwell. 'In fact, he was very kind and tactful about it, and even took the trouble to make sure that my little mare is written down as my property, for my lord Robert gave her to me.'

'Which proves nothing, save that your paragon has an eye for a female face!' Amyas scoffed. 'Who was he, this very parfait, gentil commissioner? Perhaps I know him.'

'His name is Hartwell.'

'What, Matt Hartwell? Oh, well—yes, he's not much like the rest of the breed. In fact, I can't imagine how he finds himself in that den of thieves at all! He's a quiet, dull sort of fellow, but honest and not above putting himself out to do a good turn here and there, although he's not over-clever in choosing when it will advantage him. In fact, he lent me five pounds and a horse once when I was in urgent need of them! I paid him back the following week.'

Kate noticed that he sounded surprised by the last statement, as if startled that he had done such a thing, and she wondered uneasily if he was in the habit of not paying his debts.

'I wish I might get an abbey!' he sighed, following a train of thought set off by the mention of Master Crumwell and Launde. 'You'd think abbeys and priories were to be had for the asking, wouldn't you? But it's only those in the highest favour in the right quarter who get them—the King's own favourites, and those with powerful friends at Court—at both Courts, that is, the King's and the Augmentations! My God, but it's rightly named, for it serves only to augment the riches of those who have plenty. Those who are not owed favours by the right people, or have some sort of hold over a man in power, can't get anything. Would you believe that even the King's own uncle cannot get an abbey, but only a poor priory, and that let out at some ridiculous low rent to a fellow who can't be budged from it at any price?'

'The King's uncle?' Kate exclaimed. 'But surely the King has no uncle! Old King Henry had no brothers, and Queen Elizabeth's brothers . . . Oh, you mean her sister Anne's husband, the Duke of Norfolk?'

'No, sweetheart! I mean Arthur Plantagenet, Lord Lisle, Edward IV's bastard! He's Governor of Calais, and filled with bile! It cost him a fortune in gifts to Crumwell and Rich to get his priory, and it's not worth so much as a hundred and fifty a year. Mind you, I'd be glad to get so much as that, for it would be enough, given care, to free me of my bondage to my father, and buy favour about the Court with the men who count.'

'Why must you buy favour?' Kate asked. 'And how? I thought favour had to be earned?'

'Oh, it's the common way at Court, or anywhere else, for that matter. If you want someone to act in your interest, you must ply him with "gifts", and beg him be a "good friend" to you, and if anyone does you the slightest service, he'll name the price of it in terms of "gifts" before you have time to thank him. Come to think of it, your friend Master

Hartwell didn't ask anything for lending me that money, but I've no doubt he'll be after me to remind me of it when he thinks of something I can do for him!'

'You mean, you have to bribe people for everything?' Kate thought it all sounded horribly mercenary and unChristian.

'Oh, nothing so crude as bribing, save for the lowest and most greedy! No—it's a matter of the person admiring a horse, or saying he wished he had such a dog, or a better hawk, or that quails were not so dear . . . Not money, of course, for that implies bribery and corruption.'

'It all sounds very corrupt and unpleasant,' Kate said in a troubled voice. 'Does nobody ever do anything out of love or charity?'

'Why should they? Life at Court is a continual struggle to rise to the top, and then to stay there, for there's no other way to power and fortune. They say the King is the fount of honour, but, believe me, he's the fount of all else as well, and he's hedged about by powerful, greedy, unscrupulous men who'll not easily let in another to their number. I don't hope to reach the top of the pile, but I'll make myself a safe niche as far up it as I can, and that needs every scrap of influence and interest I can win or buy!'

'But have you not enough already?' Kate ventured, feeling inwardly sickened by the hard tones of his voice and the greedy ambition expressed in his words. 'You have a knighthood, and the chance to serve the King in small ways. Does that not give you any satisfaction?'

'Faith, no! What use is serving the King, unless it brings a rich reward? I want more than a paltry knighthood, granted as a favour to my father, not gained on the battlefield, and there's no fortune or power in being a mere lackey to any man, even a King! Any one of a dozen men can tell me to do this, go there, as the whim takes them, and I must obey, or lose my place. I mean to be one of those who gives the orders, like the fellow in the Gospels—*do this, and he doeth it*—you know! I mean to have authority, like that centurion!'

'I believe he was *under* authority,' Kate said quietly and thoughtfully, for she had read the Gospels for herself in the few months since the English translation had been placed in the parish nave of the Abbey church.

'Oh, words!' Amyas exclaimed impatiently. 'You're not about to turn Lutheran, are you, quibbling over an exact word more or less?'

'An exact word can be important,' Kate replied seriously. 'Especially these days, when the wrong one can lead to—to an accusation of heresy or treason . . .'

'And what should you know of that, in this little haven of peace?' Amyas asked lightly. 'Oh, come now, Kate! Sweet Kate! Why do you trouble your pretty head with these great matters? Are you meaning to become a learned lady, a second Margaret More, to confound the great scholars in academic disputation? Come, sweetheart! Such talk isn't for a woman's lips—they were meant for kissing. I'm glad of your pretty ears to listen sympathetically while I pour out my troubles, but I want no solemn pronouncements from your sweet lips. I need to talk, Kate, for I can't confide in anyone at Court—there's not a soul I can trust there—but I don't need advice or admonition from you. I know what I'm about, far better than you could ever understand! I need comfort and—well, you know what I need well enough, don't you, eh?'

The conversation disintegrated thereafter into nothing but endearments and incoherencies, in the manner of any young lovers with no more than a stolen hour together in the evening damp of an autumnal coppice, and the afterglow had faded and the moon risen before Kate forced herself to draw away from the delight of his kisses and caresses.

'I must go, before my father finds I'm out,' she said regretfully. 'I've made an excuse to come down to the town in the morning to see my cousin. Shall I see you there?'

'I hope so, at least for a little while. The King's bad leg troubled him a little by the end of today's hawking, and he means to rest tomorrow by spending the day in discussion with the Abbot and the Archbishop, and, presumably, Bishop Gardiner. If no one orders me otherwise, I'll endeavour to be about near the house all the morning.'

'Then goodnight, dearest Amyas!' Kate whispered tenderly.

'Oh, but—let me walk with you to within sight of your door. It may not be safe, abroad in the dark!'

'Why, what is there to harm me in little more than a furrow's length to my own home? Besides, someone may see you, and tell Father! No, best to part here . . .'

And part there they did—eventually—and Kate returned home, walking in a little cloud of happiness, for he had spoken of love, and treated her with great tenderness and passion, yet respected her virtue in a manner which pleased and comforted her enormously.

It was only later, as she leaned on the sill of her bedroom window and gazed out over the moonlit valley, that she thought of the less pleasant things he had said that evening, and the memory of that hard, ruthless talk of striving for power and wealth troubled her spirits. The picture of Court life that he had drawn sounded to her like some corner of Hell. Was it really like that, with everyone striving and struggling for power and position? Were they all so greedy, selfish, ambitious, so grasping and corrupt? She had thought men like Master Crumwell and Sir Richard Rich to be exceptions, the black sheep amid the more or less snowy majority of good, kind people about the King, but it sounded, from what Amyas had said, as if they were all tarred with the same brush, and her heart quailed at the thought that dear Amyas might grow like them.

How long her sad and anxious thoughts dwelt on that vision of a world of which she knew little more than Amyas had told her she did not know, but she suddenly found that she was shivering, that the oiled linen panels were still not in place at the window, and the damp night air had been flowing unchecked into her bedroom for hours, filled with rheums and fevers and lunatic-making moonlight, and no doubt she would suffer for it in the morning.

However, she felt perfectly well when she woke, and, although it was a dull day with a threat in the clouds of rain to come, she was happily looking forward to another snatched meeting in town during the morning as she went down to the hall for morning prayers with the household, followed by a quickly-eaten breakfast of bread and small ale.

'What did you say you must do this morning?' Master Cressy asked in a more agreeable tone than usual, for today's reading from the Bible had been a particularly threatening portion of the Old

Testament, which he had delivered in a blood-curdling growl guaranteed to put a proper fear of Jehovah's wrath into the servants, and it had left him with a pleasant feeling of sanctity and benevolence.

'I must take Cousin Cecy's chain and brooch back to her,' Kate replied, trying to sound casual about it. 'And I dare say she will wish me to stay to dinner, for she and Aunt Cressy are the only ladies in the house, with all those guests . . .'

'Well, don't be wasting all day with those gadfly, worthless fellows from Court, who want nothing more of you than what lies between your legs, and will give nothing in return for your favours but a bastard, or the pox!' Master Cressy said bluntly. 'Bear in mind that your maidenhead is your only dowry, my girl, for what little money I have won't grow on whatever pittance Rich and his fellows choose to grant me for pension.'

'I'll not forget, Father,' Kate replied equally bluntly. 'I'm as well aware of my situation as you are, and I'm not a fool, for all that I'm female and not an all-knowing male!'

Master Cressy pointed an accusing and admonitory finger at her, and said curtly, 'Watch that saucy tongue, girl, or you'll go nowhere, save to the cellar, on bread and water for a week!'

'Yes, Father. I'm sorry,' Kate said meekly enough, hanging her head in a convincing show of remorse, for she had spent several weeks in the cellar during her life.

'No man wants a froward tongue in a wife! You mark my words, girl! A complaisant, virtuous body, plenty of sons, good cooking, a clean house, a careful purse and a sympathetic ear are what a man wants in a wife, not opinions and pert answers! See to that mis-darned cloth before you set foot outside this house today. I'll not be disgraced by it again without putting my stick to your back!'

Kate obediently sought out the offending table-cloth and inspected the darn. It was not, in fact, cobbled or uneven at all, for it was Dame Marjorie's work, but it was rather large, and Kate sighed over it, for most of the household linen had more darns and patches than any houseproud female would wish to see. It was all so old—older than her father, even, for most of it had come into the house at her grandmother's marriage, and it was simply wearing out.

Rather than attempt to unpick and redo the darn, she found a good piece from a really worn out cloth and made a neat patch, curbing her impatience to do the job properly. As the household had risen, as usual, before seven, it was still not nine o'clock when she had finished, and there was plenty of time to go down to her uncle's house.

A cautious enquiry in the kitchen revealed that Master Cressy had gone to inspect the ploughing of some of the demesne land, so Kate decided to ride down to the town. To her despair, even as she was saddling Jewel, her cousin Cecy appeared in the stableyard on her grey palfrey, which was trapped out in scarlet leather with bells on the reins. She hailed Kate with a lively, 'Good morning, Coz! Such news I bring! Where is Uncle Christopher?'

Kate left the saddle on Jewel's back, the girth unfastened, and went to meet her. 'I was just setting out to come to you,' she said, striving to hide her disappointment. 'I've not returned the chain and brooch you lent me, for I couldn't get away yesterday.'

'We were out with the hawks all day, and most

tedious it was! Not a gallop all day, and the King as
sour as bad wine with the pain in his leg, and so
few herons. I can't think why the heron is so highly
prized, for it tastes quite horrid, but he'd set his
heart on them, and there were no more than a
dozen to be caught. But I must see Uncle
Christopher—where is he?'

'Out in the fields,' Kate said, looking along the
ridge above the house to see if she could make out
where the ploughman was working. 'Did you see
anyone ploughing as you came along?'

'Why, yes! Just down the road, in the big piece
beside the ridge. Is that where he is? I must have
passed him and not noticed. Is your horse saddled?
Well, come with me, then, and hear what I have to
say to him.'

From the arch look which accompanied the
invitation, Kate gathered that the content of the
message in some way concerned herself, but no
amount of questioning would get any more from
Cecy than a teasing 'Ah, would you not like to
know?' and 'Wait and see, Coz—wait and see!'

They found Master Cressy in the piece by the
roadside, sitting on the headland with an ox's foot
in his lap, trying to discover why the beast had
gone lame. The Abbey's oxen were all shod with
the curious divided iron shoes which Kate thought
looked like broken horseshoes. It was a practice
that most of the local husbandmen scorned, mostly
because they could not afford to do as much for
their own beasts.

'What's wrong with Abel?' Kate enquired as the
two girls dismounted, showing a proper interest in
the work of the Grange, and correctly identifying
the ox, which contemplated her with mournful eyes

and chewed the cud in his usual stoic fashion, ignoring the probing fingers investigating his foot.

'Abel?' queried Cecy. 'Do your beasts have names?'

'Yes, of course, and all good Biblical ones,' Kate replied.

'Which is on account of they being religious beasts,' the ploughman put in solemnly. 'And all in pairs, being as oxen always works in the same couple, like. This yin be Abel. That be Cain next him, having a mark on his head.'

Presumably the oxen, despite their proverbial stupidity, at least recognised their own names, for Cain turned his head and stared blankly at Cecy, revealing a C-shaped white patch on his red-brown forehead.

'Oh, the brand of Cain! Of course!' Cecy exclaimed, to demonstrate that she did not spend all her time in church day-dreaming. 'And what are the others called?'

'Moses and Aaron,' the ploughman replied, pointing to the next couple with his stick. 'And Samson and Delilah behind.'

'Delilah?' Cecy exclaimed. 'But surely . . .' She broke off, not wishing to lay herself open to ridicule if she proved to be wrong in thinking that oxen were castrated male animals.

'Tes as good a name as any, and the beasts don't care,' the ploughman shrugged. 'The other team be called . . .'

'Yes, yes—very well!' Master Cressy broke in testily. 'Enough talk of oxen's names—sentimental frippery, and I can't think why anyone bothers with it. They'll be naming all the sheep next!' The ploughman hid a grin behind a horny hand, for he knew very well that every lamb was named at birth.

'Here's the trouble! A flint in the cleft, no more, and not even a cut. You pamper your team, Tom, and make them over-fussy about their comfort!'

He put the beast's foot down, and Abel looked at it in a bemused fashion, as if surprised to find it attached to the end of his front leg, but presently he recollected what it was for, and moved off in response to some persuasive bellows from the ploughman.

'I should poultice it with yarrow when you put him in his stall,' Kate advised the ploughman, and he gave a friendly nod of agreement, for Kate was a recognised local expert on such matters.

Master Cressy got to his feet with his usual grunts and groans about stiff joints and advancing age, although both Kate and Cecy knew he was not yet fifty, and stood watching the plough cut another unwavering furrow in the rich brown soil.

'Best to get the winter wheat in,' he said. 'Though God knows what will come of it—who'll harvest it, or if it will rot in the ear.'

'Lord Dallance will harvest it,' Cecy replied a trifle pertly, 'or someone else, as he says he doesn't want all the demesne land himself.'

'And what do you know about it?' Master Cressy demanded, sounding both angry and curious.

'Only what I heard him tell that pleasant Master Hartwell at breakfast this morning,' Cecy replied. 'So refreshing to find a man from about the Court who actually smiles with his eyes as well as his mouth! I declare, I'm quite taken with him!' She flounced her skirts a little and arched her slender neck in a most becoming fashion, which was quite lost on her uncle.

'Then you'd best be untaken! Your father has more sense than to give you to a plain Master,' he growled. 'And what are you doing about the ploughland, Niece? Not come to see how the work goes, I'll be bound!'

'No, dear Uncle! Good, kind Uncle!' Cecy said beguilingly, linking her arm in his and turning her blue eyes beseechingly up into his face. 'I'm come to beg a favour—a great favour!'

Master Cressy looked sour, but did not pull away, and said only, 'Oh, yes?'

'Will you lend me dear Cousin Kate tomorrow? I have the greatest need of her.'

'She has her duties at home,' came the unpromising reply.

'Oh, I know, but I'm sure she'll make up the time by working all the harder.' Cecy brushed aside the objection. 'You see, dear, dear Uncle—the King goes hunting tomorrow, and he's invited me, so I must go—it's a Royal Command! But my lady mother says she must stay at home, for the King means to eat his supper at our house after the hunt, and she has so much to prepare.'

'Well, of course she has,' Master Cressy admitted willingly enough, for, in his opinion, a housewife's place was in her home, not gadding about hunting in the Forest.

'And I cannot go alone, can I?' Cecy's blue eyes grew enormous at the thought. 'Imagine, all alone among the King's Court! I must have a gentlewoman with me—a servant won't do at all.'

'So you want Kate to go with you.' Master Cressy cut through the careful approach in his usual ruthless fashion. 'You'd do better to stay at home yourself, and help your mother.'

'Ah, but my father doesn't think so!' Cecy informed him coolly. 'There's a prospect of a good husband in it, if I can use my opportunities! He's already shown interest, and a day out with the hunt could be a great help. Besides, the King did invite me—truly he did.'

'You'd best be careful there, lass!' Master Cressy said, not unkindly, for Cecy was a very pretty girl. 'A King's invitations to a female don't always honour her! They're more tending to dishonour, if you take my meaning.'

'It wasn't that kind of invitation!' Cecy assured him. 'He's quite taken up with the thought of his lovely new German wife. No, it was a kindly, fatherly invitation, with a meaning look towards my prospective suitor thrown in. Oh, Uncle Christopher, I do so want to go! You will let Kate come with me, won't you?'

'Well, there's rushlights to be made . . .' Master Cressy began, casting about for duties which might be neglected if he allowed Kate a day off.

'Why, I'll go home with Kate now, and we'll make rushlights all the afternoon!' Cecy exclaimed. 'I'm sure you can give me a bit of dinner, and by working together, we can make twice as many.'

Master Cressy concealed a fondness for his niece under his usual grouchy manner, and was sufficiently placated by her charm to concede that this was a fair offer, and even went so far as to say that the two cousins might go for a canter along the ridge to the Forest edge and back for a breath of air, provided they had the rushes gathered before dinner, ready to start dipping them after the meal.

'There, now! Am I not a good cousin to you, Kate?' Cecy demanded as they reached the top of the ridge and paused to let the horses breathe before riding along it. 'You'll have a whole day in the Forest with your handsome knight, and supper with the King afterwards.'

'Oh, Cecy! You are indeed the best of cousins!' Kate exclaimed. 'But how do you know about Amyas? I thought we'd been so careful!'

'I saw you talking to him when he arrived, and I remembered that last time he came, in the spring, I noticed you looking at one another in that certain way! Make the most of it, Kate, for love lasts such a little while, and then you must think of more certain things, like marriage.'

'And can the two never go together?' Kate asked soberly.

'Not for ordinary mortals, Coz! Only for the great and powerful folk, and not often for them. We must be thankful if we get husbands who are at least kind and likeable. Come, I'll race you to the Forest edge!' She set her grey off without more ado, stealing an unfair advantage in that as in everything else, Kate thought as she laboured after her, and then felt ashamed of the thought, for Cecy had always been very kind to her, in her erratic fashion.

CHAPTER FIVE

KATE'S REGRET about her inability to meet Amyas as she had arranged was tempered by anticipation of a whole day out in the Forest on the morrow, when she would surely be able to contrive to snatch some time alone with him, and would at least spend several hours in his company. For now, Cecy's cheerful presence was a great comfort, both in sweetening her father's temper during dinner, and in lightening the burden of rushlight-making—a task which she detested.

The rushes were easily collected before dinner from a patch of marshy ground where a rill of water emerged from the hillside near the house. After dinner, when the rain arrived, it was not unpleasant to be indoors in the dry, peeling them, but then the pithy interior had to be dipped repeatedly in melted tallow, kept liquid by a candle-flame under the earthenware pot.

Its smell was unpleasant, permeating hair and clothes and hanging about the house for days after, and when, at last, they had dipped and hung a couple of hundred rushes, Kate and Cecy repaired to the wash-house to share a wooden tub of hot water and wash themselves and their hair, with much giggling from Cecy at the antics of a slippery bar of soap.

Kate half-expected that Master Cressy would

withdraw his permission for her day's hunting on some pretext or other, but Cecy's luxuriant hair was still damp by the time supper was ready, so she stayed for the meal, and kept her uncle in a comparatively sunny mood all evening. When she left, he was feeling so benevolent that he even allowed Martin to accompany her with a lantern, and gave the lad permission to stay the night with his widowed mother in the town, provided he was back by his usual rising-time in the morning.

Kate was up even earlier than that, dressed in her frieze riding-gown (another of Cecy's discards), with a short cloak over it against the chill of the autumn morning, and had eaten a crust of bread and pork-dripping and drunk her small ale before anyone else came down to the kitchen. By the time her father rang the bell to summon the household to prayers, she was already mounted on Jewel and riding down the crooked road to Woodham as the morning mists dissolved in the first rays of the sun, rising over the black, brooding mass of the Forest.

The cattle-market was a bustling scene of activity when she arrived, with horses being made ready, and a wagon loaded with provisions for the day. The King's huntsmen were discussing with a keeper which area of the Forest would be best to draw first, while the various hounds milled about their legs, sniffing the canine news of the town and obviously eager for the scents and sounds more natural to their specialised noses and ears.

Cecy came out of the house with her father as Kate dismounted, assisted by a harassed-looking groom, who already had two horses in hand, but added Jewel to them without demur at Sir William's orders.

Kate's uncle bore a strong resemblance to her

father, having the same sturdy build and rather
rugged features, but his habitual expression was
either thoughtful or judicial, rather than disagreeable, and his manner far more pleasant and polished.
He greeted Kate with an approving, 'You're in
good time, Niece! We're to hear Mass first, of
course, so we'd best be getting to church. Your
mare will be safe with Lewis, never fear! Rub her
down and walk her with the others,' he added to
the groom, then took his niece and daughter, one
on either arm, and conducted them to church.

The road by which the King had arrived came
over the causeway across the rivers and marshes
and ran on, past the cattle-market, to the cornmill
stream which ran across the road in a most
inconvenient fashion, cutting the town in two, and
it was necessary for vehicles and animals to splash
through a ford, but a narrow wooden footbridge
was provided for humans, and the Cressys crossed
this, then approached the great west front of the
Abbey church, which faced directly down the road
towards the river.

The west front was a comparatively recent addition
to the church, being only two hundred years old.
Small turrets rose at either side of it, with parapets
rising from them to carry the eye smoothly up to
the broad gable of the central nave, which was
pierced across its whole width by a great window,
with a majestic portal below it, framed between
niches which housed figures of saints. Above the
door, a quatrefoil framed a bust of St Lawrence,
the patron of the parish part of the church, the
canons' high altar being dedicated to the Holy
Cross.

The Cressys joined the flow of people into the
church, nodding discreetly to those they knew, for

many townspeople had come to join their King at worship in their own church. Kate could not resist looking about to see if Amyas was among the courtiers, dressed for hunting, who had already come to stand or sit about in the best places.

She saw Master Crumwell, sitting on the front bench on the men's side, reading a book, and Sir Richard Rich, standing near him and leaning against one of the great drum columns of the Norman building, staring about openly at the banners and altar-cloths in the chapels, the jewelled candlesticks and crosses on their altars, and the fine gilded lamps which hung from the soaring half-round arches, clearly assessing the plunder which he might expect for his office next spring.

Kate, with a sudden sickening realisation, looked at her parish church with the eyes of one who might soon never see it again, for it formed the nave of the Abbey church. It was old—built by the first Henry's queen, they said, and parts of it might be even older, from the days of the last Saxon king. The walls were of stone, a rare material in this part of England, and she knew that the pale gold blocks had been brought across the sea from Normandy, while the side-walls, hidden by plaster painted with figures of saints and patterns of vine-leaves, were of English stone from the counties south of the Thames. The roof was made of oak from the Forest, as was the great beam which spanned the nave and had carried a great stone crucifix which was reputed to work miracles, until Parliament had decreed the removal of such things eighteen months before.

It was a very beautiful church Kate thought, although she had heard people say that it was old-fashioned, cold and dark, the coloured glass in the windows blocking out the light. She wondered what would happen when the Abbey was dissolved. Would the parish be allowed to keep it? Surely the King would not deprive them of it when it had been their parish church for centuries, since long before the second Henry founded the Abbey? Presumably the rest would have to go, as most of the buildings of the abbeys and priories already dissolved had gone - pulled down for the precious stone, timber and lead which they contained, or converted to other uses. There would be enough stone in Woodham Abbey to rebuild the whole town.

She looked eastwards. Behind the parish altar, a low wall shut off the nave from the canons' part of the church, but it did not hide the higher levels of the building. First, there was a crossing with the bell-tower—eight bells, tuneable and familiar, for they signalled the events in the life of the town. One rang to rouse labourers and apprentices in the mornings, another signalled the Elevation of the Host during Mass, a third tolled for the passing of a soul, a fourth rang to signal the end of the day's work, and all eight rang to call the faithful to church, as they were doing now, or to celebrate a wedding, or the coming of the King, the birth of a prince, the King's wedding . . .

While she was looking and thinking, her uncle and cousin had moved to the front benches and taken their usual places, for Sir William was a churchwarden. Kate hastened to join Cecy, and then saw her uncle leave his place again with the other warden, and go to conduct the King into church with proper ceremony.

As she waited, she again looked discreetly about to see if she could catch sight of Amyas, and presently saw Master Hartwell, alert and spry, standing near Sir Richard Rich and looking in her direction. He nodded and smiled in a friendly fashion as he caught her eye, and, after a moment's hesitation, she gave a slight inclination of her head in acknowledgment. After all, he had been far more helpful and pleasant than she might have expected, so it would be unfair to give him the cut direct . . .

Then, at last, she saw Amyas, who was only a few feet from Master Hartwell, and she forgot all about the latter in his dull russet and green as she admired Amyas, glorious in an amber-coloured waistcoat and doublet with green netherstocks to match the velvet cap which hung negligently from one elegantly beringed hand, its curling plume brushing his shapely leg. He turned his head and looked at Kate, smiled and bowed a fraction, his free hand going briefly to his heart, and an odd sunbeam, penetrating the coloured glass of a window behind him through a broken quarry, turned his golden hair to a nimbus.

She caught her breath, feeling her colour rise, and then, before she could do more than give a little shuddering gasp, the bells stopped, a couple of trumpets blared outside the west door, and the King entered, preceded by the wardens with their staves of office, and followed by his close attendants. At the same moment, the two doors in the low wall behind the altar opened, and the Abbot entered through one, robed in mitre and cope, and the Bishop of Winchester, also robed, through the other.

It was said that the second Henry, who brought the Austin canons to Woodham, expected Mass to be said as quickly as possible, and became angry if it lasted above a quarter-hour. The eigth Henry was less impatient, but he loved his hunting, and the Abbot was tactful enough to keep the service to the minimum, so that the congregation followed their Sovereign from church in a little over the half-hour, only the King having taken the bread.

Amyas found his way to Kate's side as she was going out of the door, and said quickly, 'I waited all morning, but you didn't come. Would your father not let you out?'

'No. My cousin came to see us, to beg my company for today, and Father made me stay at home yesterday to do today's chores,' she replied. 'I'm sorry—I couldn't let you know.'

Amyas shrugged, as if it was of no moment. 'You're coming on the hunt? Are you sure you want to? I doubt you'll enjoy it much!'

Kate turned to look at him in surprise, but he had already slipped away, and was too far off to hear if she replied.

The lively scene in the cattle-market had taken on an air of frenzy with the return of the prospective hunters from church. Gentlemen were shouting for their horses, the hounds were baying, and one of the lymers had got loose and was fighting a town dog of no pedigree, but inordinate determination and presumption, which appeared to be getting the better of the fray. A well-meaning groom who aimed a bucket of water at them missed, and dampened the legs and feet of two very high-born gentlemen, then dropped his bucket in his embarrassment. It rolled a few yards, and tripped a third, even more highly born, gentleman, who sat down abruptly in a puddle left by an incontinent horse. The resulting language was amazingly coarse, and the belligerent town dog was sufficiently surprised by it to let go of the lymer's throat for a moment, and Master Hartwell, moving with remarkable speed and economy, took the opportunity to empty a bucket neatly over both combatants, without even wetting his own feet.

The King had gone to church fasting, and must needs take a light breakfast of most of a loaf of new bread, with plenty of fresh butter and a few rounds of cold beef, but he was soon ready to leave for the Forest, and came out of his house to mount the solidly built seventeen-hand horse which his height and weight required, happy in the knowledge that another dozen such mounts would await his convenience at various places about the Forest. Because of his ulcerated leg and considerable girth, he had to use a stout pair of steps to mount, but, once in the saddle, he was still as fine a horseman as he had ever been, and he set off at a good rate, his little pursed mouth smiling in the midst of his fleshy jowls, and his small, deep-set eyes quite sparkling with anticipation of a day at his favourite occupation.

The townsfolk had turned out to cheer him as he went by, the rest of the cavalcade, having mounted and followed pellmell, clattering behind him. Kate rode in the midst of them with Cecy, and thought what a grand sight they must all look, with their rich clothes and jewels shining in the sun, the fine horses and the huntsmen, with the dogs running on either side.

There were, in fact, only twenty riders to follow the King, for he was enjoying a small, private visit, and several of those who had come from London with him were here for scholarly discussion with Lord Robert, not sport in the fields and Forest. Kate noted that Master Crumwell was absent, and the Bishop, the elderly gentleman who had partnered her at supper, and the Archbishop, but she heard someone say that the latter had gone back to London about some ecclesiastical business. Sir Richard Rich was present, as close to the King's elbow as he could get, and Master Hartwell, looking about him with every appearance of interest and enjoyment, his lips pursed in a quiet, tuneful whistle and his cap on the back of his head, riding only a few paces behind her. She was surprised that he and his master were not taking the opportunity to inspect the Abbey's treasures, which would so soon be passing under their aegis.

Presently Cecy fell into conversation with a serious-looking gentleman, who was not really old, despite a scattering of grey hairs in his beard, but not as young as Kate would have wished, for she deduced from Cecy's demure manner and modest, quiet voice that this was her cousin's prospective husband. She slowed the pace of her horse a trifle and dropped a little behind, gauging her place so that she did not leave Cecy unchaperoned, yet was not near enough to listen to the conversation.

This move brought her nearer to four of the huntsmen who were riding behind, and she heard that three of them were discussing the prospects for the day's hunt with a certain professional gloom.

'John Smith's gone ahead with the lymers to see if they can sniff out a red hind,' the third, more optimistic, fellow said. 'He's sure there's half a dozen good fat beauties near Fairmaid Bottom, and he'll send them up this way when he finds them.'

'If he finds them!' one of the others corrected. 'It's a fine thing when the King's hunt is reduced to a few fallow does, or even roe deer! You can't beat a red deer in its grease for good venison. Fallow's sweet enough, though inferior to red, and roe isn't even worth the cooking.'

'Roe ain't even venison,' put in the fourth man, who had not spoken before. 'Red and fallow's venison, and wild boar, but not roe.'

'Wild boar? But that's pig-meat, not venison!' protested the optimist.

'Boar's venison,' repeated the taciturn man. 'Ask Master Hartwell. He knows Forest Law, and he'll tell you.'

Master Hartwell was appealed to at once, and he drew his black horse up level with the huntsmen quite willingly, and listened to the arguments pro and con boar-meat with smiling patience, but Kate kept her back turned to the discussion, and did not see that as much of his attention was on her as on the huntsmen.

'Is the boar a forest animal?' he asked when all the evidence had been presented. 'Is it hunted for food?'

'Why, yes to both,' the huntsmen agreed readily.

'Then it's venison!' Master Hartwell declared. 'But roe deer is not, for it's not a forest animal, but lives in parks and on grassland. Does that settle your argument?'

The huntsmen agreed that, if that was the Law, it did, but with an obvious but unspoken rider that, if that was the Law, the Law was very odd! The taciturn man adopted an irritating air of 'I told you so', and then they fell to arguing about the last known sighting of a boar in the Forest.

Master Hartwell edged his mount gently forward to Kate's side, and bade her 'Good morning', to which she replied with no more than a nod, thinking that she did not wish to associate with one of Sir Richard's henchmen, however pleasant he might appear to be on the surface, for she was still sure that he could not really be a good man if he worked for the Court of Augmentations.

'Do you enjoy hunting?' he asked sociably.

'Yes and no.'

'That's an ambivalent answer!' he exclaimed, looking at her with interest.

'I enjoy riding through the Forest on a crisp autumn day, and the excitement of the chase, but I don't like the killing when the hart or hind is brought down,' Kate replied unwillingly, not wishing to be drawn into a friendly conversation with him.

'But you enjoy eating the venison, no doubt?'

'I prefer pork or beef,' she replied shortly.

She sighed a little, wishing that Amyas would contrive to come and ride with her, and she looked ahead, to where the King was already riding up the steep rise to the edge of the trees, and saw Amyas, in his amber velvet, keeping close behind the leaders.

Master Hartwell continued to ride at her side, making an occasional attempt to draw her into conversation, but receiving only brief answers, not much short of actual rudeness, until the whole company was well into the Forest, and the huntsman with the lymers appeared, hard on the heels of a fine hart in her grease, which led them a grand chase through the denser and wilder parts of the woodland, effectively ending all conversation and splitting up the party into smaller groups. The keener hunters, led by the King, followed hard on their prey, and the less enthusiastic, which included Kate, at a slower pace, just keeping in touch with the baying sight-hounds and the cries of the close followers.

In the excitement, Kate succeeded in losing Master Hartwell but had the good fortune to come upon Amyas, who had taken a tumble through failing to notice a low branch.

'Are you hurt?' she asked anxiously, coming to a halt beside him as he sat on the leaf-strewn ground in a small clearing. The sun, filtering through the branches, illuminated his face as he looked up at her, and highlighted the puffiness about his eyes and chin and the scowl which made him look quite ugly, and Kate thought with misgiving that he looked positively unhealthy.

'Not in the least,' he replied, turning away to look in the direction which his horse had taken. 'I'm just waiting for my groom to bring my mount back, that's all.'

'I'm sorry about yesterday . . .' she faltered, thinking that he seemed not entirely pleased to see her, for he had not even bothered to get to his feet.

'That's of no consequence! I guessed your father wouldn't let you come, so I found other things to do. Mistress Cecy told me what happened when she returned in the evening.'

'I thought perhaps you were angry . . .' Kate began again, uncertainly, 'I mean—you haven't so much as spoken to me all morning, apart from a few words coming out of church.'

'It's difficult,' he replied, his eyes on the ground between his bent-up knees, and his hands industriously picking up beechmast and tossing it about. 'I don't wish to be seen with you when any of my father's friends might notice, for they'll run back to him with tales, and I'd be in great trouble.'

'Oh,' Kate said flatly, feeling puzzled and disappointed. 'Does he not know about me, then?'

'Lord, no!' He looked up at her for a moment, then returned his gaze to the beechmast, his fingers plucking it up and throwing it down at a great rate.

'I'll tell him when the time's right, but he mustn't find out prematurely, so be patient, sweetheart! Stolen kisses are sweeter, they say.'

'They may be—for men!' Kate replied a little more brusquely than she intended, and rode away, biting her lip and blinking away tears of anger and disappointment. She met the groom returning with Amyas's horse, but he did not catch her up, and she next saw him an hour or so later, when the hunting-party gathered in a pleasant glade to meet the cart with the hampers of food.

The morning's exercise had given everyone a good appetite, and, once the cloths had been spread on the ground and the cold meats, pies and crusty bread unpacked, everyone waited with unconcealed eagerness for the King to be served, so that they could begin themselves.

King Henry was seated on a massive log, his thick but still shapely legs planted well apart to draw the skirts of his doublet out in a good lap to support a napkin, on which he had enough food to keep a poor man for several days, and a page stood at his elbow with flagon and goblet to pour his wine as soon as he was ready for it.

Everyone else stood about or sat on the ground, the greedy close to the food, the more abstemious leaning against convenient tree-trunks. The one other fallen log was left, out of courtesy, for the two ladies, who had no need to scramble for their food with the men, as Cecy's matrimonial prospect waited upon her, and a couple of the younger men brought Kate a choice of meat, cheese, a pie and bread on a silver plate, and butter on a cabbage-leaf.

She could not help but notice despondently that Amyas came nowhere near her, but stood in conversation with a couple of the King's closer friends on the far side of the glade, and it was Master Hartwell who brought her a cup of wine.

'Would you like this?' he asked, looking dubiously down into it. 'It's good Rhenish, I think, but perhaps you'd prefer ale?'

'Wine will do very well, thank you,' she replied sharply, holding out her hand to take it. She was a little piqued by his question, which sounded to her as if he thought she was unused to drinking wine.

He surrendered the cup with a little bow, and said, 'May I bring you anything else?'

'No, thank you.'

Although she concentrated on her food, she was aware that he had not moved away but was still standing a little to her right, and she glanced up to see if he was watching her, but he was apparently looking at the unoccupied part of the log beside her.

'Is something amiss?' she asked pointedly.

'No—I was just wondering if that curious-looking thing there is animal or vegetable,' he replied, pointing to a smooth white blob peeping out from under the log.

'It's a small puffball,' Kate replied, hardly bothering to look at it, although she would have taken it home with her if he had not shown an interest in it.

'Small!' he said. 'I'd not care to meet a large one, then. Presumably it's vegetable?'

'Yes, of course. It's of the same kind as mushrooms and toadstools.'

'It looks rather poisonous and unhealthy.'

'Not at all! It's considered very good eating, sliced and fried. The poor people gather them when they're full-grown. That's little more than a baby yet!' She spoke crisply and unencouragingly, but Master Hartwell went down on one knee to look more closely, putting a hand on the log as he did so, and she felt that he was uncomfortably close to her, so she said, 'Your lord and master appears to be looking for you!' for she could see Sir Richard on the other side of the glade, leaning against a silver birch and looking about him in his usual smug and insufferable manner.

'What, the King?' Master Hartwell said, looking towards his Sovereign, who was laughing heartily at a joke which one of the huntsmen had just told him.

'No. Sir Richard Rich.' Kate's dislike for the man was only too apparent in her voice.

'He's not my lord and master!' Master Hartwell returned quietly, looking up into her face and frowning. 'We both serve in the same part of the King's administration, that's all. If I may advise you, Mistress Cressy, it's not wise to make your distaste for him too obvious. He never forgets a slight.'

Kate digested that, recalling that Sir Richard had a considerable slight to hold against her, then said, 'I—I think I should like some more wine,' a trifle unsteadily. He stood up, made her a bow as he took her cup, and went away purposefully towards the cart, where a sutler was drawing wine from the cask as it was required.

'What do you think of my suitor?' Cecy asked in a hushed voice, for the serious gentleman had just gone off on a similar errand.

'He seems very courtly,' Kate replied cautiously.

'He's most beautifully well-mannered, but a little solemn,' Cecy said, sounding quite calm and unconcerned. 'He's a baron, and delightfully rich!'

'Do you like him?' Kate asked doubtfully. 'Is he not a little—er—well, older than you?'

'Oh, quite old, but not decrepit, for he's not yet forty—well, not quite . . .' Cecy assured her. 'His first wife died very young, in childbed, and his second of the sweating-sickness, and both her children with her, so we shall be starting afresh, with no older children to take precedence over mine.'

'But do you like him?' Kate repeated, for this, to her, was the most important question.

'I don't find him irritating or unpleasant, and his breath is reasonably sweet,' Cecy replied with the seriousness which Kate's concern merited. 'As for anything more—that comes later, when we've had a few children and grown accustomed to one another.'

Kate thought to herself that Cecy's words might be true for most women, but she herself would not willingly be satisfied with mere absence of dislike for a man in order to marry him. Once one had known what it was like to be in love, how could one ever settle for anything less? No, she could never marry a man because he was rich, or suitable, or for any of Cecy's negative reasons!

'Your wine, my lady!' Master Hartwell said, breaking into her thoughts and presenting her cup on bended knee, as if she were royalty. With an odd feeling of *déjà vu* she noted that the light on his face showed how well moulded were its bones, and the skin fitting closely over them was clear and lightly tanned.

'Oh, get up, do!' she exclaimed in horror, looking round to see if anyone had noticed, particularly Amyas.

He offered the cup, and she took it impatiently, realising that he would not get up until she had accepted it. She jerked, and a little wine spilled on his knee.

'That's cold!' he exclaimed.

'Well, I'm sorry, but you shouldn't . . .' Kate began, still looking to see if anyone was watching, but she failed to finish the sentence, for her eyes fell on a figure, half-concealed by a thick bush, a few yards directly behind Master Hartwell.

He was a roughly-clad man, looking like a poor labourer, but it was what he was holding which caught Kate's eye and made her gasp. It was a long-bow, and it was bent, nocked and aimed, ready to loose!

CHAPTER SIX

EVEN as her eyes followed the line of the archer's aim and came to rest on the oblivious figure of the King, Master Hartwell twisted round to see what had caught Kate's attention sufficiently to stop her in mid-sentence. He rose to his feet in one lithe movement, turning as he did so and shifting his weight to the balls of his feet. Then everything happened so quickly that, afterwards, she could only remember a blur of movement and her own voice crying out, and she had to reconstruct what actually occurred by deduction from the results. As she cried out, the King looked up, and must have seen death about to wing its way to him, but Master Hartwell moved even before the archer loosed, and his outflung left hand took the arrow clean through the palm as he flung himself into its path. He fell to the ground at the end of his drive, twisted round on to his side by the force of the blow. The King stood up and shouted, a great bellow of fury, and everyone else stood frozen into shocked stillness.

One person moved. The archer turned and ran, but it was a second or two before anyone else realised what they had seen, and then most of the men present rushed after him. One of the huntsmen uncoupled a dozen hounds, but, as they did not know what they were to chase, they simply milled about and got in the way, tripping up some of the pursuers. The confusion would, in other circumstances, have been laughable and it resulted in only a dozen of the more agile courtiers actually leaving the glade to go after the would-be assassin. The rest picked themselves up, or slowed to a halt as they realised that they were too far behind, and turned their attention to the King, who was already surrounded by a few who had made no move after the archer.

Kate rose to her feet, dropping her cup and the food she had not yet eaten, and ran across to Master Hartwell as he sat up and gazed with surprised interest at the feathered shaft transfixing his hand.

'I didn't think I'd manage it!' he said calmly as Kate dropped on her knees beside him. 'I've seen a man catch an arrow in mid-air at Bartholomew Fair, but I thought it was a trick. Be careful—you'll be getting blood on your gown!'

'Let me look,' commanded a deep voice behind Kate, and a heavy figure descended laboriously beside her as the King got down on the knee of his good leg and took the injured hand in his massive paw with surprising gentleness.

'That was very well done!' he commented. 'I've seen jugglers catch even a cross-bow bolt, but after years of pracice. You must be remarkably fast on your feet, and in your wits, Master Hartwell! Do you wrestle at all?'

Master Hartwell made no reply, for he had turned very pale and his eyes had closed as he leaned rather heavily against Kate.

'I think he's fainted, Sire,' she said quietly.

'Good,' the King replied, giving her a searching look. 'Are you about to do the same? You're sure?' as Kate shook her head. Then let's get this thing out before he comes to his senses! Denny—come here and hold his wrist steady!'

Sir Anthony Denny, the King's close friend, knelt beside his monarch and laid the injured hand across his thigh, holding it by the wrist and fingers, with the projecting arrow standing upright. The King took the shaft in both hands and broke off the feathered end as easily as snapping a twig, then gripped the head and pulled the remainder through with a quick tug. There was a rush of blood from the wound, which the King stanched with a handful of clean linen napkins held out by a quick-witted servant.

'What now?' he asked, looking about him, and his eye came to rest on Kate.

'It looks clean,' she replied, thinking how lucky it was that the injured man had taken off his gloves to eat, and forgetting that she was addressing the King. 'It needs cobwebs to stop the bleeding, and a compress to help it heal.'

'Cobwebs!' commanded the King, making two or three attempts to get up, and succeeding only with the help of two sturdy grooms. 'Do you know what you're about, Mistress?' gazing sternly down at Kate, arms akimbo and feet planted well apart in his most typical posture.

'Yes, Sire,' she replied calmly, for she had some experience of dealing with injuries, and a good knowledge of ordinary remedies. 'If people will collect cobwebs, as clear of flies and dirt as possible . . .'

'How?' asked a plaintive voice in the background.

'With forked twigs,' she replied. 'And I'll need leaves of comfrey, self-heal, woundwort, or Herb Benet.' She described the plant, and indeed pointed out a fine clump of comfrey growing close by.

For a time there was a scurrying of courtiers and servants hastening about in search of cobwebs, and the sensible servant who had brought the napkins helped Kate to lay Master Hartwell down comfortably, his head on a bundled cloak, and then fetched more napkins, for the others were already soaked with blood.

'I'll need long strips of linen for bandages, and something to macerate the herbs in, and something to use as a pestle,' she said, looking about her.

'There's another cloth not been used,' the servant replied, 'and a good big goblet. A dagger-handle will pound well, and you'll need wine to moisten the leaves.'

He hastened away again, and returned with the goblet, which was of solid gold, heavily jewelled on the outside, and of a goodly capacity. If its rightful owner objected, he said nothing, although he was still standing near by, watching the proceedings closely as Kate tore a strip off one of the napkins and tied it about Master Hartwell's wrist, twisting a stick through to tighten it and stop the bleeding. Then she carefully felt the bones of the hand, to see if they were much displaced. The shaft seemed to have passed between the bones leading to the middle and the index fingers, where the gap was wide enough to let it through, pushing them aside, but they appeared to have returned to their normal places once the arrow had been removed.

When the bleeding had slowed and almost stopped, she wiped the wound clean, and, as quantities of cobwebs began to arrive, she laid them thickly across the wound, front and back, using them to draw the edges of the torn flesh together, and then spreading more on top until the whole palm and the back of the hand were covered with a

grey layer. Then she released the tourniquet
cautiously, but no more blood appeared.

'My old nurse used to do that when I cut myself,'
the King commented. 'What now?'

'I need the leaves next,' Kate replied absently,
her attention on what she was doing, and completely
forgetting the 'Sire' which should have accompanied
the words. A sharp voice supplied it, to remind her,
but was drowned in a bellowing 'Leaves! Leaves!
No more cobwebs . . . Leaves!' from the King.

Leaves began to arrive swiftly and Kate sorted
them carefully, for few were of the right varieties,
soon she had a large pile of the wrong ones, and a
small pile of comfrey, woundwort and Herb Benet,
and one spray of self-heal.

Presently she looked at the pile of useful leaves,
assessing whether she had enough, and, as she did
so, a gloved hand laid a bunch of leaves amid the
comfrey. She noted unconsciously that there was a
heavy engraved ring on one finger, worn over the
glove, bearing a crest which looked like a greyhound's head, but her conscious attention was on
the leaves.

'That's deadly nightshade!' she exclaimed. 'And
hemlock! Gracious Heavens! Would you kill the
man?' She picked the poisonous leaves out and
threw them as far away from her as possible, then
looked up to see who had brought them, but half a
dozen men were crowding round and bending to lay
their offerings before her, and she could not tell
who was responsible.

'That will be enough, thank you,' she said, and
set to work to tear up the good leaves and put them
in the goblet, where she mashed and pounded them,
adding wine to moisten the mixture, until she had a
thick green paste to make her compress.

At some point, while all this was going on, Master Hartwell had regained his senses and now tried to sit up, but Kate pushed him down and bade him lie still rather more firmly than she intended, being anxious that he should not do anything to start his wound bleeding again before she had it dressed and bandaged.

'Yes, my lady!' he murmured, smiling faintly and subsiding against his makeshift pillow. 'That feels good!' he commented as she spread the cool mush of leaves and wine over the wound in his palm and covered it with a pad of linen.

'Now, do you hold that in place while I see to the back of the hand,' Kate instructed the sensible servant, who was still helping her, and she gave her attention to completing the treatment, while Master Hartwell lay still and quiet, watching with his usual sharp-eyed interest, despite his white face and bitten lips.

Someone had ripped the clean linen cloth into strips, and Kate used them to bandage the hand once she had both compresses in place. She left the greater part of the fingers and thumb free, and, after tying the last knot, sat back on her heels and looked at them. 'Can you wriggle your fingers at all?' she enquired dubiously.

It was only then that she had time to think of the man attached to the injured hand, for she had been too much concerned before with stopping him from bleeding to death, and doing her best to help the wound to heal well. Now she looked at his face and noted the marks of pain on it with something between pity and admiration, recollecting that he had not made one sound of complaint throughout.

He moved his ring and little finger to and fro, then, very cautiously, managed a slight movement of the index and middle ones, followed by a slightly freer waggle of the thumb. 'They still seemed to be joined on,' he said encouragingly.

'Does it hurt very much to move them?' Kate asked, looking at at his face.

An interesting series of expressions succeeded one another as he said, 'Not much . . . Well . . . A little . . . I suppose it will heal . . . eventually?'

'I don't doubt that it hurts a great deal,' Kate said matter-of-factly, 'but you wouldn't be able to move your fingers if there was very much damage to whatever makes the muscles work. I'm more concerned about the bleeding, but that seems to have been stanched by the cobwebs.'

'Have you finished, mistress?' asked the King, peering over Kate's bent head at the bandaged hand.

'There's one more thing,' she replied, then hesitated, for she was unsure of the present climate of opinion concerning the final part of her treatment, but her conscience insisted that nothing must be omitted, for the magic of the spiders' webs and the healing herbs might not work without the charm, so she took the bandaged hand gently between both her own, closed her eyes, and recited:

> *When Christ came to be baptised*
> *And entered Jordan's flood,*
> *The river stood.*
> *So may thy blood,*
> *Matthew Hartwell,*
> *In the Name of the Father, the Son, and*
> *   the Holy Ghost,*
> *Amen.*

'Superstition!' hissed a voice somewhere behind

her, but the King uttered a firm 'Amen!' and crossed himself, and almost everyone else took their cue from him and followed suit. Master Hartwell's 'Amen' was a little belated, as if he was unsure whether or not he was supposed to join in.

After that, everyone lost interest in Master Hartwell and Kate and took to discussing whether the hunt should continue; the prudent considering that the King should not venture his person about the Forest until the potential assassin had been caught, and the more dashing and impatient eager to go on with the day's sport, claiming that enough gentlemen and huntsmen had gone after the archer to ensure his capture, and there could be nothing more to fear. The King resumed his seat on the log and continued to eat bread and cheese, but, between mouthfuls, he told one of the remaining huntsmen to sound his horn a few times to recall the searchers. Meanwhile, several other people recovered their appetites, and finished their meal.

Kate allowed Master Hartwell to sit up, and the sensible servant piled a couple of hampers for him to lean against and asked her if the poor gentleman might be permitted to drink a little wine.

'The poor gentleman could manage another well-buttered crust and a slice of beef, too!' Master Hartwell addded on his own behalf.

'A little of each, then,' Kate replied, contemplating the ruin of her one good riding-dress, which now had several rusty stains and mildewed-looking green streaks on its skirts.

'Will you do me a great favour?' Master Hartwell asked cautiously, balancing his buttered crust (which was nearer half a small loaf) on his bent knee while he sipped his wine.

What is it?' Kate asked, looking up to find those bright eyes gazing searchingly at her face.

'Let me give you a new gown. You've ruined that one in helping me, and it's the least I can do.'

Before Kate could reply, the King licked his fingers one by one, and between digits, announced loudly, 'While we wait for the others . . . there are some matters . . . in need of our attention . . . which are best dealt with at once!' He belched gently, and patted his midriff. 'Master Hartwell, it has not escaped our notice that the arrow which you caught so neatly was intended for another target! What reward do you seek for saving us from injury!'

Kate, rising and stepping back from the centre of attention and fading into the backround, noted with detached interest that the King spoke only of injury, not having his life saved, which would probably rate a higher level of reward, and she wondered what Master Hartwell would request.

He did not answer at once, but put down his wine cup, clutched his crust with his good hand, and looked consideringly at the King.

'Well?' Henry prompted. 'What shall it be? A duke's daughter? A barony? A place in our household?'

'A house, Sire?' Master Hartwell replied, a shade of a question in his voice.

'A house, eh! Which one, then? Nonsuch? Hampton Court? Not Whitehall, I trust!'

Master Hartwell smiled. 'Something more modest, Sire! A piece of monastic property, which I believe may pass to the Court of Augmentations before long. A smallish house, and perhaps a little land to go with it?'

'Nothing more?' The King seemed surprised.

'Well, so be it then! Russell, will you make a note of Master Hartwell's modest request?' This to the Comptroller of his Household. 'And Rich, too! Matt Hartwell is to have the house and land of his choice as soon as they become available.'

Sir John Russell produced a tablet and wrote the instruction down without comment, but Sir Richard Rich said, 'If it please Your Grace—how much land, and at what rent?'

'How much land is the King's life worth?' Henry asked coldly, his eyes becoming as dark and hard as sloes. 'The man is moderate in his asking, and will take no more than he considers his due.' The little pursed mouth snapped shut.

'Er . . . yes . . . But the rental . . .' Sir Richard stammered, risking a further set-down.

Henry considered for a moment, and then his face lightened, and he said, 'One arrow, to be delivered to us, our heirs and successors, on every seventh anniversary of this day, and nothing more!' A number of eyebrows were raised and glances exchanged—the King was not customarily so generous with the monastic lands. 'And, furthermore,' Henry suddenly added in a remarkably sharp and shrewd tone, 'there will be no gifts, or bribes, or sweeteners, or need to persuade anyone of anything. The surrender of the particular property by its present owners will be followed immediately, within twenty-four hours, by the gift receiving our assent under the Privy Seal, and the deeds will be placed in Master Hartwell's hands on that same day. You understand me?'

Judging by the sickly look on his face as he bowed assent, Sir Richard understood only too well, and was not pleased to find how well acquainted the King was with the usual procedure of the Court

of Augmentations. Kate thought, with a little smile
to herself, that he looked as if he had bitten a
comfit and found it filled with wormwood.

Unfortunately, in turning away from the King,
Sir Richard caught sight of the smile, and shot Kate
a look of extreme venom. Master Hartwell,
addressing himself once more to his bread and
meat, saw the look, and sighed, thinking that he
would have to warn Kate to be careful, but that
must wait until he felt better. At the moment, he
wanted nothing more than to retire to bed and
sleep for a week or so.

'And you, mistress!' the King said suddenly,
turning his attention to Kate. 'Mistress—er . . .?'

'Cressy,' Kate's uncle hastily supplied, stepping
forward from the throng far enough to impart the
information in a discreet tone, for Henry disliked
having to admit that he did not know the name of
someone towards whom he felt some kindness. 'My
brother's daughter, Sire.'

'Mistress Cressy—of course,' the King went on
smoothly, as if he had known all the time, 'You are
skilled in the healing arts?'

'A little, Sire,' Kate replied modestly, wondering
if she should curtsy, but finding herself too paralysed
by being addressed by the King to do so. 'The usual
household cuts and scalds and fevers, and injuries
about the Grange.'

'My brother is bailey of the Abbey Grange,' Sir
William supplied quietly. 'My niece keeps house for
him, his wife being long dead. She has a goodly
reputation as a wise-woman, despite her youth.'

'A wise-woman!' Sir Richard put in pointedly in a
acid tone, as if to draw attention to the fact that the
term was often a euphemism for a witch.

'In the sense that she has a sound knowledge of

herbal compounds and simples, and the goodwill to use them in the service of anyone in need,' Sir William countered in an unhurried but decisive fashion.

'Yes,' the King said flatly. 'As we have seen, Our purse, Russell!'

Sir John stepped forward with a purse, but whether it was in fact the King's or his own was not clear to Kate. The King dipped into it, took out some coins, and sent Russell to her with them.

'I can't!' she said in an agitated whisper. 'I may not take money for using my gift!'

'What is she saying?' asked the King, who had excellent hearing.

'She says, may it please Your Grace, that she may not take money for using her gift,' Sir John said in a neutral voice. He had reached and retained his present position by keeping his thoughts to himself, and this had, over the years, made his voice singularly lacking in expression.

'I know,' said the King without hesitation or change in his benevolent tone. 'It is to buy a new gown, in place of the one she has spoiled!'

Kate recollected herself and her manners and managed a proper little speech of thanks to both the King and Sir John, adding a creditable curtsy, and tucked the four gold angels into her glove, where they cut painfully into her fingers, but were safe from possible loss.

'Master Hartwell had best be taken home to rest,' the King went on, after smiling agreeably upon Kate. 'Take him in the cart, and someone have a care to his horse.'

The sensible servant recruited two of his fellows to help lift Master Hartwell into the cart, where he was made comfortable amid the hampers, which had been hastily packed with the remains of the meal. He kept a firm hold on his bread and meat all the while, as if determined not to be deprived of his dinner, although Kate noticed that he hardly did more than nibble at it. She suspected that he had asked for it in an attempt at *sang froid*, and probably really felt too sick to eat it. His horse was tied to the back of the cart.

While this was going on, the erstwhile pursuers of the archer reappeared in twos and threes, disconsolate and winded, having chased about for some time without so much as sighting their quarry. The dog-keepers were at odds with each other, the keeper of the lymers blaming the keeper of the brachets for spoiling the scent, and the keeper of the sight-hounds snarling at both for balking his greyhounds. The gentlemen were equally out of temper, for the whole pursuit had been badly bungled through everyone getting in the way of everyone else, or distracting attention from the archer's course by crashing about in the undergrowth, making far too much noise. The one thing that they all agreed on was that there would be no deer within miles now, after all the disturbance and shouting, so there was no point in continuing the hunt.

While they were all arguing, and the King was listening to the huntsmen's more reasoned report, Kate took the opportunity to tell Cecy that she meant to go back with the cart.

'But you are supposed to be attending me!' Cecy protested automatically, although not with any great vehemence, for she had been much impressed by the way Kate had taken charge in the emergency. 'Still, I suppose it will be in order, as Father is here, and he can make your excuses if the King misses you. Will you be all right, though?'

'There are three servants,' Kate pointed out, 'and I doubt if the assassin is within four miles of here by now! I should go with my patient, you know, for the bleeding may start again if they're not careful with him, and he's already lost so much blood . . . It's a nasty wound.'

Cecy winced at the mention of blood, and said hastily, 'Well, yes—of course—and you'll want to wash all that . . . your hands, I mean.' She looked with distaste at Kate's gown and hands, for, although she had scrubbed at both with a napkin, the stains were very apparent.

Kate recovered her horse, which she had left tied to a bush, and a gorgeous young gentleman in crimson satin gave her a hand to mount, no doubt thinking her worth the trouble now that the King had taken notice of her. She looked about for Amyas, who had been one of the pursuers brought down by the hounds, but he continued to stay well away from her and did not so much as glance in her direction, so she followed the cart with a hollow feeling of disappointment.

Master Hartwell seemed unaware of her presence until the cart had lurched and jolted itself over the rough ground and reached the road, which was kept in reasonably good repair. He had not eaten any more of his bread, but it had nevertheless appeared to occupy his concentrated attention in a manner which made Kate suspect that the numbness of the first shock had worn off, and his wound was now extremely painful. As the cart began to bowl along on the smoother road, however, he looked up and saw her riding beside the cart.

'I've not thanked you for your skilled attention, Mistress Cressy,' he said.

'I'm surprised that nobody else seemed to know

what to do,' she replied evasively. 'Several of the gentlemen there must have seen service on the battlefield, I believe, yet not one seemed to have the faintest idea how to deal with a wound!'

'Oh, they'd all be too important to bother with such matters,' Master Hartwell assured her. 'Officers are much too occupied with commanding to bother with minor matters like soldiers bleeding to death. I suppose you've grown used to dealing with injuries about the farm and house? And fevers, too, I gather. You seem to know a great deal about herbs and so on.'

'We once had a dog which lost a leg, torn off in a trap.' Kate wondered even as she spoke why she was telling him this, for she could not recollect ever having told anyone about it before. 'He died because none of us in the house knew what to do. After that, I went to an old wise-woman in the town and asked her to teach me her lore.'

'And she did?'

'At a price.' She did not add that the price had been her hair, which the woman had cut off with a stone knife, leaving short jagged ends which had taken an age to grow back to a presentable length. She suspected that the wise-woman, who had recently died, was also a witch, and wanted the hair for some ancient and arcane purpose. 'Father Humphrey, the Infirmarian, has taught me a great deal as well,' she added.

There was silence for a while, broken only by the creaking of the cart, the clop of horses' hooves, the rumbling of wheels, and the intermittent whistling of one of the servants, who was wandering along the edge of the road, picking the occasional blackberry from the hedgerow. Then Master Hartwell said hesitantly, 'What—er—what do you think will happen to my hand?'

'I expect it will be stiff, and maybe ache in bad weather, but you should be able to use your fingers as well as ever, if you persevere in exercising them.' She sounded more confident than she felt, for she wondered if anything had been smeared on the head of the arrow to make doubly sure of its purpose.

'Thank you.' Master Hartwell lapsed into silence again, nursing his bandaged hand in the crook of his other arm, having unobtrusively dropped his buttered crust over the side of the cart. He moved his fingers an infinitesimal amount, and winced before he could stop himself.

'You must let the wound heal for a few days first, or you'll start the bleeding again,' Kate advised sharply.

'Yes, of course. I wonder—I was feeling a little odd at the time, and not paying much attention— did you say spiders' webs?'

'Yes. They hold the edges of the wound together and help it to close, and to stop the bleeding as well. Old, dusty cobwebs are best, provided they're not full of dead flies, but there were only clean ones in the Forest. I expect they'll do well enough.' She spoke a little impatiently, thinking he was making some sort of criticism of her method.

It did not take long to reach the town, for the road ran downhill, and there was no more conversation, for Master Hartwell seemed to have dropped into a light doze. As the cart rattled and jolted over the cobbles of East Street, he woke and said a trifle plaintively, 'I suppose I'll not be able to ride for a few days?'

'No. You must rest. In fact, you must stay in bed

in the quiet for a couple of days, for no doubt you'll have a fever after losing so much blood,' Kate told him firmly.

'At the moment, I hardly have a bed to stay in. I've laid claim to a truckle in the attic of your uncle's house, but it's dark there, and a half-dozen others share the place. I'm like to be trampled to death in their comings and goings, I fear!' He seemed to be making a rueful comment, rather than complaining.

Kate thought he was probably exaggerating, but she realised that her uncle's at present crowded and noisy house was no place for an injured man to recuperate, so she diverted the cart to the Abbey, and gave her patient into the charge of Father Humphrey at his neat little infirmary in the enclosure.

'You'd better tell me exactly what treatment you've given,' the elderly canon said, frowning a little, for he misliked the sound of such a wound, with all its implications for the King's safety and possible trouble in the Woodham area if the archer were not caught.

Kate described exactly how she had treated the wound, while a burly lay-brother was helping Master Hartwell out of the cart and into the infirmary, and Father Humphrey gave her a look of approval as she finished.

'I'll not disturb the wound for the time being, then,' he said. 'You've done exactly as I would have done, and it's best left alone until the initial inflammation has subsided and the veins knitted again. Now, what can you tell me of the patient? I know who he is, of course, for he's been here before. Is he a man of good sense?'

'He seems to be,' Kate replied, trying to think

how she should describe the man's character, for she found herself in considerable confusion about it. 'He seems a kind and considerate person, but he belongs to the Court of Augmentations . . .'

'At my lord of Winchester's behest,' Father Humphrey finished the sentence impatiently. 'That tells me only that he's a lawyer, which I already knew. If he develops an infection, will he fight it, or succumb? Is he tenacious? Does he complain unnecessarily? Come now, daughter Kate! You know what information I require.'

Kate collected her wits, and summed up Master Hartwell as an uncomplaining person who appeared sufficiently tenacious to survive a reasonable amount of infection, and recounted how she had found it necessary to tell him to stop trying to move his fingers too soon.

'Good! Then there is every hope for him!' Father Humphrey exclaimed.

'What about Master Hartwell's horse, mistress?' the sensible servant enquired, looking dubiously at the animal, which seemed agitated at seeing its master disappear into a strange building with a scent of sickness about it, half-carried by a man in monkish robes.

'It can stay here, in the Abbot's stable,' Father Humphrey said, showing a more lively interest than was usual in him at the sight of such a glossy black beauty. 'You'd best have the rest of his belongings sent over as well, for I've no doubt they'll disappear if they're left among the Court gentry!'

Kate had known Father Humphrey ever since he dosed her for whooping-cough in her childhood, and his somewhat jaundiced view of the honesty of men in the world outside the Abbey walls did not surprise her, for she suspected that a priest working

among the people, as all the canons did, saw and
heard a great deal of the worser side of human
nature. She thanked him for taking charge of Master
Hartwell, thanked the sensible servant for his help,
and then hastened away to her uncle's house, where
she found her aunt in a state of distraction,
everything, apparently, having gone wrong.

'Oh, Kate!' she exclaimed. 'Thank Heaven you've
come! Cook has dropped the pastry on the floor,
and the cream for the syllabubs is gone sour, and
all to do again, and the meat won't roast properly
because the firewood is too green. I don't know
which way to turn!'

Kate called from the window to the groom who
was holding her horse, telling him to stable her and
give her a good rub-down, sent a trusty servant to
collect Master Hartwell's belongings and take them
to the infirmary, then went to the kitchen to scrub
her hands and set to work. She found the scullery-
boy about to put dry wood on top of green in the
hearth, and just stopped him in time, then helped
him to remove the damp log and relight the fire
with dry wood. Then she rolled up her sleeves, put
a large holland apron over her ruined gown, and set
to work to make several pounds of pastry,
simultaneously instructing the boy to put faggots in
the bread-oven and fire them, so that there would
be a hot oven for the pastry as soon as it was made.
By then, Lady Cressy had recovered her wits
sufficiently to send various messengers about the
town in search of fresh cream, and soon amassed
enough to remake the syllabubs.

What with the fire roasting the meat, the glowing
walls of the bread-oven and the effort of making
such a large quantity of pastry, by the time the
hunting-party made its leisurely way down into the

town Kate's hair was plastered to her head by
sweat, and drops of it were running down her nose.
Lady Cressy rushed away to oversee the laying of
the tables in the hall and to change into her best
gown, and Kate remained in the kitchen to finish
the last few jobs and see the supper safely on its
way to table.

'Oh, Mistress Kate! Thank goodness you came
back early, or the Holy Virgin only knows how
we'd have got all done!' cried Cook. 'But what'll
you do now? There's the trumpet sounding for
supper, and the King coming, and you not changed!'

'I should like to wash myself, and then creep
away home,' Kate said, and was delighted by Cook's
prompt offer of a tub of warm water in the wash-
house, where the copper had been lit long ago in
expectation of a deal of washing-up.

Kate was able to take her second bath in two
days, which made her wonder if so much immersion
would do her any harm. She decided that, provided
she did not make a habit of it, she would probably
not suffer any lasting ill, and sluiced her body with
relief, then washed her hair, and felt much the
better for it. Someone kindly slipped up the back
stairs to Cecy's room and brought her a clean shift,
so that her soiled outer clothes did not feel so
horrid to put on again. She took the King's gold
angels out of her glove and carefully tied them into
part of the skirt of the shift, where they made a
heavy little lump, which knocked reassuringly against
her leg as she walked but was invisible under her
wide, stiff skirts.

When she returned to the kitchen, she found that
Cook had kindly made her up a platter of meat and
worts, and kept back a syllabub and a dish of
flummery for her, so she sat down at the kitchen

table and made a good supper, for she had eaten very little at dinner, and the day's events had left her feeling tired and dispirited.

When she had eaten, she sat quietly, sipping the wine that someone had brought from the hall for her, and remembered something else—the gloved hand which had put down poison herbs among the healing ones, and the distinctive ring it had worn, and she resolved to call at the infirmary on her way home, to warn Master Hartwell.

CHAPTER SEVEN

SHE WAS disconcerted to find that Master Hartwell had been put to bed, but Father Humphrey seemed neither surprised nor shocked that she still wished to see him. He took her to one of the small cubicles in the infirmary hall, ushering her in, and went away, leaving the door open for propriety.

It was like she imagined a monk's cell might be, with wooden partitions and a bare, white-washed wall pierced by a small, high window with real glass in it. A wooden crucifix hung on one panelled partition, and the little shelf below it supported a small pot of marigolds, presumably to keep flies away. Master Hartwell was firmly tucked into a narrow, hard-looking bed, and propped up on a couple of pillows. Surrounded by such an expanse of spotless linen, he appeared only a little pale. He looked surprised to see her, but then, she noticed with no great interest, smiled as if with pleasure.

'How kind of you to visit me!' he exclaimed. 'I thought you'd be enjoying the royal supper at your uncle's by now.'

'Oh, I didn't go,' Kate replied off-handedly. 'There was a crisis in the kitchen, and by the time I'd made the pastry, I was too floury and hot to appear. I've remembered something I have to tell you.'

'But have you not supped?' he interrupted, frowning. 'You had no dinner to speak of, and now no supper . . .'

'I had a very good supper,' she said impatiently 'and while I was eating it, I remembered . . .'

'And you've not changed your gown!' he interrupted again. 'Could not Mistress Cecy have lent you one? I don't like to think that you've had to go on wearing one stained with blood and—and whatever that green stuff may be . . .'

'Oh, do be quiet and listen!' Kate snapped, her manners overcome by sheer fatigue and exasperation that he would not let her deliver her warning and go home. 'Whom do you know who wears a heavy gold ring carved with the crest of a dog's head?'

'What breed of dog?' He was suddenly very still and sharp-eyed.

I'm not certain—I only caught a glimpse—but I think a greyhound.'

'Yes, I know it. Why?'

'When the gentlemen were running to and fro with herbs to make a dressing for your wound, I saw someone's hand lay down poison herbs among the good ones. The ring was on that hand!'

'And?' as Kate paused.

'I fear that its owner saw an opportunity to be rid of you.'

'Or to bring trouble on you!'

Kate was considerably taken aback. 'What—kill you and lay the blame on me? Why should anyone wish to do that? I don't even know whom the man was. How could anyone think to risk poisoning you? If I hadn't noticed, and those leaves had gone into your dressing, you would have been very ill, and maybe even died! Surely no one would do that to you, just to make trouble for me? I don't understand!'

'Perhaps you will if I tell you that Sir Richard Rich's crest is a greyhound's head, and he wears just such a ring as you described!'

Kate was silent, staring at him, as she tried to comprehend the implications.

'He's a vindictive man,' Master Hartwell went on quietly. 'To be fair to him, I don't think he always thinks of the possible ultimate results of his actions, but he enjoys taking revenge, and is not overtroubled in his conscience if it all goes too far. You refused his advances in a manner which made him appear ridiculous, and he'll not forgive, or forget.'

'How—How can you know about that?' Kate demanded, knowing at once to which incident he referred.

'I followed you after I'd—er—met you on the stairs, and saw him stop you. I was about to gallop to the rescue, but you dealt with him yourself, so I retired discreetly behind a bush. I don't go out of my way to make an enemy of a man like Rich!'

'Only to follow strange females about!' Kate said angrily. 'I suppose you had the same intentions as your master, and thought better of it when you saw him take a ducking!'

'Rich is not my master,' he said quietly. 'As I told you before, I have the misfortune to work with him in the King's service, that's all. I don't make a habit of following anyone about, but I wished to talk with you.'

'About what?'

'Immediately after we parted on the stairs, I realised that you must be the bailey's daughter, and I wanted to talk to you about the Grange house, and your father's future.'

'Then why did you not catch up with me after I left Sir Richard?'

'I thought best to wait behind my bush until he had climbed out of the water and retired from the scene, and by then you were already talking to—to someone else. Kate, be careful! Rich is a dangerous man.'

'I did not give you permission to call me by my Christian name, nor to spy on me!' she flared at him. 'If your friend thinks he can demand kisses from any female he chooses with impunity, he must take the consequences! I don't believe even he would try to poison a man to put the blame on me just for revenge over something so trivial. No—you look to yourself, Master Hartwell, and don't presume to question me about my father, or his future plans—they are none of your business!' With that inconsequential speech she swept out of the cubicle, banging the door behind her and bringing an indignantly shushing lay-brother out of an adjoining cubicle to frown at her.

She was still feeling ruffled and annoyed when she reached home on Jewel, although she had to admit to a certain amount of apprehension, for it was quite true that Sir Richard was known to be an unforgiving man. Had he not given the evidence which led Sir Thomas More to the block out of sheer spite over some petty grudge against him? She certainly had given him cause to dislike her, but surely he wouldn't risk another's life to take his revenge for a mere ducking . . . Would he?

Her father happened to be in the stableyard when she arrived, and he looked at her with some surprise. 'What are you doing home so early?' he asked. 'I thought you'd be making the most of your chances among the King's Court!'

'What chances, Father?' she asked as she dismounted and gave her reins to the groom who came to take Jewel.

'Of finding a husband, of course! Your cousin's all but settled, I hear, and it's time you made some effort in your own behalf, for God knows I can do

nothing for you! Why are you not still at supper at
your uncle's?'

'I didn't stay,' Kate replied briefly.

'Why not? Did they put you in too low a place for
you honour?' he demanded, ever ready to detect an
insult if anything like one appeared.

'I didn't go into supper,' Kate explained. 'I was not
dressed for such an occasion, and I had no time to
change, for Aunt Cressy needed my help in the
kitchen.'

'The kitchen! Who does that fine lady think she is,
to use her husband's niece as a scullery-maid? How
dare she rob you of a chance to sup with the King?'
Master Cressy's face took on a lowering and apoplectic
appearance, and Kate cut in quickly, before he could
work himself into too great a fury to listen.

'It was not like that at all! There was an—an
incident in the Forest, and a man was hurt. I soiled
my gown with blood and with a mash of herbs in
treating his wound, and then poor Aunt Cressy was
in such a state, because so much had gone wrong
with the supper, and the King came back early, so I
offered to help her . . .'

'Treating a wound? What, with the King's huntsmen
there? How dare you put yourself forward in so
immodest a fashion, girl? Your little knowledge may
be enough to deal with petty cuts and scalds in the
kitchen, or a yoke-gall or a sore hoof, but hunting
injuries should be left to those who know what
they're about. What was it? Did a stag gore someone?
Surely not a boar—there's not been a boar seen
about here in years!'

Kate sighed to herself, and briefly described the
attempt to kill the King. She was suddenly very tired,
and longed for bed and the peace of her own room,
but Master Cressy wanted details, and kept on

demanding to know exactly what the would-be assassin looked like, where he had been heading when his pursuers lost track of him, and a dozen other things she could not tell him.

When, at last, he accepted that she did not know the answers, he began to speculate, and had soon convinced himself that the culprit must be the brother of the man from the far side of the Forest who had been hanged for taking part in the Pilgrimage of Grace. From that deduction, he went on to talk himself into expecting that the villain would now wish to eliminate anyone who might identify him, and would therefore probably come to the Grange house during the night to kill Kate and murder them all in their beds.

While he was rushing about the house, ordering the servants to bar all the shutters and doors and barricade them with furniture, Kate went quietly off to her bed, and slept soundly all night, undisturbed by fears of the unknown archer, but dreaming vaguely of riding in the Forest with a greyhound and a man who was sometimes Amyas, and sometimes that irritating Master Hartwell. She woke late in the morning, and went downstairs to find her father already consuming his morning bread and ale, and full of the news, brought by one of the farm labourers, that the archer had been found hanged, presumably by his own hand, from a tree in the Abbey orchard. 'And he *was* the brother of that fellow who was involved in the rebellion, just as I said!' he informed Kate triumphantly. 'Quite mad, it appears, since his brother was hanged!'

Kate privately felt sorry for the man, and said a silent prayer for him, although she knew that suicide meant certain condemnation to Hell. She doubted if anyone else would spare him a moment's pity, but she was proved wrong, for when she met Lord Robert a few days later, walking peacefully alone by the river as he was wont to do, he spoke with sorrow of the man.

'I deeply regret that he did not come to the Abbey first,' he said. 'He had only to ask, and one of us would have heard his confession, and perhaps helped him to settle his poor, tortured mind. I think he must have been seeking our help, or he'd not have come to our orchard.' He sighed, and was silent for a moment, and then said, so quietly that Kate hardly heard his words. 'What will they do when we are gone? Who will help them then?'

'I—I suppose we'll have a parish priest?' Kate ventured.

Lord Robert looked at her sadly. 'I don't know. I'm told that what comes after is not my business. Presumably the new Lord of the Manor will give someone the living, but that will be his affair, not mine. By then, I shall be but a parish priest myself.'

'But, my lord . . .' Kate began, shocked by the sorrow and loss already apparent in the eyes which met hers.

'No more "my lord", but plain Sir Robert, parish priest,' he corrected her gently. 'I must get used to it, for we have but five months left to us here. You have not been to see your patient since the day he was hurt.'

Kate was taken aback by the sudden change of subject and the implied reproof. 'I gave him into Father Humphrey's care!' she protested. 'I have no skill to deal with such a wound.'

'And you do not care how he does?' the Abbot enquired gently, but went on without waiting for her reply. 'He's an interesting man. You'd think, to judge

of some of those who serve with the Court of
Augmentations, that he'd be hard, concerned only
with earthly matters, but he was most upset by that
madman's death, and begged me to say a Mass for
the poor fellow's soul, despite the fact that, but for
you, he might have lost his hand, or even his life,
from the fellow's arrow!'

'And—And did you?' Kate asked before she could
stop herself, then blushed to think that she had asked
such a question of the lord Abbot.

'Of course,' he replied gravely. 'I would have done
so, in any case. Your friend Matthew is doing well.
He has one stiff finger, but the wound is healing
cleanly and well, and Father Humphrey sings your
praises every time he attends the young man! He says
you have the gift of healing. Have you, daughter
Katherine?'

'I—I don't know . . .' Kate replied, embarrassed. 'I
have a little knowledge, and a meed of sense, I
think.'

'Use them well and freely, and the Lord will bless
your endeavours,' Lord Robert said gently, 'and call
on your friend, for he watches for you daily. A truly
charitable man is a *rara avis* in these days of greed
and self-interest!' With that, he gave Kate a blessing,
and went serenely on his way, walking slowly along
the cornmill stream bank, pausing from time to time
to watch the ducks or the cattle, or to read in his
breviary. Kate watched him for a few moments,
feeling an awful coldness within her, and a sense of
impending loss. What would they all do, all the
people of Woodham, when the Abbey was closed and
all the good Fathers departed? The town had come
into existence because of the Abbey. Everyone in it
was employed, directly or indirectly, by the Abbey.
How could the town, the people, continue without it?

She was on her way to her uncle's house again, to
see her cousin, but had a message to deliver to the
neat-herd on the way, which she would have forgotten,
walking deep in troubled thought, had she not met
him by the day-house.

'Your father will be pleased, mistress!' he exclaimed.
'The little brown cow calved last night, and dropped
just such another as herself. Like as two pease, they
be, or will be when the calf's grown.'

'When the calf's grown . . .' Kate echoed, wondering
where they would all be, neat-herd, Father, herself,
the brown cow and the new calf, when that time
came. Then she pulled herself together, delivered her
message, and went on her way.

When she reached the Abbey gate, she hesitated,
wondering whether to visit the infirmary. The Abbot's
reproof had made her feel guilty, but she still had
that lingering doubt, despite Lord Robert's good
opinion of Master Hartwell, about the man's character.
After all, he was a colleague of the infamous Sir
Richard, however much he disclaimed any closer
connection . . . Before she could decide one way or
the other, Master Hartwell himself emerged from the
small wicket gate and came across the bridge towards
her.

'Good morning, Mistress Cressy!' he said, as calm
and unembarrassed as if she had not lost her temper
and slammed out of the room at their last meeting.

'I was just coming to see you!' she announced a
shade defiantly.

'That was kind of you.'

'I wished to know how you do.'

'Very well, thanks to you.' He held out his
bandaged hand and wriggled his fingers at her, only
the index finger failing to move normally.

'I—I'm glad,' she said lamely, then added reluctantly, 'I fear I was a little short with you the other day.'

'It's in the nature of the eglantine to be prickly,' he said abstrusely. 'It's of no matter. I hope to return to London tomorrow.'

'So soon? Does Father Humphrey think you well enough?'

'No. He had the dressing off the wound this morning, and found it clean and healing well, but he'd like me to stay another week. The King left yesterday, and time and dissolutions wait for no man.'

'I suppose you'll be back again before long?' Kate was unaware of sounding more sour than she intended.

'I fear so. The King is still considering advancing the Abbey to cathedral status, but unfortunately it's in the wrong place—too near London—so I believe he will choose Peterborough instead. A pity, but . . .' He shrugged, and had the grace to look apologetic.

'Well, you'll get your house, then.' Kate had not consciously thought about the reward to which he had laid claim, but she had a sudden conviction that she knew exactly which house he had in mind.

'You don't think your father will claim the tenancy?' he asked, those alert eyes on her face again.

'He has no money,' she replied curtly. 'He'll lose his livelihood and his home together, and God knows what will become of us! But that is not your concern. I hope your hand will heal well, Master Hartwell. Good day to you.'

She walked away quickly, before he could reply, and dismissed him from her mind, for her thoughts were busy with what he had said earlier. She had not realised that the King had already left Woodham, and she wondered why Amyas, who presumably had gone with him, had not sent her any word. She hoped that perhaps he had left a note, or at least a message, with Cecy.

Her cousin, however, had nothing to talk of but two impending marriages—the King's, for it seemed all but settled that he was to marry the Lady Anne of Cleves, and her own, for her serious-faced suitor had made his offer and been accepted, and the settlements were now in process of preparation.

'And I expect to be married before the beginning of Lent!' she declared. 'You shall be my attendant, Coz!'

Kate made every effort to show interest and enthusiasm, but with a melancholy feeling within her heart, as she wondered when, if ever, she would be able to announce her own impending marriage. How could Amyas have gone away again without so much as a word or a token? Could she be sure that she would ever see him again? Unless . . .

'And do you still hope to go to London when the King weds?' she asked when the opportunity arose.

'Yes, of course! And you shall come with me.'

The promise was kept, and on a chill January day, Kate stood with Cecy, Lady Cressy and Sir William in a crowded courtyard at Greenwich Palace to watch the King go out to his fourth wedding, looking more like a thundercloud than a happy bridegroom. The spectators had spent the long time of waiting talking idly and with ill-concealed levity about the King's reaction to the sight of his new bride, who might be considered a beauty in her own country, but did not, apparently, appear so to English eyes.

'But surely Master Holbein was sent to paint her portrait for His Grace!' exclaimed Cecy, agog at the scandalous comments flying about. 'And did not the picture make His Grace decide to marry her?'

'Ay, and there's some say that beauty is in the eye

of the beholder,' replied a worldly-wise and sharp-featured lady amid the assembled gentry, 'and a man paints what he sees, if you take my meaning!' The nods and winks and significant looks which accompanied this remark would have conveyed her meaning to a slow-witted elephant, given time. Everyone waited for the bride to appear with all the more interest, to judge for themselves whether the King or Master Holbein had the truth of the matter.

Kate thought, from the brief glimpse that she caught of the Lady Anne, that they were both right, for the lady look kindly and patient, with a sweet smile, but, had she not been the sister of the Duke of Cleves, most men would not have given her a second glance. Her glimpse was, however, very brief, for she was so busy looking for Amyas that it was a wonder that she saw the bride at all.

It seemed that all London, as well as all the Court, had come to Greenwich for the wedding. The common folk were kept outside in the road, but there were more than enough gentry and lords to fill the courts and halls of the King's favourite palace with a colourful throng, yet nowhere could Kate see Amyas, although his height, his bright hair and his handsome face should have made him easy to spot. Instead, she found the thrushlike eyes of Master Hartwell regarding her above a lively smile, and he came over, pulling off his glove to show her how well his hand had healed. The scar on his palm was no more than a pink, puckered area the size of a silver shilling, and a little larger on the back of his hand.

'I was afraid it might mortify,' Kate admitted, interested, in spite of her urgent wish to see Amyas.

'No, it healed cleanly and quickly, thanks to you.'

'Is it stiff, or weak?'

'A little of both, but improving steadily. Luckily,

I'm right-handed. But tell me—what may I do for you?'

'Do for me? Why should you do anything?'

'My dear! Had it not been for you, I'd have lost my hand, if not my life!'

'Oh, hardly . . .!' Kate began in a scornful tone, thinking he was exaggerating.

'Father Humphrey assured me that I'd have bled to death had you not stopped the flow, or lost my hand if you had not dressed the wound before it could become infected. Is there nothing I can do for you in return?'

Kate hesitated, then said in a low voice, embarrassed and unwilling, yet desperate to know if her journey to Greenwich had been wasted, 'You could perhaps tell me if Sir Amyas Calton is here?'

'Calton?' The unusually expressive face was suddenly sympathetic. 'No, I'm sorry—he isn't. His father sent for him just after Christmas, and he's gone into Worcestershire—or was it Wiltshire?'

'Warwickshire,' Kate said impatiently. 'Was his father ill, do you know?'

'Er—no. Angry, I think! Calton said something—in his cups, you understand—about news of his debts having travelled home, and he was to be called to account. I've no doubt he'll be back soon, once his father has read him a lecture. May I give him any message?'

Kate turned away despondently, her eyes filling with tears, and said, with assumed indifference, 'No, I thank you. It's of no importance.'

She did not see the look of pity and concern on the man's face, or hear his murmured, 'I'm sorry. If there is anything I can do, at any time . . .' He did not finish the sentence, for she was already wandering away, and had obviously forgotten about him.

Kate was bitterly disappointed, of course, that Amyas was not there. For almost three months she had heard nothing from him, had waited and hoped for today, sure that he would be here, and now all her hopes and dreams had come to nothing. Added to that, there was this worrying news that he had been summoned home, and that he was in debt. If he had not yet established a reasonable livelihood at Court, when would he be able to do so? Until then, there was no hope that his father would allow him to marry her, dowerless and with no prospect of ever having more than those four gold angels which the King had given her—and which were still unspent, hidden in a secret place in her bedchamber.

Luckily, Sir William put his niece's abstraction and pale face down to standing about too long in the cold, and hurried her and the others away, despite Cecy's protests, first to an inn for hot broth and mulled wine, and then, when they were well warmed, on their homeward way. It was seventeen long miles to Woodham from Greenwich, even by the shortest route, which involved the mild excitement of crossing the river to the Isle of Dogs on a flat ferry-boat, poled expertly by two burly men between the multitudinous craft plying up to London or down to the sea.

Kate's next hope of seeing Amyas depended on the King making his usual spring visit to Woodham before or during Lent, when he often came for a few days' hawking along the river, and serious discussion of religious matters with the Abbot. This year, however, he was too busy seeking the means to rid himself of his new wife, who was already known throughout the country as 'the Flanders Mare'. Cecy, who had seen her better on her wedding-day than Kate, admitted that she was a large-framed female, but thought her ill-done-by, and was very concerned that she might follow the other Anne, Henry's second wife, to the block. She found time to pray assiduously for her, despite the time-consuming preparations for, and the actual celebration of, her own marriage, which proved to be the only happy event in Woodham that sad spring.

Because Lent began quite early that year, Cecy chose to marry on St Valentine's day. She expected that the ceremony would be performed by the Dean of Woodham, Father Hugh, but a few days beforehand Lord Robert went himself, alone and without ceremony, to the Cressy house, and asked, as if he were seeking a favour instead of bestowing an honour, if he might marry Cecy to her sober bridegroom himself.

'I think it will be the last wedding in the church before . . .' he said in explanation, and had no need to say before what, for everyone knew by now that the Abbey was to be surrendered before the end of Lent.

Of course, both bride and groom were happy to accept his offer, and, Cecy being a popular figure in the town, there was a determined air of festivity about her wedding-day. The church was decorated with wreaths of ivy and old-man's-beard, festooned between and wound round the great columns, and posies of snowdrops, aconites and Christmas roses, the only flowers to be found in that ironbound season, were laid on window-ledges and column-bases. The groom, despite his solemn appearance, sent a surprisingly romantic gift to his bride on her wedding-morning of a dozen crimson roses, bunched in a silver holder and decorated with white satin ribbons.

'Wherever can he have found them, at this time of year?' Cecy exclaimed, sniffing their rich perfume.

'He must know someone who has a stove-house,' Kate said, admiring them with a show of enthusiasm, as she had admired all Cecy's gifts, from Sir William's rope of pearls to the kitchen-maid's dozen carefully stitched cambric handkerchiefs.

'Red roses for true love!' Cecy saïd sentimentally, although neither she nor her groom, nor anyone alse save Kate, thought that there was any reason for her to be in love with her husband, or he with her. That would come later, when they had a growing family and were used to one another.

So Cecy went to her wedding in white brocade, with white fur to turn back her sleeves and edge her bodice. All her guests thought it was ermine, and only Harry Warrener and Lady Cressy knew the truth! She had gold and pearls on her french hood, her beautiful hair flowing loose from under it to mantle her shoulders, and she carried her red roses. Kate followed her in a new gown of rose with a sky-blue petticoat, trying to look as if she expected to be the next to marry, as everyone said she would be— although no one could seriously have believed it! She danced at the wedding-feast afterwards with the serious, middle-aged friends of the groom, and joined in the hilarity of the bedding ceremony, throwing Cecy's stocking over her shoulder and hitting the groom in the face with it in the traditional manner, thus ensuring that, if the tradition were true, she would be wed herself before the year's end, and could have wept for the unlikelihood of it.

Afterwards, going very late to her own narrow bed at home, it being still St Valentine's night, she put bay-leaves under her pillow, hoping at least to dream of Amyas, but, instead, she had a strange, confused nightmare in which Sir Richard Rich and Master Hartwell hunted with her through a forest of golden trees with a silver greyhound, which cried like a cat. Their quarry appeared at first to be a thrush, and later, a small brown mouse.

She woke suddenly, before the hunt had come to any conclusion, and felt so disturbed by the strange dream, and its echoing of the other she still remembered from several months before, that she got out of bed, wrapped a blanket about her, and walked up and down her room, making brave resolutions to put Amyas out of her heart and mind, to stop pining for a man who would probably never be able to marry her, and to set her mind to . . . To what? Seeking a husband? Where? Her relationship to Sir William made her eligible as a bride for any of the local gentry, but there were few unmarried men among them. All the grown men of the Colte family were already provided with wives, and their sons were too young. Lord Dallance was at least fifty, and had recently married his third wife. The Grevilles had a son, but he was barely fifteen—too young for her, Sir Robert Hook was a widower, but he was past sixty! Even if she could find someone suitable, there was still the insuperable problem of her lack of a dowry, and there was nothing she could do about that.

It was, of course, pitch dark in her room, and she had to feel her way back to her bed. She knelt beside if for some time, praying in a confused and hopeless way for a solution to her problems, some hope for a future more bright than a gradual growing old in poverty, tied to her cantankerous father, without the prospect of ever having a home and children of her own.

She was shivering with cold by the time she crept back into the comparative warmth of her bed, where she half-consciously slid one hand under her pillow and grasped the bay-leaves as she drifted off to sleep again. This time, she dreamed she was dancing at her own wedding—or was it the King's? Certainly he was there, huge and in a hearty good temper, as he used to be when she was a child and had first seen him, leaping with the liveliest of the dancers, and singing his own song, 'Pastime With Good Company'. The dancers moved like figures in a tapestry brought to life by the flickering of firelight in a draughty hall, and she could hardly make them out, but nowhere could she see Amyas—only the King, the haughty face of Sir Richard, and the bright, interested eyes of Matthew Hartwell.

CHAPTER EIGHT

TOWARDS THE END of Lent, it became known, by some undercurrent of rumour, that the Abbey was to be surrendered to the King's commissioners on the Tuesday of Holy Week. It was only the presence of those commissioners already to be seen about the town that prevented a more open demonstration of protest than the comparatively mild murmurs of 'What a shame not to let them have their last Easter!', and similar expressions of the people's sentiments.

To Kate, it seemed unthinkable that the good Fathers should be denied a last celebration of the holiest festival of the year in their own church, so, when she was told the news by her aunt, she went straight to the Abbey to find out the truth.

At that time in the morning, the canons were about their normal business, either saying their individual daily Masses or attending to the particular duties of each one's office, so only the Almoner was available to answer her question, and he, with a deep sigh, told her sadly and quietly that it was true.

'How could he!' Kate exclaimed indignantly, immediately putting the whole blame on that petty-minded, uncharitable monster, Sir Richard Rich, who had by now assumed the role of Principal Villain in her estimation.

'It depends on the identity of "he",' Father Miles replied cautiously. 'If you mean Our Lord, it is not for us to question His Will. If you mean the King . . .'

'I mean the Chancellor of the Court of Augmentations!' Kate replied in her sharpest tone, not wishing to be accused either of heresy or of treason.

'Oh! Well, Lord Robert says that even he has some good in him, although I can't at the moment recall what it is,' Father Miles said judiciously. 'I doubt if it was his personal decision, you know. More likely it was some petty clerk decided that March 23rd would fit in well with his own plans, or those of someone else, and it will, of course, leave just enough time for them to finish with us before Lady Day. Perhaps it's as well. It would be difficult for us to celebrate the Resurrection as we should with our expulsion hanging over our heads . . . I hope to reach my new parish in time to keep the feast as a fitting start to a new life.'

'You have a parish to go to?' Kate asked, struck with guilt, for she had not thought about the future of the individual canons, only of the effect of the Abbey's passing on the town.

'We all have, dear child, thanks to my lord Abbot, excepting Father Thomas and Father Humphrey, who feel that they are too old to start again in their profession. They are to go with Lord Robert as his chaplains.'

'I'm glad to hear that you all have somewhere to go,' Kate said sincerely, 'but I still think it cruel to choose Holy Week!'

'My dear child!' Father Miles said gently. 'You must guard against overmuch finding fault in others. Your voice takes on a sharp tone, and I almost expect you to unsheath talons when you speak so! Even if we had no cures of souls awaiting us, we would still have the generous pensions which the King's Grace has granted.'

Kate bit back a sharp reply to that, for she did not

think six pounds, thirteen shillings and fourpence a year overly generous payment, and that was what she had heard that most of the canons would receive, only the Abbot and the most senior Fathers having been allocated more, and the young men even less.

'What will your father do?' Father Miles asked, seeming more concerned about that than his own future.

'I don't know,' Kate sighed. 'He is to have thirteen shillings and fourpence pension, which I suppose he could just manage to live on, with great care, but he says he'll not take a labourer's job after being bailey, and no one hereabouts needs a steward or a bailey.'

'What of the house?'

Kate shook her head. 'I don't know that, either. The Court offered it to him, to rent or buy, but he could afford neither, and, in any case, how could he keep it up, with all the servants, without land to go with it? I believe Master Hartwell will be given it, and half the demesne, in payment for saving the King last autumn. I don't know what we shall do.'

'Trust in the Lord,' Father Miles said, his attention already turning to some new arrivals, a travel-worn couple with a young baby, who were hovering hopefully in the doorway. 'Be of good cheer, dear child! I shall pray for you, as for all the good people of Woodham.'

After bowing her head to receive his blessing, Kate went home, wrestling with her mingled despondency and anger as she walked along the bank of the stream. Despite the Almoner's words, she still felt that Sir Richard probably chose the timing of the surrender out of spite, for he seemed to hate the monasteries and all manifestations of the Old Faith. She suspected that he was probably a Lutheran at heart—if he had a heart!

Remembering what the Father Almoner had said, she wondered if she were turning into a shrew. Well, small wonder if she was, with her father grown even more morose ˙ and unpredictable, no word from Amyas, no Cecy to confide in, now that she had gone to her new home with her husband, and her own future nothing but a great question-mark.

Her feet dragged up the steep slope to the Grange house, and she braced herself before entering, wondering what mood her father would be in this noon—it had been a silent and scowling one when she left after breakfast.

Dame Marjorie met her in the screens passage, and, between little outbursts of clucking and hand-wringing, told her that Master Cressy had been asking for her for the past half-hour, and 'the gentleman' was come and had dined with him.

'Dined?' Kate exclaimed. 'Already? I'd not thought it so late!'

Dame Marjorie's little murmurs, without a clear sentence among them, somehow conveyed that Master Cressy had demanded dinner at a quarter before eleven, and it was now half-past the hour. Kate was welcome to come to the kitchen at any time for meat and bread, but first she had best go to her father in the parlour. She took Kate's cloak from her and shooed her gently in the right direction.

Master Cressy's greeting was a crabby, 'What time do you call this, Kate? Mooning about full of daydreams, I'll be bound, like a green girl, and you past eighteen, and should have been married long ago! A husband and half a dozen children would soon put your fanciful nonsense out of your head.'

Kate, who prided herself on not being fanciful or given to mooning, or anything but a sensible and practical woman, was stung to reply sharply, 'My

Aunt Cressy kept me, and you will not let me ride Jewel to the town above once a week.' She was conscious that her irritation was not so much due to her father's accusation as the fact that it was uttered before a guest, and the interfering busybody Master Hartwell at that.

'Good day, Mistress Kate,' he said, making her a bow, having risen as she entered. His eyes twinkled and his lips twitched a little.

To be laughed at by him was the last straw for Kate, and she snapped, 'I wonder you dare show your face in any house in Woodham, sir! The news is out that your office has decreed the Abbey's surrender in Holy Week. Of all the weeks in the year!'

'I did try to have it altered to the following week,' he replied equably, 'but the decision was already made, and the arrangements in train.'

'So you did nothing, in fact!' Kate retorted, unmollified.

'I resigned,' he said quietly.

Kate stared at him in blank astonishment, rendered quite speechless by the implications of the two words.

'To be honest,' he resumed, 'I had intended to resign in any case, as I've had more than my bellyful of the Court of Augmentations, and mean to devote myself to the cultivation of my mind and my new estate in future, but it seemed a good idea to kill two birds with one stone, and make my protest by that means. It was fairly dramatic, and I must take a little credit for rendering an old friend of yours quite crimson in the face and spluttering for a few minutes. In the King's presence, too! His Grace laughed quite loudly!'

'Nonsensical ideas!' snorted Master Cressy. 'What difference does it make, one week or another, if it has to be? Best do it and have done, I say! We've more important things to discuss. Listen, Kate! Master Hartwell brings the solution to all my problems.'

'Er-hm,' Master Hartwell interposed in a discreet cough. 'May I, perhaps, speak privately to Mistress Cressy first, sir?'

'Privately? Rubbish, sir! What's to speak to her about? It's all decided, and I can tell her better than you.'

'Tell me what?' Kate asked in a cold, suspicious voice. She had encountered this mood in her father before, and fully expected that whatever had been decided would be to her disadvantage.

'About the house,' Master Cressy replied, almost affably. 'Sit down, Master Hartwell! Sit down, girl!'— waving them impatiently to seats while he sank into his own carved armchair. 'It seems that Master Hartwell performed some service for the King, who promised him a house and land . . . (Kate realised with a start of surprise that, somehow, she had never told her father that it was Master Hartwell who had saved the King from the archer's arrow in the Forest.) . . . and he's chosen this house! Of course, there's no estate attached to it, but it seems that Lord Dallance is to have the Manor, and he doesn't want all the demesne, so all that part of it lying to the north of the Abbey precinct is to be Master Hartwell's. A tidy parcel it will make—a good mixture of meadow, ploughland, pasture, grazing and wood. I couldn't have chosen better myself!'

Kate listened, puzzled by the rare note of enthusiasm in her father's voice. How could he sound so pleased to recount the good fortune of the man who was about to turn him out of the house where his family had lived for three generations—four, counting herself?

'And he'll keep on all the servants, indoor and out.

I've been worried about Dame Marjorie, poor soul—
I don't suppose you've given her a single thought!—
but it's not easy for anyone like her to find a living,
for all she's a good housekeeper as any in the county,
but her funny little ways . . . And there's Martin.
Who'd employ a half-wit? Yet he manages well
enough, in work he's used to doing.'

Thinking how often her father had snarled at
Martin for his slowness and lack of comprehension,
and mocked at Dame Marjorie's affliction, even to
her face, Kate could hardly manage to keep silent,
but she sat on her hands and scowled, all of which
was noted and stored for future reference by the
ever-interested Master Hartwell.

'Master Hartwell is very good,' she said woodenly,
Master Cressy having paused expectantly. She meant
what she said, but, somehow, the words sounded
sardonic rather than sincere.

'Indeed! I can honestly say that I've never met a
more considerate and kindly man!' Master Cressy
exclaimed with even more inexplicable enthusiasm.
'But you've not heard the best, Kate!'

She looked with deepening puzzlement from her
father to the object of his eulogy and back again, a
feeling of trepidation growing so rapidly within her
that she felt like to choke with it. 'And what may
that be?' she asked, lowering her chin and glaring
suspiciously at Master Cressy's face, which was creased
in an unaccustomed smile, ill-suited to the lines drawn
by his usual look of sulky discontent.

'Why, that I'm not to lose my old home!'

She gave a little gasp of relief. 'You mean, he
needs a bailey after all?' she exclaimed, her face
lighting up and giving her a look of joyous beauty,
which the bright, near-black eyes also noted, this
time with a faint, wry smile.

'Not exactly,' their owner put in. 'By your leave, sir—I think I should . . .'

'Nonsense!' Master Cressy cut him off. 'It's my privilege to tell the girl of her good fortune!'

'*My* good fortune?' Kate's suspicions returned, reinforced, and her voice sharpened.

'The best of good fortune!' her father declared, his face now positively wreathed in smiles. 'This excellent gentleman has need of someone to keep his house for him, of course, and you being familiar with the running of it in all respects . . .'

'Dame Marjorie is the housekeeper,' Kate cut in swiftly, 'and you've already said that Master Hartwell means to employ her.'

'Not a housekeeper, you fool!' Master Cressy returned to his usual impatient manner, recollected himself, and continued more graciously, 'He has chosen you to be his wife, which means, of course, that I, as his good-father, may continue to live here without the embarrassment of accepting charity.'

Kate rose slowly to her feet, and, to Master Hartwell's perception, at least, continued to rise until she seemed considerably more than her mere average height. Her temper rose also, to a state of cold fury, bottled up within tightly pressed lips as she looked at her father in contemptuous silence. Then, after what seemed a very long pause, she said in an icy voice, 'So you would sell your only daughter's body to purchase your own comfort. A fine man you are! A father to be proud of! Would you not do better to sell me to a brothel-keeper in London? As I'm a virgin, he might even give you enough to buy your house and land outright, and then you need not put yourself to the trouble of being civil to Master Hartwell. I'm sure the effort at politeness must be very painful to you!'

Master Cressy's face lost its alien smile and turned to a black thundercloud.

'How dare you speak to me like that!' he spat at her. 'Sell you, indeed! What's a daughter for, but to be married off to advantage? Think yourself lucky, you empty-headed, useless, shrewish *female*, that any man thinks you worth the taking, in or out of wedlock! It's your duty to provide for me in my old age, and what other means do you have of doing so?'

He had remained seated in his chair, and he was gripping the arms so tightly that the veins stood like cords on the backs of his hands. His face had gone an ugly, mottled red which, in a more sanguine man, might have warned of approaching apoplexy.

'Useless, am I?' Kate riposted, her eyes flashing. 'There are those who think otherwise! And shrewish, you said? Then consider who makes me so, with his eternal carping and fault-finding! And female? I had no choice in that, I think, but you begat me, and they say that it's the father's seed determines the sex of the child. As for providing for you in your old age . . . Had you saved your money, instead of spending it as it came, you'd have no lack of it now!'

'Money? What money have I ever had?' Master Cressy was diverted into an accustomed self-pitying channel of complaint, which Master Hartwell, prudently sitting very still and trying to merge into the furniture, noted with another twitch of his lips, and discreetly lowered his eyes to hide their gleam of amusement.

'Oh, no great fortune, but enough in gifts and little remembrances to see a man's cottage gets repaired, or his hiring renewed, or one carter preferred over another.'

'And what's wrong with that?' her father demanded truculently. 'My brother grew rich in the City and at

Court by that means, for it's common practice. Why should I not do, in my small way, what every great man in the land does, and thinks it no more than his due? God knows, there's no profit to be made from the stipend the Abbey pays me!'

'I say nothing about how you got the money—only how you spent it!' Kate tossed her head and flung out a hand in a wide gesture. 'You threw away good furniture to buy things which suit neither the house nor your station, and you've a press full of new clothes you've never worn. I say nothing of the woman at Horsing, or the other at Beetley! Don't blame me that you've fallen on hard times, for you've spent nothing on me, save my board and lodging, and you've done nothing to find me a suitable husband!'

'Well, I've found you one now!' Master Cressy declared triumphantly. 'For God's sake, girl! Don't be a complete fool! Here's a young, handsome man come to offer you a better marriage than you could have hoped to make, and to solve all my problems into the bargain! It's not an offer you'll ever get again, so take the chance while it's there.'

Kate drew breath to continue her onslaught on her father, but was neatly forestalled by Master Hartwell, who suddenly stood up and asserted an authority which neither of the others had ever realised he possessed, yet he spoke with such firmness and confidence that Kate, at least, was sufficiently impressed to pay him close attention, thinking half-consciously that he seemed merely quiet and pleasant, yet there was certainly more to him than at first appeared . . .

'By your leave, Master Cressy, Mistress Kate,' he said, 'or without it, if you insist, but this has gone far enough! I do not make my offer with any intention of buying a wife, or merely finding an honourable means of providing for a man who has suffered as a result of the dissolution of a monastery. Neither purchase nor charity enter into the matter. I make my offer to Mistress Kate because it's my wish to share my life here with her. All else is incidental and peripheral.'

Kate looked at him earnestly and searchingly, and his dark eyes met hers with the open, honest directness which had struck her the first time she saw him, and sparked an answering directness and honesty in herself.

'You know where my heart lies,' she said.

'Yes, and if I thought for one moment that there was hope in that direction, I'd not have spoken. I do not ask for your heart—not yet, at least.'

Kate hesitated, something within her admitting that he was right, that Amyas would never be able to marry her, and that she would be wise to forget him and try to build a future with this man, who was honest, kindly, considerate.

'For Heaven's sake! What foolish chatter is this of hearts?' Master Cressy demanded, breaking into that crucial, silent pause with all the disruptive, ill-timed effect of an explosion of gunpowder. 'Marriage is a business matter, and it's your business, girl, to do your duty by your family!'

Master Hartwell's eyes held Kate's for just one breath longer, and something indefinable passed between them, then Kate turned to her father and said quietly, sounding reasonable and almost kindly, 'I cannot agree to be sold by you to any man in order to buy what you want, Father. I am a free woman, not a slave! Master Hartwell,' turning to him, 'I thank you for your offer, which I'm sure was indeed well meant, but my father and I do not need, and cannot accept, such a kindness. I bid you good day, sir, and beg you'll excuse me.' With that, she walked out of the room in a silence which was almost tangible, with a calmness and dignity which startled her father, and caused Master Hartwell to put his hand to his heart and bow to her receding back as if she were a queen. He did not appear to be particularly downcast.

Kate's calmness—indeed, an uncanny, cold lack of feeling—carried her out of the house in something like a trance, in which she picked up her cloak in passing from the chest on which Dame Marjorie had absent-mindedly laid it, went to the stables, saddled Jewel, and rode out of the yard and up the steep rise behind the house to the top of the ridge.

It was only gradually that normal feeling returned to her, bringing a jumble of conflicting emotions. There was still anger with her father for thinking to use her as an object of barter to get what he wanted, but there was also surprise at finding Master Hartwell so suddenly unveiled as a forceful personality, a man to be respected and given more consideration than she had allowed him in the past. There was, too, an aching sorrow, a strange feeling that she had lost something important, but whether that something was the chance to stay in her old home, or a tacit admission that Amyas was lost to her, or something else which she could not yet grasp, she was unsure.

She rode unseeingly along the ridge towards the Forest, and presently found herself at the Selvedge, the path which ran along the very edge of the trees, like a boundary, linking the tiny hamlet of Cob End to the main road. There, Jewel slowed to a halt, having come so far without direction. Kate looked vaguely about her, then urged the mare on into the Forest, ducking down low over Jewel's neck to avoid the low branches, and leaving the mare to pick her own way between the thick trunks of oaks and beeches and the bushes and briars which struggled for life under the canopy of the great trees.

The leaf-buds had hardly begun to break yet, so early in the year, but she gradually became aware of new life stirring about her. There was a sensation of green mistiness high up in the treetops, and little clumps of aconites and snowdrops peeped between the gnarled roots or pushed through the carpet of dead leaves.

Presently she came upon an open glade, thick with wood-anemones and primroses, where she allowed Jewel to come to a standstill while she gazed at the delicate beauty before her.

'Oh, Jewel!' she whispered. 'Why do men make the world so ugly, when God made it so beautiful? Why are they so greedy, so cruel? Look—even the Forest is decked for Easter, but those grasping men about the King won't allow our church to be beautiful for the Lord's rising! The doors will be locked, and the church bare and empty.'

She slid from the saddle and sat on a root of a great oak, her arms clasped about her bent knees, and let her tears run unheeded down her cheeks. It was very peaceful in the Forest. A few birds, busy with their nesting, flew about collecting twigs and leaves, a thrush sang high up in the treetops, out of sight, and there were stirrings amid the dead leaves as little animals scurried about, intent on their own small affairs. A squirrel unearthed a cache of nuts and sat eating them with brisk efficiency not five yards from where she sat, watching her with bright, candid eyes, which reminded her of Master Hartwell and made the tears run all the faster, until, eventually, there were none left to flow, and she simply sat there, feeling drained of all emotion, her throat aching and her eyes feeling hot and swollen.

Somewhere, whether near or far she could not tell, for sound is deceptive among trees, she could hear the sounds of people chopping wood, and she assumed that some of the townsfolk were lopping the pollarded trees before their right to do so expired for the winter on Lady Day. In her returning consciousness of her situation, she realised that she had no idea of where in the Forest she was, for she had taken no heed of direction on her ride between the trees, so she took Jewel's bridle in her hand and led the mare towards the sound.

The wood-choppers were further away than she had realised, but eventually she came upon them, and found that they were not townsfolk at all, but charcoal-burners who had made their huts of branches and ferns in one of the runnings or long clearings. They were busy building up one of the dome-like mounds in which they burnt the pollard-wood to make their charcoal.

They were a silent, self-contained group of some half-dozen men, grimed by their craft, and used to spending weeks at a time in the Forest, seldom seeing anyone but their fellow-workers, and regarded by the townsfolk as strange, alien creatures, akin to hobgoblins or worse. They all stopped work as one man when Kate emerged from the trees, and stared at her in silence.

'Good day,' she said a trifle nervously. The man at whom she happened to be looking as she spoke nodded briefly, but said nothing. The rest continued to stare.

One man, clearly the eldest present, for he was gnarled like an old tree and had a white beard, surprisingly snowy against his grimed face and clothing, walked towards her and said abruptly, 'Be you in trouble, mistress?'

'No, only lost,' she replied, wondering if she should have kept clear of the camp.

'You'm been a-weeping,' the old man said, studying her face with pale blue eyes which were not in the least dimmed by age.

Kate bent her head, embarrassed that the signs of her tears should be so obvious. 'I was troubled and upset about something,' she admitted, 'so I came to the Forest to think, but I've strayed into a part which I don't recognise.'

'Oh, so you know some parts?'

'I come here to gather herbs.' Kate found it impossible not to answer him, for he had an air of authority, and clearly led this band of colliers.

'Herbs? Be you wise, then?'

'Yes. I have some skill.'

'Happen you'll look at Young Billy's finger, then. A has a whitlow won't heal up.'

'By all means,' Kate replied, for she had been told by the old woman who taught her that she must never refuse a request for help, or take money for it.

Young Billy, who looked nearly as elderly as the old man, bashfully came forward, unwrapping a dirty rag from his hand. The swelling, which had a handsome cream-coloured head on it, was not by his fingernail, but between the second and third knuckles of his middle finger, which was swollen as thick as a sausage.

'You've a splinter in that!' Kate exclaimed. 'Have you any clean water?'

The colliers gathered round, deeply interested in the proceedings, and one of them fetched a leather bucket of reasonably clean water. Kate washed the injured hand as clean as she could get it, so that she could see the swollen finger better. The area in the middle of the swelling looked almost ready to burst, and Kate could make out a tiny black speck in the heart of it, so she asked, 'Has anyone a sharp knife?'

There was a little shuffling among the men, and some sidelong glances from one to another, and then Young Billy himself delved among his clothing with his free hand, and produced, not the steel knife which Kate expected, but a delicate object about the size and shape of a young beech-leaf, and a pale translucent brown in colour. It was a flint arrowhead, and its edge was as sharp as any knife.

'This will hurt,' she warned, and drew the edge hard and smartly across the swelling. A great gout of yellow matter welled out of the cut, and, amid it, a long black thorn, and Kate rinsed all away in the bucket.

'I told you not to cut blackthorn without gloves!' the old man said with some satisfaction. 'What now, mistress?'

'If you mash up some bread in boiling water, and put it on the wound a little hotter than you can bear,' Kate instructed Young Billy, 'it will draw out the poison. Leave it on until it grows cold, then take it off, make a fresh lot, and put that on, and go on doing that until the swelling goes down and no more matter comes out. Then put a thick layer of cobwebs over the cut, and leave it for three days to heal.'

'I'm obliged to you, mistress,' Young Billy said with great dignity. 'I'll be pleased if you'll keep the elfstone as a gift. Happen it'll save you from the lightning-stroke or the thunder-storm while you're about the Forest.'

'Thank you,' Kate replied with equal dignity. 'It's a fine and generous gift, and I'm very glad to have it.'

'You should thread silk through the little hole and hang it about your neck,' the old man advised. 'We're beholden to you, mistress, and if it's Woodham you seek, your way lies yonder.' He pointed. 'Your pretty mare will know her way to her stable, I shouldn't wonder.'

He allowed the briefest of smiles to appear in the midst of his beard, and Kate realised, with a feeling of foolishness, that he was right, and Jewel, at least, had not been lost at all, for they must be within half a dozen miles of home at the most.

She bade the colliers good-bye, and received nods and cautious smiles in return, but no offer of help to mount Jewel—not that it was really necessary, with the footboard to act as a step, but it was customary for a man at least to offer to help a lady to mount.

On the way home, she inspected the elfstone carefully, and wondered if such things were really the work of wood-spirits, or if they had been made by men long ago in the past, as Lord Robert had once told her. Long, long past, she thought vaguely— perhaps even as long ago as the Romans, although she had only the haziest idea how long it was since they were in Britain, and thought of it only as an extraordinarily long time ago, when perhaps people had greater skill, and could work ordinary stones into things of such jewel-like beauty.

It was only when she came in sight of her home that she was overwhelmed for a few moments by fear of what she would find there, but she summoned up her courage, and rode down the steep end of the ridge to the stableyard, where the lad came running out to take Jewel.

'Master's in the parlour, and Dame Marjorie says there's food in the kitchen for you,' he informed Kate, giving her a curious, flickering sidelong scrutiny, as if he could not believe what he must have heard of her defiance of her father.

'Thank you,' Kate replied, sounding more calm

than she felt, and went indoors. Thinking it best to get whatever was to come over and done with, she went straight to the parlour.

Master Cressy was still sitting in his carved chair, alone and apparently brooding. He looked up, scowling, as Kate entered and stood just inside the door, waiting for the storm to break.

To her surprise, all he said was, 'I don't know what the world is coming to, when a mere chit of a girl rebels against her own father and defies him as you've done! I've a mind to lock you in the cellar on bread and water until you learn to obey, but Master Hartwell pleaded your cause—a damned good lawyer he is, I can tell you. He reckons you'll come to your proper senses in time, and realise your duty and your advantage lie together. Well, then—we'll see if he proves right, but I tell you, you ungrateful wretch, that I'll never speak to you again until you learn obedience!'

CHAPTER NINE

MASTER Cressy kept his word, avoided Kate as much as possible, looked past or through her when obliged to be anywhere near, and communicated with her through Dame Marjorie, or by means of curt little notes in his neat secretary hand, which were almost entirely brief orders to do this or that.

Naturally, Kate was troubled by the rift between them, yet she could not bring herself to change her mind and do as her father demanded, although she had to admit privately that, did she not think love important in marriage, and had she not given her heart to Amyas, Master Hartwell might have suited her well enough as a husband. He seemed kind and considerate, and not so badly tarred by the brush of greed and corruption as his former confreres in the Court of Augmentations. She sometimes found herself wondering why he had asked her to marry him, for he had denied that it was out of charity, but she could form no conclusion on the question.

There were few things in her life of sufficient importance to drive the imminent loss of her home and the quarrel with her father to the back of her mind, but the events of Holy Week succeeded in doing so.

Most of the townsfolk attended Mass on Palm Sunday, crowding into the parish nave until it was uncomfortably full. The service followed its usual course, with no indication from the Dean or his acolytes that this was the last Sunday in the life of the Abbey until the very end, after the priest had blessed the palm crosses and the acolytes had distributed them. Only then did the Dean come to the sanctuary rail and announce, in a clear, unemotional voice, that Vespers would be sung on the following evening as usual.

'This will be followed, also as usual, by the procession to the parish altar, where the choir will sing an anthem—a setting, composed for this occasion by Master Thomas Tallis, our talented organist, of the Lamentations of Jeremiah, which are usually sung in Holy Week.' He then proceeded with the final blessing of the service, and returned immediately through one of the doors in the reredos to the canons' choir beyond, leaving a silent congregation to its private thoughts and fears.

'Nearly four hundred years!' a woman next to Kate whispered. 'That's how long the canons have been here, and goodness knows how long the ones before them! What's to become of us? Who'll take the services and give us the sacraments when they've gone?'

Kate was unable to answer her, for she knew from various remarks made by her uncle that the churchwardens had still not succeeded in getting a satisfactory answer to that question, nor in discovering whether the commissioners were counting the parish nave as part of the Abbey.

The men from the Court of Augmentations who were to receive the surrender and carry out the dispersal of its property were already in the town, staying at the Bell inn, which formed one side of the lychgate arch from the market square to the churchyard, and, consequently, the townspeople were

very wary of saying anything about the dissolution.
What comment there was consisted of significant
glances and nods, and yet proved adequate, as
everyone who could manage to do so gathered in the
church the following evening at the hour of Vespers,
when usually only a couple of dozen attended. The
service formed part of the monastic horarium, and
was sung in the canons' choir, out of sight beyond the
ten-foot wall of the reredos. It was not, however, out
of earshot, for the clear, beautiful voices of the choir
soared to the roof and threaded between the arches
of triforium and clerestory, seeming to gain an
unearthly beauty from the acoustics of the building
and the invisibility of the singers.

Kate listened, as did everyone else, in an entranced
stillness. Some of the rowdier element of the town
had come intending to mock the canons, now that
they no longer owned the town and could not
retaliate, and some had come to celebrate what they
considered to be the end of a corrupt and outmoded
institution, but all were caught by the spell of the
music and the sorrow, the finality of the occasion.
For nearly four centuries, Austin canons had sung the
monastic hours here, day by day, without a break,
but this was the end, and even the most Lutheran or
the most pagan could feel the poignancy of it. Many
were openly weeping, and even the roughest, the
most insensitive, felt a lump in the throat and an
unaccustomed appreciation of the soaring voices which
sang the age-old words as if to carry them up to the
gate of Heaven itself.

After the last notes of *Deo Gratia*, the two doors in
the reredos opened, and the procession came through
in two files. First came the acolytes with censers, then
the singing-boys and the choirmen, followed by the
Cantor, and the rest of the canons, each carrying a

lighted candle, which caused a stir of surprise in those who frequently attended this aftermath of Vespers, and had never before seen all the canons attend, or lighted candles carried at it. Usually several of the Fathers were away, attending the outlying parishes, but tonight all were here. Apart from the Cantor, there were sixteen, each in black robe and white cotta, the candles shining on their faces so that the features of each stood out clearly, from the lined, sad face of Father Thomas, the Prior, to the youthful countenance of Father Edmund, as yet but a Deacon, who was to be sent to Cambridge at the King's expense to continue his education.

At the last came Lord Robert in the purple cope and mitre appropriate to the funereal aspects of the service, yet worn quite properly, from the point of view of any Augmentations man present, because it was still Lent. He did not carry a candle, but his elaborate gold-headed crozier, which was normally only used on the Great Festivals, and the big gold-set amethyst ring, granted to his predecessors by Pope Celestine III, glowed on his gloved hand. This, too, was only seen on Great Festivals, for the Abbot preferred a more modest stone set in plain silver for everyday wear.

The choir was chanting a plainsong setting of the Psalm for the day, but after it, when they were all grouped about the altar, they sang the new setting of two verses from Jeremiah.

It was quiet, melodious, and very beautiful, and provided a necessary release for the tensions of sorrow and fear for the future which had built up in the nave during Vespers. It was not a long anthem, but, by the end of it, all the women and most of the men in the congregation were weeping, and tears were running down the cheeks of most of the canons as well.

After the last *Amen*, there was another departure from custom, for the Abbot lifted his arms, his cope spreading like wings on either side of him, the crozier blazing and the amethyst glowing in the candlelight, and he pronounced a long and comprehensive blessing on the parishioners, the town, the King, and all the people of England, in a clear, ringing voice which resounded through the church like a trumpet-call.

Most of the congregation had fallen to their knees for the blessing, and the Abbot waited at the end, his arms still flung wide, until all had scrambled to their feet again, many crossing themselves repeatedly. Then he dropped his arms to his sides and bowed solemnly. All the canons then also bowed, as if in farewell, and pinched out their candles in unison, a dramatic gesture which Kate remembered for the rest of her life. The choir began to chant again, and the acolytes swung their censers, stepping forward to lead the two lines back through the doors to the Choir.

The voices receded gradually as they progressed slowly to their places beyond the eastern tower, and then, as the Abbot passed through the northern door, the voices ceased suddenly, and both doors closed together with a decisive bang which echoed with note of finality through the building.

A subdued and silent congregation left the church, and the west doors were closed and locked behind them before the canons began Compline, the last service of their day, and, presumably, of the monastic life of the Abbey.

'In some places,' said a reflective voice quietly to Kate, who was jerked suddenly out of her thoughts by it, 'the closing of the local monastery was greeted with bonfires and feasting, or with relief, but not here. There were still some houses fulfilling their purpose, and this was one of the best.'

It was, of course, Master Hartwell, and Kate strained to see his face in the gathering darkness, wondering that he should speak so calmly to her after the drama of their last meeting.

'Yes,' she said briefly.

'I gather that your father has found a lodging for you both,' he said after a slight pause, during which Kate thought that she should walk away, yet did not do so.

'Yes,' she said again, for she had received Master Cressy's note that morning, informing her that he had taken rooms for them both from Lady Day at the Three Tuns. Lady Day fell on Maundy Thursday that year, so she added, 'We shall be out of your way by the end of the week.' There was resignation, rather than bitterness, in her voice.

'I wish, in some ways, that you did not have to lose your home, although I've longed to own the house since I first saw it,' he said. 'Of course, if you should change your mind, my offer remains open.'

'If you mean that you intend to wait for me to "come to my senses", as my father puts it, you'll wait until you're too old to think of marriage at all!' Kate snapped irritably. 'I'll not be sacrificed to preserve my father's comfort!'

'There are other considerations, if you'll allow yourself to think of them,' Master Hartwell observed cautiously, for Kate's voice had sounded positively cutting in its sharpness.

'I don't choose to do so!' she said dismissively.

He made a sound which might have been a sigh, then risked another snub by saying, 'Well, meanwhile, if there is anything I can do to serve or help you, you have but to ask. Goodnight, Mistress Kate.' Then he was gone, disappearing into the darkness. Kate wept all the way home, and was not altogether sure that this was because of the emotional tension of that last service in the Abbey church.

She was back in the town early the next morning, standing amid the silent crowd outside the Abbey gateway, waiting for the canons to emerge after signing their deed of surrender. It appeared, from the news put about by the knowledgeable ones amid those waiting, that Sir Richard Rich had not condescended to come and receive the surrender himself, but had sent Dr Petre and a dozen clerks to make the inventory, so that unwanted goods and the least valuable of the church fittings could be sold off before Easter.

Presently Kate was joined by her uncle, who came out through the gateway with his fellow churchwarden, both looking tired but not unhappy.

'Is everything all right, Uncle?' Kate asked quietly.

'Yes and no,' he answered equally quietly. 'Dr Petre tried to argue that the nave was part of the Abbey, and must be closed along with the rest, but your friend Master Hartwell made an unexpected appearance, and persuaded him otherwise. A most admirable young man! I was greatly relieved by his intervention, for I have little knowledge of the legal aspects of dissolving religious houses, my practice having been concerned almost entirely with straight-forward matters of estates and inheritance. He had all the facts and the legal precedents at his fingertips, and put his case in the most irrefutable manner, cutting the ground from under Petre's feet at every turn. Why, he knows more of the history of our church than I do myself!'

'What has happened, then? Are we to lose our parish church or no?' Kate asked anxiously.

'No, for Master Hartwell proved that it belonged to the parish before ever the Abbey was founded, and the canons' part of the church was built on to it, all in the most beautiful Latin which would have delighted Cicero himself! And, for good measure, he talked Petre into agreeing that the two chantry priests might act jointly as parish priests until the gift of the living is allocated to someone. I had feared that we might have no priest for months.'

'And what of the bells?' Kate asked, sharing her uncle's relief that the parish was not to be bereft after all, and feeling a curious, almost proprietary, pleasure at his praise of Master Hartwell, which was, of course, quite ridiculous, as she disliked the man for his outrageous proposal of marriage. Presumably her pleasure was due to the thought of the Court of Augmentations having been defeated by one of its former members! To be fair, however, she had to admit that it was a good thing for the parish that the new owner of a substantial part of its land should already be taking an active part in ensuring its well-being.

'The bells!' Sir William exclaimed. 'Oh, God and Our Lady forgive me! I'd clean forgot about the bells! Of course—they belong to the Abbey. They'll be melted down for gunmetal!'

He looked about wildly, seeking the other church-warden, but, before he could locate him, the wicket gate opened again, and the departing canons came out.

They were still wearing their black robes—Kate had half-expected that they would have been required to don ordinary clothes at once—and they came in their usual order of procession, with young Father Edmund leading. A murmur passed through the waiting crowd, but no more than that. Only one person spoke aloud, and that was the miller, who was widely suspected of being a Lutheran. He said loudly, 'Well, the carrion crows take flight at last! Good . . .'

Presumably, the next word would have been 'riddance', but, before he could utter it, John Plomer the blacksmith and Harry Harvey the horse-coper, the two largest men in the town, suddenly moved up, one on either side of him, and lifted him off his feet.

'I only said it because the Augmentations man paid me to!' he whispered hoarsely.

'Thirty pieces of silver?' John Plomer enquired in an interested tone as he and Harvey carried the struggling man over to his own millstream and dropped him into it, everyone else taking no apparent notice at all, as they were too busy watching the canons.

They all had their hoods up, shadowing their faces, but they looked to left and right as they walked slowly along in single file, nodding gravely to familiar faces, and murmuring blessings. Father Humphrey paused briefly before Kate, thrusting a small, fat leather-bound book into her hands and saying, 'I trust you will find this useful. Use your gift generously, good Kate, for there will be no one else to help the sick and the injured.' Then he passed on, before Kate could reply, leaving her with the sudden realisation that the infirmary must now be closed, for she had assumed that, like the Guild chapel, it would continue its work, being a separate foundation from the Abbey—but how could it, with no Infirmarian? The book was Father Humphrey's own manuscript herbal containing invaluable receipts and information about treatments and dosages. It would seem that he did not expect ever to have any use for it again.

The lord Abbot—plain Sir Robert now—came out last, bareheaded. He crossed the bridge, then stopped and looked at all the faces turned expectantly towards him. Most were sad, and many had tears running down their cheeks as they watched him, and they saw an old man, suddenly shrunken and bowed in his plain black, where before they had always seen an upright, commanding figure, apparently ageless.

'I may not address you, my friends,' he said, his voice still steady and clear, 'but I may give you my last blessing.'

He spread his arms wide, hands turned upwards, and everyone, even the dripping miller, sank to their knees as if they were one, although some were so stiff and rheumaticky that they knew they could not rise again without help.

The blessing was long and full, encompassing every aspect of their lives—the welfare of their souls and bodies, their work, their homes, their marriages, their children, their lives on earth and their hopes of Heaven, and it was given in English—a departure from the normal which somehow reached their hearts and made these few minutes the most momentous of an historic day. The final *Amen* was echoed by voices choked with tears.

Sir Robert's hands dropped to his sides and he bowed his head, then drew his hood up to shade his face, as his brethren had done, and he paced slowly after them, hands concealed in his sleeves and his eyes on the ground, to where Father Thomas waited with that same recalcitrant mule which had brought the Abbot to the Grange house to introduce Master Hartwell on a day which now seemed to Kate very long ago.

The crowd dispersed in silence and sorrow, yet, on Maundy Thursday, most of them returned to cross the bridge and enter the enclosure in a different frame of mind, coming to attend the sale of much of the portable property of the Abbey which had not been appropriated for other purposes, haggling with the Augmentations men for sharper bargains, and generally failing to meet with much success, as those men now had several years' experience of such sales behind them.

Kate went, clutching one of her gold angels, determined to obtain as many articles as possible of use to her in her healing work. She was accompanied by one of her uncle's serving-boys, pushing a stout wheelbarrow to hold her purchases.

Most of the women were interested in kitchen equipment, and the men in the tools from the forge and the other workshops, or wood and stone from wherever any might be available. Some hurried to the Choir and presbytery of the church, only to find that the King had ordered that the building be stripped of its lead roof, but otherwise left standing for the time being, and they had to be content with demolishing the flimsier structures in the enclosure for whatever they could salvage from them.

Kate was almost the only one to go to the infirmary, where the man in charge looked at her shrewdly and enquired if she were Mistress Cressy.

'Yes,' she replied, disconcerted.

'The former Infirmarian asked that we might save this for you, if you should want it,' he said, gesturing towards a small coffer, barely three feet long and nearly as wide, and four feet high on its stubby feet. It had three drawers, each with a plain but good iron lock, and three different keys to fit them. Kate pulled out the top drawer, and found that it was full of stoneware and glass pots, each with a well-fitting lid with the name of a herb or root painted across it. It was Father Humphrey's medicine chest!

'How—How much is it?' she asked anxiously.

The man looked at it sidelong and sniffed disparagingly. 'Considering what it is, and what use you'll be making of it, you can have it for a shilling,' he said.

Kate produced her angel, and wondered where she could get it changed, but the man delved into a leather pouch and gave her the change in silver shillings, which Kate took a little doubtfully in exchange for her gold, and was surprised to find that they were good, true coins of the old King's time, not the debased rubbish of the present reign.

'The Abbey kept a good money-chest,' the man volunteered with a grin, 'which was to the canons' advantage, for their reward money was paid to them out of it! Every coin in it was old and full weight. I helped to count them, so I know it's true! What else would you like?'

Father Humphrey had used a marble mortar and pestle, which Kate had long coveted, for her own was but ordinary stone and contaminated her salves and compounds with grit. It was standing on a small, stoutly-made oak table near by, and she pointed to it. 'How much is that?' she asked.

'Twopence,' the man said, giving it a cursory glance. 'Too small to be much use in the kitchen.'

'But it's not meant for kitchen use!' Kate exclaimed.

'So it's of no value to anyone but you. You can have the table as well for another twopence.'

Kate expended the fourpence without hesitation, before he could change his mind, and the boy helped her to load her acquisitions into the barrow. Having made her intended purchases for a fraction of the sum she had expected to pay, she went round looking for other bargains, and bought a small pair of scales, a measuring-jug, a dozen pairs of splints of various sizes, and a stout linen bag to carry them in, all for another penny the lot.

As he put them in the bag, the man asked off-handedly, 'Do you know aught good for kybes? My wife has them cruelly on her hands and toes in winter.'

'She should boil a white beetroot to a paste and spread it on the chilled flesh as hot as she can bear,' Kate replied briskly, 'and try to dry her hands well whenever she wets them, and rub goose-grease or wool-fat into them when they're sore or chapped. Best of all, she should try to keep hands and feet warm, for it's getting numb with cold causes the kybes.'

'Ay—I'll tell her. She'll be grateful!' the man said, adding a dozen fat rolls of good linen bandage and a very small, carefully sealed, glass phial to Kate's bag. She discovered afterwards that the phial contained poppy-juice, and was worth more than all the other things she had bought put together, which puzzled her, as she was sure that the man knew very well what it was, and its value, and he did not appear to be overcome with gratitude to that extent for her advice.

Leaving the infirmary, she sent the boy to her uncle's house with the barrow, giving him a penny for his trouble, which unexpected windfall filled him with delight, while she went to see what else might be useful. Apart from the infirmary, the Abbot's hall and the almonry, she had never seen the other domestic buildings, so she wandered about looking at them. Having heard all her life of the wealth and luxury of the monasteries, she was surprised how old and shabby everything seemed to be. The tables in the refectory were plain scrubbed deal, like any in the poorest kitchen, and even the Abbot's bedchamber

had old, faded, ill-darned hangings and a plain pallet
bed without posts or curtains, scarcely less hard than
the floor it stood on.

In the church, she was startled to find the vestry
goods being sold, and she had qualms about even
going near them at first, wondering if the sacrilege
would bring Christ to cleanse the Temple as he had
done in the Gospel story, but everyone seemed to be
buying and selling as easily as if they were in the
market square, so she went to look, meaning only to
satisfy her curiosity.

Master Hartwell was there, buying books from the
Abbey library by the barrow-load, and squabbling
amicably with a gentleman, whom she believed was
Dr William Petre, over an armful of them, but she
moved to the other end of the aisle, well away from
him, without him seeing her.

It appeared that everything of obvious value had
already been packed up and sent under guard to the
Tower of London, to be added to the King's very
considerable store of monastic treasures, and the next
best of the vestments and altar vessels had been
allocated to the parish churches formerly owned by
the Abbey, but there was still plenty left, an
accumulation of centuries in a foundation for twenty-
four canons, each of whom had to say his daily Mass,
so there had been at least a dozen altars. The hopeful
purchasers were turning over piles of old vestments,
frontals, altar-cloths, veils, banners and stoles, and
some were buying silver chalices for secular use at
mealtimes.

One of the sellers offered Kate a prettily engraved
little silver chalice for five shillings, saying it would
make her a fine caudle-cup or a wine goblet, and,
after a long hesitation, she decided to buy it, thinking
to save it from such a fate and keep it herself until

she could perhaps restore it to its proper use. Her hesitation was misunderstood, and resulted in the man offering to 'throw in' a single candlestick which had lost its partner and an old cope, all for the same price, which she hastily accepted.

She retired to one of the side-chapels, which was bare, its altar stripped and dark, probably for the first time since it was consecrated, and there considered her purchases by the light streaming in through a great window which had already lost most of its glass, despite the King's orders about the building.

The cope was made of silk damask which had once been crimson, but it had faded to a deep rose-pink. It was embroidered with seraphim, each with his six wings properly arranged as it said in Revelations. The work was done in soft, pretty silks, and the feathers of the wings were outlined in gold thread, which was tarnished black but came up like new when Kate rubbed it with a licked finger. A broad band of cream silk along the straight side was embroidered, too, with Latin letters which she made out to mean, 'To Thee cherubim and seraphim continually do cry.'

'I shall sponge you carefully with a clean, damp cloth,' she said to the cope, 'and use you for a bed-cover. You'll be warm in winter, and what better protection could I have while I sleep than a dozen angels?'

She took the rest of her purchases to Sir William's house, for she had arranged to leave there whatever she bought until she moved with her father to their new home, and he locked the chalice away in his strong-box, saying that an inn was no place to take anything of such value, for it might be stolen.

The move was eventually made, after various hitches, on the Monday after Easter Day, which had been almost as sad and drear as Good Friday, despite the efforts of the chantry priests, the churchwardens, and the women who had scoured the meadows and gardens for Lenten lilies for decoration, the bright yellow of which seemed to mock the sadness of the congregation, who could not even manage to proclaim their Risen Lord with any cheerfulness, such was the pervading feeling of loss and mourning.

Master Cressy had sold all his expensive furniture at a considerable loss, apart from his bed and one of his big carved armchairs, for the rooms they were to occupy at the Three Tuns were already furnished. They were conveniently arranged to give a degree of privacy, for the ground floor of the building was split by a cart-arch to allow access to a long, narrow courtyard, and their rooms were in the smaller part of it, while the public rooms of the inn were on the other side. They had a small stable, which was to be occupied by Jewel, and their own access through a door beyond it. This opened on a narrow, ladder-like flight of stairs to the room above, which was their parlour. Master Cressy's bedchamber was beyond that, towards the front of the house, and Kate was to have a small garret above the parlour, reached by a ladder. There was no kitchen for them, for the landlady, a stout, middle-aged widow called Mistress Golding, would provide their meals from her own kitchen.

Kate managed to get her coffer and her small table safely up to her room with the help of two of her uncle's men. She made the end of the room furthest from the ladder into her still-room, for it was well lit by a casement window containing little lead-glazed panes of real glass, albeit thick, green and flawed, giving a very odd view of the jumble of little courts and gardens behind the shops and inns. She had not much room left for anything else once the coffer and table were in place, but the furniture of her old room at the Grange house had been sold, without explanation or apology from her father, and she had not even a shelf for her books, only a simple pallet bed and a clumsy wooden chest for her clothes.

Through his brother's good offices, Master Cressy had been appointed Parish Clerk, which was an honourable employment where his ability to write well, keep accounts and make inventories would be of great value. He thought he was not very well paid, but it was better and far less degrading than labouring in the fields with the common men whom he had formerly employed on the Abbey's behalf, a humiliation which he had dreaded. The money, which was nearly twice the amount a labourer might hope to get for half the hours of work, was, with his pension, enough to pay for their food and lodging, and leave something over to be saved for necessities. Both he and Kate had enough clothing to last for some time, with care, and soon she too was able to contribute, much to her own as well as her father's surprise.

The departure of Father Humphrey and the closing of the infirmary had left the townsfolk with no one to turn to for help and advice about their injuries and ailments, and, with Kate now living in the town instead of nearly a mile away, they began to come to her when their own knowledge proved inadequate, and she soon spent much of her time gathering herbs, drying and pounding them for ointments, draughts and compounds in her little garret, and visiting her patients. She tried at least to ease those she could not cure, admitted at once if she could not help, sent for one of the two chantry priests early rather than late if there was no hope, and coped more than adequately with the rest. She steadfastly refused to accept coin, or, indeed, any metal, for her services, but was paid well enough in eggs, honey, worts, fruit, butter, pots of conserve, shoe-repairs, and anything else her patients' families could manage and thought she might need.

It was less than a month after she and her father had settled in at the Three Tuns when she returned one mid-morning after sitting up half the night to see a child through the crisis of a fever. She was content when she turned in under the arch, satisfied that the child would recover, and, as usual, she paused by the stable-door for a few words with Jewel. The stable was empty.

After the first shock, she was quick to realise what had happened, for the saddle, footboard and harness were gone too, and the stable was as bare as if it had never housed a horse. Even the hay and oats, which she had earned herself by treating Master Harvey's wife's shingles, were missing.

She leaned against the doorpost for a few moments, trying not to dissolve into tears, half angry, half torn with anxiety about the fate of the mare. She was such a fine-boned little creature, and the thought of her put to the plough, or harnessed to a cart too heavy for her strength, was heartbreaking.

'Mistress Cressy?' Mistress Golding called from her kitchen door across the courtyard.

Kate went over to her, and asked anxiously, 'Do you know where my father has taken Jewel? He's sold her, I know, but where? Who bought her?'

'Well, you can't expect Master Cressy to keep a horse for your pleasure, when he's at his wits' end to get money for his own keep, let alone yours! I suppose you'll be expecting a meal now, having missed your supper last night?'

'I had some bread and ale,' Kate replied dismissively.

'Please, Mistress Golding, please tell me where Jewel has gone!'

'If you must know, first thing this morning, Master Cressy took your little horse and all the bits and bobs along to Harry Harvey, and got a good price for them, so he said when he came back. You be thankful that your father's a good business-man, and Master Harvey wouldn't dare cheat him, you can be sure!'

'Thank you!' Kate exclaimed, and ran from the kitchen door and back out through the arch, narrowly missing being run down by a heavy wagon which was toiling up the slope to the market square. This made her slow down and proceed in a more fitting manner to Master Harvey's stables. From the street, it looked like a cornchandler's, but there was a cart-arch at the side, and through this, a cobbled entry led to the yard at the back.

There, Master Harvey was sitting on a stool, plaiting the tail of a fine cart-horse, which stood like a rock, looking at nothing in particular under its long eyelashes and chewing at something pleasant in a well-filled nosebag. A large tabby cat was asleep on its back.

'Good day, Mistress Cressy,' the horse-coper said, glancing up from his work. 'I can't stop—the carter's coming back for him in ten minutes, and I've the mane to do yet. Are you wanting to know about your little mare?'

'Yes! Oh, please . . .' Kate clasped her hands tightly together, hardly daring to ask, yet compelled by her need to know. 'Where is she?'

'Why, sold straight away! The gentleman said a week ago—no, a fortnight, it'd be! Anyways, he said he thought Master Cressy might be selling her, and he'd buy, no questions, no quibbling, so I sent the lad, and he came back hisself to get her, the price in his hand, a shilling for the lad, and ale-money for me as well. A shilling for the lad, mind you! He said to tell you that you're welcome to go see her or ride her whenever you please. I must say he's a most generous gentleman, though no fool, I can tell you! He told me to a penny how much I was overcharging him, and warned me not to make a habit of it, but as pleasant as you like! I enjoyed dealing with him.'

'You overcharged him?' Kate exclaimed.

'Well, he said no questions asked! Anyways, I offered him back the difference, but he said I could keep it this time.' Master Harvey grinned up at her unashamedly, still plaiting red ribbon into the tail as fast as his fingers would go.

'And who was he?' Kate asked breathlessly, already half-guessing.

'Why, the gentleman what the King give your house to. Master Hartwell, o' course!'

CHAPTER TEN

KATE RETURNED to the Three Tuns in a confused state of mind, half-annoyed with Master Hartwell, and half inclined to think him very kind, for she could not work out why he had bought Jewel. Although he was not a big man, she was too small to serve him as a riding horse, and he would surely realise that she was no use for farm work. Had he just taken her because she 'belonged' to the house, so to speak, or as some sort of retaliation against her for refusing his offer of marriage? Could it possibly be simply an act of kindness? But why? What advantage could it bring him?

She could not imagine, after what Amyas had told her about life at Court, that anyone used to that dog-eat-dog striving for position and influence, which necessitated a constant flow of gifts or services to gain useful 'friends', would ever do anything without ulterior motive, yet Matthew Hartwell had done several things, to her knowledge, that were unlikey to bring him any return save gratitude, but the man was no fool.

As she turned in under the arch, she was still abstracted and puzzled, and would have walked straight by the kitchen door if Mistress Golding had not called her.

'Mistress Cressy, come in, do! There's two men come seeking you, strangers, and one on 'em in a mighty hurry.'

'Two men?' Kate looked at her in astonishment. 'What men are they? What do they want?'

'The one in a hurry's here, in the kitchen. Best see him first. The other can wait—he's in the little parlour, for I'd not wish any of my customers to see him. I don't know what they want—'tis none of my business.'

Kate gathered from her acid tone that she had failed to find out, despite questioning. She re-entered the warm, scrubbed kitchen, and a thin little man rose from the stool where he had been sitting by the fire, and came to meet her, looking impatient and none too pleased.

'Mistress Katherine Cressy? I was about to give you up and be on my way.'

'I've not been above a quarter-hour!' Kate protested.

That's as may be, but I've got to get to Ware and back to London this day, and Woodham's well out of my way, whatever my master says. I've to deliver this packet to you, and have your mark made on my docket here.'

He held out a small packet wrapped in a piece of cloth, which was stitched firmly all around with fine twine. It had a paper label stitched on it, with the direction 'To Mistress Katherine Cressy at the sign of the Three Tuns in Woodham in the County of Essex.'

'What is it?' asked Kate, taking it and turning it to and fro. It felt like a small box.

'How do I know? I'm but the messenger. The stitching's not broken anywhere?'

'No,' Kate agreed, looking at it.

'Then do you make your mark here, then, and I'll be on my way.'

He laid a slip of parchment on Mistress Golding's

scrubbed table (which made her hiss indignantly), produced a travelling inkhorn and a quill, and pointed to a blank space on the slip.

Kate picked up the slip and started to read it, but the man snatched it and said angrily, 'I've no time to waste while you spell it out! It says just that you've received this here packet unopened.'

Kate raised her eyebrows, twitched the slip from between his fingers, and deliberately read it. It said exactly what he had said it did, so she took quill, which was ill cut and spluttered, and wrote her name in her usual neat, firm handwriting. The man stowed away his inkhorn and pen, took the slip and left, waving it about to dry the ink, and muttering about getting to Ware and back before nightfall.

'Whatever can it be?' enquired Mistress Golding with elaborate casualness, handing Kate a thin-bladed knife.

'I can't imagine,' she replied, frowning. She cut the stitches and pulled off the fabric covering. Inside was a small, hinged wooden box, and inside that, wrapped in a square of silk, a brooch.

'My, that's a pretty thing!' Mistress Golding exclaimed, peering over Kate's shoulder. 'A love-token, I shouldn't wonder! From London, did he say? I'll warrant one of them Court gallants took a fancy to you while the King was here, and he's sent you a fairing. Is there a note?' She managed to sound disagreeable, despite her curiosity.

'No, nothing,' Kate replied, quite at a loss, for, apart from the silk and the brooch, the box was empty, and there was nothing on the cloth wrapper but the direction. She examined the brooch, thinking that something about it might give her a clue.

It was made of some sort of yellow metal which looked quite like gold, and it was circular, about two inches in diameter. In the centre was a rose, a wild briar rose, painted a delicate pink on the petals, with tiny metal stamens in the centre. It was wreathed about, caged almost, with stems bearing thorns, which were painted just the red of briar thorns. Round the edge was a posy, an inscription, cut into the metal and filled with black to make it easily legible. *SPINAS TRANSIREM UT ROSAM CARPEREM*, Kate spelled out.

'And what may that mean?' Mistress Golding asked tartly—she could not read, and considered it an unnecessary accomplishment for a woman.

'*Spinas* is thorns, I think, and *rosam* is something to do with a rose,' Kate said. 'I haven't enough Latin to make out the meaning, though.'

An idea was forming in her mind as she looked at the gift. It came from London—perhaps Mistress Golding was right, and it was a fairing from a Court gallant—from Amyas! No one else would send her a love-token, and that must be what this was! He must have seen it at a fair, or somewhere like that, and thought it pretty and suitable for her. It was well made, and must have cost him a shilling or more, for the painting was carefully done, in accurate colours, and the maker had even taken the trouble to put some sort of a mark on the back, as if he had some pride in his work. She could make out a crowned, bearded head, and letters—a T and a W, she thought, but she had no idea what, if anything, they signified.

Dear Amyas! She could guess what the brooch meant! The rose was hemmed in by thorns, and it must mean that their love was surrounded by difficulties, but at least he had thought of her, and sent her this pretty thing.

'The other man's still waiting,' Mistress Golding

prompted, noting for further reference that Kate's normally over-firmed lips had softened to a faint smile, and her eyes were shining.

'Yes. In the little parlour, you said?' Kate pinned the brooch securely inside her wide sleeve, out of sight, and went to seek her second visitor.

The small parlour was a dark little room, its one window under the shadow of the arch, and at first she could hardly make out the figure which rose from a seat at the table as she entered, and stood looking at her in silence.

'You wanted me?' she asked, moving closer.

The man was tall and thin, and as she drew near, he half-turned away and the light from the window fell on him, catching his profile and something odd about the top of his head. When Kate was within an arm's length of him, she realised that he was a monk—no wonder Mistress Golding didn't wish her customers to see him! He was clad in his black robe, the hood thrown back, and the crown of his head, where his tonsure had been, was sprouting a circle of new growth, so short that it stood up straight, looking very odd. His face was hollow-cheeked, with a beaky nose and deep-set eyes which burned as he gave her one searching look before dropping his gaze. It was her brother.

'Why, John!' she exclaimed. 'How good to see you! How are you?'

'How would you expect, sister?' he asked in a quiet, bitter voice. 'How do you feel after losing your home? Content with the world?'

'St Alban's was dissolved last December!' she exclaimed. 'Why did you not come straight home? Where have you been these four months?'

'Trying to live in the world,' he replied, sitting down abruptly on the chair from which he had risen. 'I had a home, and wanted no other in this world. What was there for me here? Your father wouldn't take me back, you know very well.'

'Our father,' Kate corrected, although she knew that Master Cressy had disowned John before he entered religion. 'Have you not come to see him, then?'

No. I hoped I might see you, but I came to consult Uncle Cressy, to seek his advice, and maybe his help, but they said at his house that he's away to London about some bells, and not expected back for a few days.

'Yes, that's true. When the Abbey here surrendered last month, he didn't realise that the bells in the tower would be lost to us, and he's gone to the Court of Augmentations to try to buy some of them back.'

John continued to look at the floor, and made no reply, but his thin shoulders sagged as if his last hope had gone.

'What did you want of him? Can I help at all?' Kate asked gently.

'Not unless you know a lawyer who would give advice without payment,' he replied, the bitterness so apparent in his voice that Kate guessed that he had been refused more than once.

She bit her lip, thinking. 'Advice about what?'

'Leaving England.'

'Leaving . . .? Why? Where would you go?'

John put his elbow on the table and rubbed his hand over his face, than half-covered his mouth and said, very quietly, 'Can we go somewhere else to talk?'

Kate glanced over her shoulder towards the door, wondering if Mistress Golding were listening at the keyhole. 'Will you walk by the cornmill stream with me? I need to gather some peppermint.'

John nodded mutely, and followed her out of the inn and down Church Street, his hood over his head and his hands concealed within his wide sleeves. He moved silently in his worn sandals, and said nothing at all as they crossed the footbridge by the ford and turned up the lane past the mill, and on beside the stream.

Kate paused occasionally to pick a sprig of water-peppermint, or a few stems of eyebright, until they were well away from the town and the Grange buildings, and then she stopped and turned towards him.

'Let's sit on the bank and talk. No one can overhear us here.'

John looked about him, not at the meadows, which shone green in the sun, spangled with flowers, or at the Forest, dark in the distance, but only to see that there was no one nearer than a man cutting osiers by another stream in the distance.

'There's little to say,' he replied. 'I entered religion because God called me. I was content, my life all that I wanted in the this world. Now, I have nothing but a little money, which I don't want, save to keep life in a body grown weary of this world. All I want is to return to the ordered life of the Rule. I want to follow St Benedict for what time remains to me, to pray and comtemplate, to sing the Offices, to work with books, or in the gardens.'

'But there are no monasteries left,' Kate said sympathetically.

'Not in England, but elsewhere—France, or Flanders, or even Spain . . . I want to find out how I may obtain a pass to go abroad, but no one will tell me! I know it can be done, but how? I'm no traitor—I'm loyal, I took the Oath willingly, but I can't live in the world!'

Kate looked at him, and thought that she had never seen anyone so burned up by misery. 'Oh, John! I wish I could help! Who would know . . .?'

The answer sprang into her mind even as she asked the question. Who but a lawyer, a man who had served the Court of Augmentations?

'Master Hartwell! Of course!' she exclaimed. 'Come, John. We're going to see the very man you need.'

John gave her one searching glance from those deep, unhappy eyes, which briefly showed a faint glimmer of life, then his disciplined gaze returned to the ground, and he followed her in silence again.

She thought it best to approach the Grange house from the back, which entailed a roundabout route and brought them eventually to the kitchen door, where Dame Marjorie welcomed them both with delight. Kate was surprised by the change in her, for she seemed to have lost most of her nervous mannerisms, and hardly clucked or stammered at all, but talked volubly of the changes Master Hartwell had already made about the house, with the obvious implication that it was all much better than it had been in the old days.

She plied her vistors with ale and food, for it was past dinner-time, and this, too, surprised Kate, for she knew that Dame Marjorie had never entertained anyone in the old days without first nervously and humbly asking leave of Master Cressy.

'You'll find the master in the garden,' she said when Kate explained that she had come to seek Master Hartwell's aid for her brother.

'Garden!' exclaimed Kate, for such an amenity had not existed in her father's day. The Dame

explained that Master Hartwell was turning the
rough field between the house and the road into a
terraced garden, so Kate went there to find him,
leaving her brother to rest in the kitchen.

There was little sign as yet of the results of
Master Hartwell's plans, apart from some trenching
in the lower part of the steep field near the road,
and a row of what looked like thorny green twigs
stuck in the ground at the edge of the track which
led up from the road to the house. Master Hartwell
was sitting on the grass under a large oak, bareheaded and in his shirtsleeves, patiently feeding
pieces of bread to a squirrel which sat facing him,
taking each piece between it paws and eating it
quickly but neatly before reaching for another.

Both man and squirrel looked up as Kate
approached, then the man rose in one fluid
movement and the squirrel ran up the tree and sat
on a low branch, ready to return when all was safe.

'Good day, Mistress Kate! Have you come to see
Jewel?' Master Hartwell asked pleasantly.

'Jewel?' Kate was disconcerted, having forgotten
about the mare in her anxiety about her brother.

'Did Harvey not tell you I had her safe? I guessed
your father would sell her, and I'd not like to see a
fine little creature like that broken by ploughing or
too heavy a cart.'

'But she's of no use to you,' Kate said, puzzled
and feeling at a great disadvantage, coming to ask a
favour of a man, only to be reminded that she was
already deeply in his debt before she had even
started.

'Luckily I'm sufficiently well with the world not
to have to limit my purchases to things that are of
use,' he said, his eyes twinkling. 'Have you not
heard of my extravagance? Why, I'm even trying to

make this little desert bloom like the rose. You see, there will be terraces, like giant steps down the slope, where I shall grow roses and sweet herbs, so that I may walk among them and savour their perfume in the morning, or the evening. That,' indicating the row of green twigs, 'I'm assured will soon be an impenetrable thorn hedge, to keep the deer from eating my garden as it grows. Not that even a thorn hedge is completely impenetrable, to a determined soul . . .' He gave Kate an enigmatic smile, which she failed to see, for she was walking in his garden in her imagination.

'We never had a garden,' she said wistfully, seeing in her head how the slope would look with stone-paved or gravelled terraces and roses clothing what was now a rough pasture.

'You could help me to make it,' he said softly.

Kate took his meaning this time, and her lips tightened into a firm line. 'I'll not waste your time when you're busy,' she said in a business-like manner. 'You said that you would help me if I needed it . . .' Her whole being was flooded with embarrasment at having to ask a favour of him, but he *had* offered. 'I can pay!'—thinking of her remaining angels. 'It's my brother, John.'

'Who is—was—a monk at St Alban's?'

'Yes. He's so unhappy!' She found that it was not easy to explain to a hard-headed lawyer about her brother's deep feelings and emotions. 'It isn't that he opposed the dissolution, and he's loyal to the King—he took the Oath of Supremacy without reservations—he signed the surrender willingly— he's tried hard to live in the world . . .'

'But his vocation is too strong.' Master Hartwell finished the sentence for her quite matter-of-factly.

'Yes.'

'Then he should do as several others have done before him—apply to the Court of Augmentations for permission to go abroad to follow his vocation. He'll lose his pension, of course, but he'll have no difficulty entering a Flemish or French abbey. I take it that Sir William hasn't returned yet?'

Kate thought she followed this apparent *non sequitur*, and said stiffly, 'I'd not have troubled you otherwise.'

Master Hartwell regarded her with a slight frown. 'You've not troubled me—I meant what I said. It's lucky that your uncle is still in London. Brother John must go to him with a letter which I shall write, and Sir William will see that he and the letter find their way to the right secretary, who will give him his pass. Where is he now?'

'In the kitchen.'

'He'll have to take an Oath of Loyalty, but I take it he'll not object to that?'

'I think not,' Kate replied, feeling more confused than ever about this man, who should, she felt, have been hard-hearted and uncaring about the spiritual problems of an ex-monk, yet had seemed to understand at once just how John felt, without even seeing him. He had no reason, apart from possibly a little gratitude to her for treating the injury to his hand, to be so kind to her, yet he had not hesitated to help her when she asked—or, in the case of Jewel, without being asked. He had not mentioned anything about payment, so did he expect some 'gift' for what he was offering to do? She braced herself, and waited for the apparently casual mention of something, and, since she had no hunting-dogs, no quails' eggs. no hawk which he might desire, and very little money, she had an unpleasant feeling that she could guess what he might want. A woman with nothing had still one thing to give.

Master Hartwell looked at the heel of a loaf which he still held in his hand, as if not sure how he had come by it, then recollected and held it up to the squirrel, which seized it with a chattering that might have expressed pleasure, or surprise, or 'About time too!', and disappeared up into the tree with it.

'Come, then,' Master Hartwell said briskly. 'The sooner your brother is on his way, the better!' He put a hand on Kate's elbow to guide her back towards the house.

'There is one more thing,' she said, stiffening at his touch. 'I am well aware that, in Court circles, it's not the custom to do anyone a favour without expectation of some return. I have a little money . . .'

'Keep it, then,' he replied. 'We're not moving in Court circles, are we? I still owe you a great deal for saving my hand. Father Humphrey assured me that I'd have lost the use of it, if not its physical attachment to me, but for you. Besides, we're not discussing a business arrangement but a little exchange of problems and help between friends.' With that, he hurried Kate indoors, leaving her feeling more perplexed and confused than ever, with the feeling deep inside her that she would be foolish to continue to judge this man by comparison with anyone else she knew, for he was different. In what the difference lay, she could not tell, but she did know that there was something about him which was making him unexpectedly important in her life.

His interview with John was quite short, for the two of them seemed to understand one another at once. He asked John a few searching questions, which John answered without hesitation, mostly in Latin, as if he found it easier to express himself in that language. The letter was written, careful instructions given to John about where he was to go, for whom to ask—and, equally important, whom to avoid—and exactly what he was to say to Sir William, and then he was sent on his way on a good horse, with enough money and to spare for his simple needs. He accepted Master Hartwell's generosity with a calm dignity, not as if it were his due, but more as if it were the due of Someone Else, Who required it for His use. He gave his blessing to his benefactor, to Kate and to Dame Marjorie in a quiet, unemotional manner, as if, in spirit at least, he had already left the world again. 'I shall pray for you,' he added, and then rode away without a backward look.

'Will he be all right?' Kate asked uncertainly, watching him go down the steep track. She could hardly claim to know him well, for he had entered the monastery when she was only nine years old, and she had not seen or heard from him since, until today. In fact, it was a marvel she had recognised him, after so long! Nevertheless, he was her only sibling, and he had staked his life on her judgment.

'Surely. He's a prudent man, filled with burning sincerity. With your uncle's help he'll have no difficulty in obtaining his passport. To tell the truth, the Augmentations office would rather give a man a piece of paper and be rid of him than go on paying him a pension, perhaps for the rest of his life. You realise that only death, or preferment to a benefice worth more than his pension, will end the payments while an ex-religious remains in England?' Master Hartwell smiled encouragingly down into her anxious face. 'By the way—there is a favour I would ask of you—one of my horses has a small saddle-gall.'

'Where is it?' Kate asked, perversely relieved that there was something she could do in exchange for his help, for she was too proud to accept charity with equanimity.

The horse was in the paddock, and came to its master's whistle, then stood to have the sore examined. It was a very small gall, and Kate asked Master Hartwell to send one of his grooms back to Woodham with her to fetch a pot of salve of agrimony and liverwort—a receipt that Harry Harvey had given her in return for curing his sore throat last winter.

Jewel, too, was in the paddock, and Kate, looking sidelong at her, thought how much better life must be for her, with the paddock to graze and run about in with other horses, instead of a narrow, dark stable, but she said nothing and pretended she had not noticed the mare, and it was not until they had left the paddock and were walking back across the yard to the house that she said 'Thank you' in a small, tight voice.

She did not usually have any difficulty in expressing gratitude with dignity and grace, and it was not that she did not feel grateful to him, but some rebellious spirit still begrudged her being indebted to this man, to whom her father had been prepared to give—to sell—her in exchange for the chance to keep his habitual position and comforts.

Master Hartwell replied with a slight bow, his bright eyes looking amused, as they so often seemed to do, but he said nothing until they had entered the kitchen and rejoined Dame Marjorie.

'Perhaps you would like to show Mistress Kate round the house, and see if she approves of the changes I've made?' he said to the Dame, then, without waiting for a reply, bade Kate a courteous goodbye and went out again.

Dame Marjorie seemed very pleased with the idea of showing her how much the house was already improved, and she chatted away quite freely and confidently as she took Kate round the familiar rooms of the ground floor, about Master Hartwell's plans to build a proper brick, or even stone, wing with more modern rooms, and to put another floor into the roof of the hall.

Familiar? Certainly, the structure was unchanged as yet, but the furnishings . . .! Master Hartwell's furniture was plain and solid. Instead of rough trestles for the servants and an over-ornate, bulbous-legged high table, the hall now contained three plain oak tables, old and well cared for, which glowed with polishing, and there were stout oak stools instead of flimsy benches. The master's own chair was carved, but with a simple design of leaves and branches, and the walls were hung with tapestries such as Kate had never seen before, of forest scenes with animals and flowers among the trees, and a group of hunters who did not, in fact, seem much interested in chasing anything, as they were sitting about eating and drinking, with deer wandering among them, apparently quite unafraid. And there was glass in the windows!

In the parlour were two well-made chairs, one on each side of the fireplace, with cushioned seats to match another fine tapestry, this time of a unicorn galloping across a meadow so full of flowers that there seemed no room for grass. The fabulous beast looked alive, gracefully dancing amid the flowers, his golden mane and horn gleaming in the sunlight.

Dame Marjorie wanted to take Kate through the

whole house, but she declined, making the excuse
that she must return home, as she had much to do,
but really because she was shaken by the evidence
of good taste and comfortable means which she had
already seen. Why, the man had the very furniture
she would have chosen herself for this house; and
those beautiful hangings! He must have feathered
his nest well in the King's service to have such
lovely things!

'The tapestries were a gift from his father,' Dame
Marjorie said, stroking the unicorn with one finger.
'Are they not fine? The family owns much land in
the West Country, but Master Hartwell, as a
younger son, chose to make his own way in the
world. Are you sure you wouldn't like to see your
old room? It's just as you left it, for he bought the
furniture at Master Cressy's sale, and he's had glass
put in that window, too.' Kate shook her head, and
made no comment, but, as she rode pillion back to
the town behind Master Hartwell's groom, she
thought irritably that the man seemed to have made
a point of acquiring as much of her former property
as possible. Did he think to bribe her to marry him
by offering her all the old, loved things she had
lost?

On arrival at the Three Tuns, she left the groom
in the narrow courtyard while she fetched the pot
of salve from her garret, and sent him off with
instructions for its use, conscious that Mistress
Golding was hovering just inside the open kitchen
door.

'Well, Mistress Cressy, you're much in demand
today!' the woman cried, darting out to catch Kate
before she could escape. 'And too late for your
dinner, which went to waste, you not being here to
eat it.'

'Yes, I'm sorry, Mistress Golding,' Kate replied patiently. 'But I was called away, as you know.'

'And nothing in return for your trouble, I'll be bound!' Mistress Golding caught her up in a sharp tone. 'Eggs and worts are all very well, but what's the point of being at everyone's beck and call, and no coin to show for it, quite apart from bringing all kinds of ragtag and bobtail into my respectable inn. You'll get the place a bad name, and ruin my trade, so you will!'

'I can't imagine what you mean,' Kate replied stiffly. 'I'm sure the townsfolk who seek me out are quite as respectable as your inn, and as for those who have called here today, as I collect that you refer to them—the last was Master Hartwell's groom, as you very well know, and the first was a messenger from London, as you also know, for you heard every word he said to me!'

'And what of the other?' Mistress Golding demanded. 'What about him? I want no Pope's spawn hanging about my inn, up to no good. What did that devil's messenger want with you, eh? That black-robed son of Beelzebub, that *friar*!'

'He was not a friar, but a Benedictine,' Kate snapped, 'and what he wanted was my business!'

'Oh, very grand, ain't we! Not my business, weren't it?' Mistress Golding jammed her hands on her hips, and her voice rose in pitch and volume. 'A very fine lady, ain't you! And one growing older by the minute! No dowry, but you've turned down the one good offer you're ever likely to get, and robbed your poor old father of a chance to live out his days in his own home. Call yourself a wise-woman? You've no more wisdom or sense than my tom-cat!—less, for he can tell which side his bread's buttered, I can tell you, which is more than you do!

You disobey your father, 'spite of the Commandments, but yet expect him to keep you, while you play the fine lady, mincing about with your pots of this and your draughts of that, poisoning poor souls who don't know no better, I wouldn't wonder. The Lord'll give you your deserts, my girl, or my name's not Martha Golding! You'll change your tune when I'm your stepmother, I can tell you, or you'll be out in the street, with your herbs and rubbish after you.'

'My stepmother!' Kate exclaimed, ignoring all the rest.

'Yes!' The woman's face recomposed itself into a smug, complacent smile, still with a touch of venom. 'Your father and me're to be wed, and then you'll earn your keep, or get out!'

'How may I earn my keep?' Kate asked coldly. 'I know but one way, and that is by tending the sick and injured, for that is the gift that God has granted me.'

'Then charge for your healing! Make them pay in good coin.'

'You know I cannot. It's against custom, and if I take money, for all I know, I may lose my gift!'

'Then sew shirts, or pick up stones in the fields! You can earn a half-penny a day at that, if you work hard enough. Or you can wash greasy pots in my scullery for your keep. Whatever way, once your father and me are wed, you'll pay you way or leave, for I'll give no lily-handed young lady free board and lodging in my house!'

Kate looked Mistress Golding in the eye, standing up straight and tall, with her chin held high, and gave her a long, calculating stare. This obviously unnerved the woman, for she ceased to bluster, her high colour subsided, and her eyes began to move shiftily. At length, Kate said frostily, 'I wish you joy of your marriage to my father. You should accord well together, being of a similar mind and disposition!'

With that she turned on her heel and went indoors, marching up to her garret with ramrod-straight back and a determined set to her features. Once upstairs in her own private domain, however, she shed a few silent tears of anger and wretchedness, then sat on her pallet, twisting her fingers together and wondering what to do. Soon she realised that her mind was almost blank, with only stray odds and ends of thought wandering through it, and she got up, intending to sort out the jars in medicine coffer. Then she remembered the brooch.

It was still pinned inside her wide sleeve, and she took it out, carried it to the window and looked at it more carefully than before. Undoubtedly it was a briar rose, set in the midst of its own protecting thorned twigs, and very pretty—more than that, beautiful—and she wondered about the craftsman who could have made something so lovely just as a fairing. Obviously he must have been proud of his work, or he would not have put his mark on the back, for that was what she assumed the tiny punched signs must be.

'How odd of Amyas not to send a message with it,' she thought. 'Unless the posy is the message— he does so hate to write anything! Well, I know "thorns" and "rose", and I think *transirem* must have something to do with crossing or passing . . . I suppose he means that we must go through briars to reach the rose—pass through a time of difficulty to reach our happiness, in other words. Oh, dearest Amyas! When will that be? And what can I do meanwhile?'

It was then that a plan began to form in her mind, a mad plan, yet one which, by its boldness, might cut through all those briars and bring her to her marriage to Amyas sooner rather than later.

One of the rafters in the garret was made from a re-used timber, and Kate had found, several days ago, that there was a deep slot cut in its upper surface, and she had concealed the remains of her reward from the King in it, wrapped in a little cloth bag. She pulled out the bag, counted the money, then added the brooch, after pressing the lovely thing to her lips, and returned the bag to its hiding-place.

Then she sat down again on the bed, and began to calculate how best to carry out her plan.

CHAPTER ELEVEN

THE NEXT few days were showery, and then came May Day, when Kate had promised to go with some of the young ladies of the local gentry to gather may-blossom along the edge of the Forest.

By tradition, the branches must be cut at dawn, so groups of giggling girls set out from Woodham in the dark, clutching one another and uttering shrill little cries of excitement and mock fear as they stumbled along the long slope towards the massed trees of the Forest. Others passed more quietly over the open fields and the pasture-land, bound in the same direction, but these were young men, often going singly or in twos and threes, each hopeful of catching one particular girl (or, in some desperate cases, any of them) away from the rest, although most of them were not too sure what they would do if they had such luck, as few had marriage in mind as yet, and any over-passionate dalliance was bound to lead to the banns being put up, by irate parents if necessary!

Kate's four companions had stayed the night with Lady Cressy in order to be assembled in time. They were sensible girls of good family, and not likely to give Kate any trouble, for they considered the young men of the town much beneath their notice. Nevertheless, she thought best to take them well away from the Forest road, and headed across-country by paths well known to her towards a great hawthorn which grew by the Selvedge, quite near to the Grange house.

They reached the tree a little before dawn, and stood under its branches, waiting. Far down in the valley, a few lights gleamed faintly in windows, where servants were already at work, and the last few brightest stars still hung in the sky. The may-blossom was thick on the tree this year, and its sweet, almondy scent fell about them so heavily that it made Kate feel oddly languid and dreamy.

Already birds were stirring in the Forest trees, and a sleepy blackbird tried some preliminary chirps, but the first music they heard was not that of the birds, but of human origin. Someone, not far off among the trees, plucked a few notes on a lute, and began to sing softly. They all knew the song well—it was very popular, and rumour said that the King had a hand in the writing of it.

> *Alas, my love, you do me wrong,*
> *To cast me off thus discourteously,*
> *When I have loved you so long,*
> *Rejoicing in your company.*

The next line, however, began wrongly—the singer had changed the words, for instead of the expected *Greensleeves* . . . he sang,

> *The Eglantine is all my joy,*
> *The Eglantine is my delight,*
> *The Eglantine is my heart of gold,*
> *And who but my own sweet Eglantine!*

The words did not fit the tune properly, but the singer changed the notes, and the whole ran smoothly enough.

'Who can it be?' whispered one of the girls. 'Does anyone know the voice?'

'No,' another replied. 'It's too soft and far away—only just loud enough to hear! I wonder which of us he is serenading?'

'He must have followed us all the way from the town,' said a third, 'for I'm sure no one could have known we were coming here, so far away from the road.'

The voice and the lute fell silent at the end of the next verse, and the first light began to streak the sky with palest pink, growing steadily and rapidly stronger. The dawn chorus burst forth from the Forest after an introductory solo from the blackbird, and the girls ran, laughing, to bathe their faces in the dew, then joined hands to dance round the old tree, pulling Kate into the ring, until they were breathless with laughter and prancing.

'What must we do now, Kate?' cried the youngest, who had never been a-Maying before.

'Now we cut some branches of blossom to make a garland, and add to it any other flowers we can find,' Kate replied, producing a sharp clasp-knife for the first part of the job. 'See if there are any bluebells among the trees, but don't stray too far away.'

'Perhaps we'll find the mysterious singer!' whispered one to another, and they went off quietly among the trees, as intent on discovering the man as on finding the flowers.

Kate cut half a dozen boughs well-laden with blossom, and sat down on a great root to weave them into a garland with some long rushes she had plucked on the way to the tree. She was thinking of other May mornings, for this was the fifth time she had come a-Maying, and that thought brought a bitter reminder of Mistress Golding's words about her growing older. She would soon be too old to be considered a girl any longer! Eighteen already, and not wed! She could just imagine the gossips saying it behind her back, and she sighed, resolving to put her plan into operation the very next day, if it were fine, for there was no sense in taking her death of a chill by getting soaked to the skin on her way.

She was so preoccupied that the soft notes of the lute crept on her almost unnoticed at first among the birdsong, but eventually she took notice, and began to wonder whom the singer might be. She knew no one in Woodham who could play the lute as well as that, or adapt a tune to fit his own words, for that matter. Perhaps it was a gentleman from Court, come back to serenade one of the girls—he could have met any one of them on the King's last visit, and perhaps been attracted to her.

Then, suddenly, her mind made a connection between the brooch, hidden in the slot in the rafter, and the word which the singer had substituted for *Greensleeves* . . . *Eglantine*—the briar rose! Could it possibly be?

'Amyas?' she called softly. 'Is it you? Amyas?'

Instead of replying, the man began to sing again, and once more he altered the words to suit himself.

I sowed the seeds of love
When the leaves of autumn fall,
I'll gather the flowers when my time comes round,
While the small birds sweetly call.

The violet I do not like
Because it fades so soon,
The lily and the pink are not for me,
For I vow I'll stay 'til June,

For in June there's the eglantine,
I'll choose it for my part,
I'll strive and I'll strain to pluck my rose,
Or die with her thorn in my heart!'

'Did you hear it?' said an excited voice after the last note had died away. The girls came running out from among the trees in a group, carrying a few bluebells between them, their faces flushed and their hoods pulled awry by the twigs and brambles.

'We searched, but we couldn't find him!' the eldest girl panted. 'I'm sure he must be further away than we thought.'

'He's probably not singing to one of us at all,' said the plainest of the four dampeningly. 'I suppose there are some other girls away over there somewhere,' she gestured vaguely, 'and he's singing to them, but the sound carries such a long way amid the trees.'

'It's all very exciting, though!' the youngest girl said, refusing to be disappointed. 'He might have been singing to us, just like something in an old story, and it sounded so beautiful and romantic among the trees.'

'I think,' said the girl who spoke the least and seemed the most intelligent, 'that he was actually up in a tree—high up—and quite some way away; but he seems to have gone now. Shall we help you with the garland, Kate?'

More flowers were gathered from the field at the Forest's edge and woven into the garland, which eventually formed a sphere of flowers, and the five girls then carried it, taking turns two by two, along the Selvedge to the Forest road, where they joined the other groups of young folk in an informal procession, each group with its garland, and individuals carrying posies or bunches of flowers, or wearing them in wreaths about heads or necks, as they returned, singing, to the town.

Many of the children then went round the town, knocking at doors, singing and showing their garlands in the hope of a reward of food or money, and the older lads and girls went to dance in the market square, where the little town band was playing country tunes as hard as it could go between pauses for draughts of ale from the Bell, the Wyvern or the Three Tuns.

Kate's charges begged to stay and dance for a while, and she allowed them to do so, but not, she warned them, for long, as Lady Cressy would expect them in good time for dinner. She intended to watch, feeling herself perhaps a little too old to join in, but she was soon seized by a passing youth in search of a partner, and pulled into the ring about the biggest garland, which had been hauled to the top of a tall pole. She fell to setting and turning with the best of them, for she was nimble and light-footed.

At some point in one of the set dances she found that the red-faced miller's son who had been partnering her had suddenly been replaced by Master Hartwell, who clasped her waist in a firm grip and swung her down the middle with such vigour that her feet left the ground. It was a pleasurable sensation, not unlike flying, and she laughed aloud, her pale cheeks flushed and her normally rather sad brown eyes sparkling.

'I've always thought you'd be beautiful if you were happy!' Master Hartwell said, smiling down at her. 'I wish you all the joy of summer, Kate!'

The band, growing thirsty, brought the dance to an end on a long chord, and Kate bent her head in a curtsy. When she raised it again, her usual contained, tight-lipped expression had returned, and she said formally, 'Thank you, sir. I wish you the same.'

'Your brother is safely on his way to Flanders,' he said quietly. 'Your uncle returned an hour since with my horse and the news . . . Oh, and the assurance of keeping the bells! He rode down to Dover to see him off on the way to Calais. But I'm sure he'll wish to tell you all about it himself. Is that your garland? It's a very fine one! May I help you carry it?'

Kate looked round her for charges, and found they were not far off, apart from the youngest, who was inspecting another group's garland, but she came running when she was called.

'They have a doll in their garland,' the child reported. 'They say it's the Lady, and that everyone used to have one in their garland at one time!'

'Yes,' Kate replied with a glance at Master Hartwell. 'But we're not supposed to any more, because it's superstitious! Come, we must take ours home to Lady Cressy now, and hang it above her door.'

Master Hartwell did help to carry the flowery sphere, but not with Kate, who let the girls have the honour while she walked behind, thinking about her brother and praying that he might find a haven of peace in some foreign monastery. Sir William's grooms hoisted the garland on to the hook above the house door which normally supported a lantern, and Kate slipped away while everyone's attention was on the manoeuvre.

She was met by a sharp comment from Mistress Golding about young ladies who had time to go a-Maying and prancing about with the children in the market-place when they should be attending to their own households and raising their children, instead of coming home at all hours, expecting to find a meal prepared and ready for them. Her father gave her his customary inimical glare, and then ignored her throughout the usual uncomfortable meal.

That night there was a fine, red sunset, but not too red, and Kate made ready to leave in the morning, laying out a plain russet gown and a linen cap, her strongest shoes and a light cloak. She pulled her bag of treasures out of its hiding-place and considered her small hoard of coins, eventually deciding to take only the small ones, which amounted to several shillings, and leave the two remaining gold angels, for she could return for them later, sometime. The brooch she fastened inside the top of her corset, where it would rest between her breasts and she could feel that it was safe, and the money she meant to take with her went in a leather purse, which hung on two straps from her girdle. The rest she put back into the bag and hid again in the slot in the rafter.

She prayed long and earnestly before she crept between the sheets, and lay waiting for the hour before daybreak, not expecting to sleep, but, in fact, dozing off after a while, and waking just as the first sparrow under the eaves began an irritable chittering at the approach of dawn.

Swiftly she arose and dressed, made her bed by feel rather than sight, for she did not wish to light a taper for fear of attracting attention. She left no note of explanation, in case her plan, which she knew to be desperate, should go wrong, forcing her to come home again, looking foolish, and laying herself open to Mistress Golding's sarcastic tongue. It would be some hours before she was missed, and, if all went as she hoped, she would send a message to—to her uncle, she decided, not her father, as he had chosen to cut himself off from her.

The stairs and the floorboards of the house all creaked of their own accord, and, by moving slowly, gently and shoeless, she managed to get downstairs and outside without any noticeable addition to the

usual amount of sound from them. She waited until
she had passed under the arch and into the street
before putting on her shoes, and then set off
westwards, just as the first notes of the 'prentice bell
sounded from the church.

West Street, beyond the ford, ran out of the town
and across the meadows, marshes and various streams
of the river on a raised causeway, and already the
first carts were on their way to and fro across it. Kate
kept a lookout for familiar faces, pulling up the hood
of her cloak to hide her face, lest she be recognised
and her being abroad and going this way mentioned
in the town, but she saw no one she knew, and
reached the far side of the causeway unnoticed.

A little further on, and not much above a mile
from Woodham, stood a great stone cross, where the
lane joined the old road which ran north towards
Ware and Cambridge, and south to London. She
turned to her left and began to trudge Londonwards,
listening for the rumble of a heavy wagon going to
the City markets, and before long she heard one
coming, and stopped to wait for it.

It was a great, lumbering vehicle drawn by eight
horses, with broad-rimmed wooden wheels with iron
tyres, which made a considerable noise on the stony
road. A canvas hood, stretched over wooden struts,
protected its cargo of vegetables, sacks and bundles
of goods from the weather and the dust.

Kate hailed the driver, an elderly, sleepy-looking
man wrapped in what looked like several old blankets,
with a stocking-cap pulled down to his eyebrows.

'How much to ride to London?' she asked.

The man looked at her, apparently decided that
she looked clean, respectable and sober, and replied,
'A ha'penny.'

Kate already knew that this would be the probable

charge, and had the coin ready in her hand. The man took it, looked at it carefully, found it was good, and gave her a hand to scramble up, via one of the shafts, and get into the wagon, under the hood.

'Best go towards the back,' he said. 'Keep to the side, and don't walk on the worts—they're mostly cabbages and carrots. There's some sacks of grain behind them. Don't mind the dog.'

Kate edged along the wagon-bed, crouching under the awning, and found a fairly comfortable seat where she could see out of the back. A large, wolfish-looking dog turned to inspect her, but the man called out something to it, and, after sniffing the hem of her skirts dubiously, it thumped its tail a couple of times in a perfunctory fashion, then ignored her, being more interested in guarding the vehicle from possible invasion by thieves from the rear.

The wagon rumbled and jolted along slowly and noisily, but the road, being one used frequently by important folk, was in good repair, and they maintained a steady pace—something over four miles an hour, and faster than Kate could have walked over the distance. It left a cloud of dust behind it, so she saw little of what lay on either side of the road, save when they passed through a village with a paved street, and neither did she see much of other vehicles or riders, for they tended to stay well back behind them to avoid choking in their dustcloud.

Considering that it had rained several times in the past week, Kate was surprised at how much dust there was, but she noticed that the puddles at the sides of the road were just as great an inconvenience, for the wide wheels sent up a splash of muddy water over any unfortunate pedestrian who was near by when they rolled through one, and she was glad that she had decided to expend a precious coin on riding, rather than trying to walk all the way.

It was about twelve miles or so from where she had joined the wagon to its destination, and the journey seemed interminable, for she had nothing to do but think, her efforts to talk to the driver having proved useless because of the noise of the wheels and the creaking timbers, and his indisposition to conversation. Neither was it any use to talk to the dog, for its only response to her, 'Good dog, then,' was to roll a jaundiced eye in her direction, then sit with its back to her, gazing out on the thief-ridden world astern.

She passed the time in rehearsing what she must say and do, and in worrying. 'What if he's not there?' she thought. 'Oh, but he must be, to have sent the brooch . . . But that was a week ago, and he could have been sent off somewhere meanwhile . . . Why could he not have written a few words, to say how he does and what he is about?' She sighed deeply, knowing that her wishes were idle, for Amyas had never written to her, always saying dismissively that he had no fist for a quill and left letter-writing to clerks. She sometimes had a disloyal thought that perhaps he was illiterate—very many men, even well-born ones, were unable to read or write!

By the time the wagon eventually rumbled through the outer suburbs and passed under the arch of Bishopsgate into the City, Kate ached with the jolting, and had thought herself into an uneasy and depressed state of mind, wishing she had not come. But the amazing noise and bustle revived her, and she looked about her with interest and excitement, for she had only been into the City once before, many years ago.

The wagon was held up by an overturned cart outside St Helen's church, so Kate took the opportunity to get down, thanking the driver and bidding him farewell, as he would shortly be turning left for the granaries at Leadenhall, whereas she needed to go right, through the City and on to Westminster.

She soon found that viewing the City from the elevation of a wagon or horseback was quite different from being on foot amid the bustle. The footways were narrow and crowded, and the roadway filled with carts, wagons, horses, pigs, dogs, refuse and mud. If she paused to look around her, she was jostled about, and several times only just managed to save herself from falling into the mire or under the wheels of a passing vehicle. She kept a firm hand on her purse as she was carried along by the crowds.

The noise was deafening, and the atmosphere close and smoky. She soon had a headache, and felt lost and bewildered, unsure of her whereabouts or her direction, although she was sure that she had turned the right way out of Bishopsgate. The street she was in was narrow and straight; but there were too many people, and she could not see far ahead, and did not recognise any of the buildings. The tall, narrow houses were jettied out over the street, shutting out sunlight and fresh air and closing in the noise and smell of the filthy kennels. Narrow side-streets turned off on either side, but they were like dark, noisome tunnels.

It was with great relief that she eventually emerged into a much wider thoroughfare, so wide, in fact, that rows of stalls were set up in front of the shops and houses, and there was room to walk more slowly and look about her. Halfway along on her left, she could see a large church rising above the tall timber-framed houses and standing straight amid their drunken angles.

'This must be Cheapside!' she thought. 'Now, I've but to find St Paul's, and I'll know where I am.'

She paused by a stall selling fresh bread, the scent of it cutting through the stink of the street, and realised that she was hungry, having eaten nothing since yesterday's supper. She opened her purse cautiously, fished out a little silver halfpenny, and bought a small loaf.

It was not good bread. In fact, she suspected that it had much else in it beside wheat flour, despite the regulations, and she pitied the Londoners who had to eat such stuff all the time. However, it was better than nothing, except that it made her thirsty, and she wondered where she might get a drink, other than in an alehouse, which she preferred not to risk. Then she noticed a tall, ornate structure in the middle of the street, where people were going and coming with buckets and jugs. Guessing that it was a conduit, she managed to get safely through the traffic to it, and took a drink of the water in her cupped hands. By now, she was sufficiently used to the noise and bustle to be less bewildered, and she rested for a few minutes, looking about her, but carefully avoiding catching anyone's eye, lest she be taken for a prostitute seeking custom.

There were several grades of people about, distinguishable by their dress. The majority were neatly-clothed working folk—journeymen hastening to their work, or busy at their crafts in booths and shops; apprentices, shouting their masters' wares; messengers hurrying importantly along, darting through the crowd; housewives doing their shopping, fetching water, gossiping with their neighbours. Among them, the very poor, the beggars and vagabonds, moved, apparently aimlessly, beseeching hands held out, often with one hand ready to snatch a carelessly-held purse if the opportunity arose. These were ragged; some, particularly the children, barely decent, barefoot and filthy. At the other end of the scale, rich merchants moved in stately fashion, soberly dressed, with only the quality of the fabrics showing their wealth. They were usually attended by one or two servants, and some were accompanied by their wives, equally soberly but richly dressed. Kate noted that they did not follow Court fashions, but a style of their own, far more restrained in cut and colour.

Presently she became aware that an idle young man near by was eyeing her speculatively, so she moved on, crossing the street to the side opposite the one on which she had been walking, and began to look out for St Paul's.

She knew, vaguely, that it was at the western end of Cheapside, and she wondered for a moment if she had already passed it, for there was that tall-towered church she had noticed earlier, rising even higher above the houses than she had realised from a distance, it was midway along the street, though, and did not appear to have much of a churchyard, whereas the cathedral, she knew, was surrounded by one—oh, and it had a spire! She looked up, thinking that perhaps she would see the spire above the buildings, but Cheapside, for all its width, was yet too narrow, and the houses too high.

'Are you lost, mistress?' asked a young voice behind her.

Kate turned, and found the apprentice lad from the shop outside which she had paused was looking at her with an enquiring lift to his eyebrows. He looked a friendly boy, with his snub nose and the downy beginnings of a moustache, so she replied, 'I'm looking for St Paul's.'

'Along there,' the boy said, pointing, 'and off to

the left. You'll see it as soon as you reach the right turning.'

Kate smiled and thanked him, then hurried on her way, thinking that she must still have a long way to go, and time was passing. She peered down each close and street on her left as she passed it, and then, suddenly, saw the cathedral!

The sight made her stop in her tracks and gasp, then stand staring, her mouth open with amazement, for she had never seen anything so huge! She knew that the Abbey church at Woodham was considered one of the longest in England, but this was immense. The roof rose to twice the height of Woodham's—so high, in fact, that, as she was quite close to the building, she had to tilt her head back to see the eaves. The tower rose to twice that height, and above that was the spire, soaring up until Kate thought the tip must scrape the clouds.

As she stared, she thought for a moment that the whole great structure was moving, leaning, about to fall on her, and then she realised that it was, in fact, the clouds that were moving, giving this frightening effect, and she pulled herself together, darting little glances to either side to see if anyone had seen her behaving like a country bumpkin, but, as seemed usual here, all the people in sight were too busy about their own affairs to notice her.

She walked slowly along the north side of the cathedral, admiring the Gothic beauty of it, and wondered if she might venture inside, but, she reminded herself, she still had to find her way to Whitehall, and that was another couple of miles at least, so she contented herself with a good look at the outside.

By the time she had walked the length of the immense building—chancel, transept and nave—some of the wonder had evaporated. She still thought it an almost unbelievable creation of men's hands, but it was dirty, crusted with soot from the seacoal fires of the City which turned the sky such a curious greyish-blue, dimming its brilliance, and dulled the green of the trees in the churchyard. The ornate carvings, blunted by the coating of black, were battered and broken in many places, and there was an air of decay about the whole great edifice. She was glad to leave it behind and head down the slope of Bowyer Street towards Ludgate, knowing that at last she had traversed the City and was well on her way to Whitehall.

It was, she supposed, about a mile from where she had left the wagon, but she felt as tired as if she had walked twenty miles in the country, what with the noise, the close atmosphere, and the rough cobbles, which were painful to the feet. She had to watch all the time where she was walking, for there were filthy puddles, patches of mud and decaying rubbish everywhere. Others were not as fastidious as she, and thought nothing of splashing her as they passed or jostling her into the mire, and she needed constant vigilance to keep her feet and skirts reasonably clean. In addition, her shoes had rubbed her heels, and already she had a blister.

The smell of London was nauseating to one unused to it, but the stench of the Fleet ditch was appalling. She held her nose as she passed over the bridge and for as far as she could manage beyond, and hurried on as fast as her sore heel allowed to get clear of it, but the smell still seemed to hang about her for a long time.

Fleet Street was little different from the City streets, but beyond Temple Bar she came to the more wealthy area, where noble mansions stood in walled gardens with fine trees, and the scent of flowers replaced the stink of smoke and dirt.

At Charing, she stopped to think of her next move, sitting on the steps of the Eleanor Cross and looking down King Street towards Westminster. She could see that, halfway down, the road appeared to be blocked by the massive gateway of the palace of Whitehall, and she wondered if she would be able to gain admittance without a pass of some sort, and, even if she did, would she be able to find Amyas?

It had seemed a simple proposition when she had first thought of it at home to go to Whitehall, ask for him, and tell him her plan, but now, having seen what a bewildering ant-hill of people London and Westminster were in reality, she began to fear that she had been foolish to think of such a thing. How could she possibly find one man among so many, in such a warren of buildings as Whitehall appeared to be? Even if she could find out where he lodged, would he be there? He might be away on the King's business, or his own, or gone home to his father again, or simply out—riding, playing tennis, at the cockpit . . . There was no sense in sitting about wondering, so she got up and walked the last quarter-mile to the great gateway, and stood looking at it for a few moments.

It was massive, and most elaborate, being decked with carved and painted stone representations of the Royal Arms and the various badges of the King and his ancestors, and those areas which were not carved were diapered in dark and light stone. There was a great central arch, through which a succession of carts, wagons and horsemen passed to and fro, and on either side was a smaller arch for pedestrians, each of which seemed to open on a dark tunnel.

Kate summoned her courage and entered the left-hand opening. Immediately, a stern voice said, 'State your business!' echoing under the vaulted roof.

'If you please,' Kate replied in the direction of the voice, 'I have business with Sir Amyas Calton.' She could now make out a stout porter, sitting at a counter in a sort of hatch at the side of the passage. He looked her over, apparently decided that she was respectable, and, after consulting a rather tattered sheet of paper, gave her directions for finding Amyas's lodging, which was across the Privy Garden, near the Royal Apartments by the river.

Heartened by the ease with which she had got his direction, Kate entered the palace, and was amazed, for it was nothing like she had imagined. She had expected a single great building, but this was more like a small town. A public highway ran through the middle of it, with a walled garden to one side, and a jumble of buildings of all shapes and sizes crowded round the garden and filled the right-hand side of the main street, with narrow lanes running between to give access to still more buildings behind. There were people hurrying in all directions—servants bearing bundles and baskets of supplies, all mixed up with elegant gentlemen, fine ladies, clerks with letters or rolls of accounts, and grooms leading horses.

The buildings, although there was no uniformity of design or material, were all highly decorated with strapwork patterns in wood, plaster or terracotta on every flat surface, all painted in bright colours, and a statue of one of the King's Beasts sat on a tall pedestal wherever there was space for one.

Kate boldly entered the Privy Garden through an open gate in its wall, and walked across it on a gravel path between elaborate knot-gardens of low hedges and clumps of aromatic shrubs and herbs, interspersed with yet more King's Beasts on pedestals. She would have liked to slow her pace and try to identify some of them, but she was afraid that one of the gentlemen strolling about the garden might ask her business if she lingered, and, having come so close to finding Amyas, she thought best to go on and get over with the next part of the proceedings, which, she suspected, might be far from straightforward.

Once through the garden, it took her some time to locate Amyas's lodging, and twice she had to ask for further directions, but at last, after climbing four flights of stairs, she stood in a dark passage before a carved door, her stomach fluttering with nervousness, and said a silent, fervent prayer before she knocked on the panel.

There was a sound of hurried footsteps across a creaking board floor, then the door was flung open and Amyas stood there, scowling at her.

CHAPTER TWELVE

'WHERE THE DEVIL have you been?' he began in an angry tone, which changed to sudden bewilderment as he recognised his visitor. 'Kate? Oh, my God! Kate, what are you doing here?'

'I came to see you,' she replied. 'I have to talk to you.'

He glanced over his shoulder, then came out of the room into the passage, shutting the door behind him.

'What do you want?'

'Things are impossible at home,' she said, forgetting all the careful little speeches she had rehearsed. 'I can't bear it any longer, so, after you sent the brooch, I thought I must come to you.'

'Brooch? What brooch? I sent you nothing!'

'But—But you did! A wreath of briars with a rose within them, and a posy . . . You must have sent it—no one else could have done so.'

'I sent you nothing,' he repeated. 'What are you about, Kate? Is this some trick, some play to trap me?'

'What do you mean?' She was bewildered, confused by his denial and his obvious suspicious hostility.

'Has someone got you with child, and you mean to try to foist the bastard on me? Is that it? Well, I'll not stand for it! You know very well I never lay with you. I've always been damned careful not to give you that hold on me!'

'Nothing of the kind!' Kate was angry now, as well as bewildered. 'I came to ask your help, for I'm at my wits' end to know what to do!'

'Why bring your troubles to me? Haven't I enough of my own?'

'We love one another, Amyas! We should share our troubles, and solve our problems together.'

'Love! What has love to do with anything? I've nothing to give you by way of help. If it's money you're after, I haven't any.'

'I don't want money!'

'What, then?'

'I thought we might be married now, and face your father together. I'm sure he'd relent if he realised how much we love each other.'

Amyas gaped at her in blank astonishment, then gave a grim, humourless bark of laughter.

'You're run mad, girl! I can't marry you! You're nobody, with no fortune, no influence, no important relations. My father would have you whipped from his door for your presumption to talk of marrying me!'

'But you love me!' Kate persisted, clinging to what seemed now the one bright thread in her life.

'Love? What's that? You're a pleasant companion for an idle hour, but marriage? That's something else! No, I wouldn't marry you, even if I could. In any case, I'm to be married next week, to a niece of the Duke of Norfolk.'

Kate stared at him in stricken silence, and he obviously mistook her reaction, for he went on boastfully, 'Yes, you may well be dumbfounded! What a triumph for my father! Here's the King to be married, as soon as he's free of the Cleves cow, to one niece of the Duke, and I'm to marry another! I'll be cousin to the King himself, and good-nephew to the most important subject in the land, now that Crumwell's fallen! You think I'd give all that up to marry you?'

'I see,' Kate said quietly. 'Then you never loved me at all?'

'Well—I suppose I did, at the time, but love isn't anything much. It doesn't last—it's but a passing fancy, nothing important.'

'Not as important as power, land and money,' Kate said flatly.

'Of course not! Now, look—you go home and wait, and later, when I'm married and settled down, I'll try to come and see you, and we can enjoy our little flirtation again, just as we did before . . .'

'If you ever come near me again,' Kate said in a quiet, down-to-earth tone that carried immense conviction, 'I'll probably scratch your eyes out! Goodbye, Amyas.'

She turned and walked away from him, back the way she had come.

'But, Kate!' he called, starting after her.

She stopped and looked back. 'I wish you joy of your money and your power, and your niece of the Duke of Norfolk,' she said. 'And I pity her, with all my heart!'

With that, she went down the stairs, hardly conscious of where she was or what she was doing, feeling nothing but a numb, bitter emptiness. Somehow her feet took the right path and she walked slowly along, turning at last into the main street through the middle of the palace. It was more crowded than ever, but she passed unseeing through the throng, unconscious of being pushed and elbowed, unaware that a thief with a sharp knife cut the thongs of her purse and vanished with it into the crowd.

As she approached the great gateway, a hurrying

porter thrust her aside, and she would have fallen under the wheels of a passing wagon had not another passer-by shot out a hand and pulled her to safety. She stumbled and fell against him, and he seized her shoulders to steady her, looked into her pale, dazed face, and exclaimed, 'Kate! Why, Kate! What are you doing here?'

She looked up into the bright, concerned eyes of Master Hartwell, and then her own eyes filled with tears and she sobbed, 'Oh, Matthew!', buried her face in his shoulder, and began to cry.

Master Hartwell looked about him distractedly for a moment, then led her out of the crowded street, through a narrow arch, and into the Privy Garden by another entrance. There were still too many people, so he went on, his arm protectively about Kate's shoulders, and took her through a maze of courts and alleys to a balcony over the river, where he sat her gently down on a stone bench, himself beside her, and patted her soothingly on the back while she still sobbed against his shoulder.

'I suppose you've been to see young Calton?' he said tentatively.

Feeling rather than seeing that she nodded, he went on, 'And I suppose he told you he's to be married? You have to try to understand his position— his family is one of those which hangs on to the fringes of wealth and power, and they think that nothing else matters. This marriage is of immense importance to them, and your Amyas hasn't the strength to stand against the combined pressure of all the Caltons, even if he wanted to. With the Cleves marriage a failure, and soon to end in divorce, Crumwell and his party are out of favour and Norfolk, Bishop Gardiner and their supporters are in the ascendant, all the more as the King is in love again, and with Norfolk's young niece, Katherine Howard!'

'If he wanted to!' Kate echoed in a muffled, bitter voice. 'He doesn't want to. He never meant to marry me! He never loved me! I was just an amusement for an idle hour. He doesn't think love even matters!'

'Oh, he loved you, after his fashion, and at the time,' Master Hartwell assured her. 'He's of the breed of men whose passions are shallow, save for money and position, but he loved you as much as he was able.'

Kate sat up, pulling away from him, and fumbled in her sleeve for a handkerchief. Master Hartwell silently handed her his own, a large, clean well-ironed square of cambric, with his crest embroidered in one corner in scratchy gold thread, and she wiped her eyes and blew her nose is a somewhat unladylike manner.

'What made you come?' he asked. 'Was it the news that he's to be wed?'

'No. I didn't know until he told me. Things are so difficult at home.' She spoke jerkily, in disconnected sentences, winding the handkerchief to and fro between her fingers and staring unseeingly at the river, which teemed with craft in the bright spring sunshine. 'My father never speaks to me, and Mistress Golding is forever prying and poking, and nagging at me to take money for my simples and unguents, or go out earning! She said the other day I should go out picking up stones in the fields, and I think she'd force me to do it if she could! To hear her, you'd think I lived on her charity, but I don't. My patients give me all sorts of gifts—edibles, mostly—which go to her kitchen. I'm sure they more than cover the cost of my foods and lodging. Now she says that she and my father are to be married, and she'll not have me there with them unless I earn my keep in coin! I don't know what to do.'

'So you thought you'd come to Whitehall and ask Calton to marry you?'

'Yes. I thought . . .' She trailed off, realising for the first time that, if Amyas had not sent the brooch, someone else must have done so, but who could that be?

'Well, it seems to me that you have three choices,' Master Hartwell said, stretching his legs out before him and contemplating the rosettes on his slashed, square-toed shoes. 'Either you can do nothing, but wait and see what happens, or you could ask Lady Cressy if she would allow you to live with her, or . . .' He paused, and looked sidelong at Kate.

'Or what?' she asked quietly.

'Well—at the risk of being slain on the spot . . . My offer still stands, but it hardly seems appropriate to press my suit at the moment,' he replied, the first in a half-jocular tone, the rest more soberly and very matter-of-factly.

'No,' said Kate expressionlessly.

'Hardly—er—delicate, or—er—tactful?'

'No,' Kate repeated, still without expression, but wondering why the fact that he had mentioned the subject at all had lit a little glimmer of warmth in the emptiness which was all she could feel inside her. For that matter, why did she not feel a terrible, aching sorrow, or at least a sense of loss? Why was there only leaden nothingness? It was not at all as if her heart were broken, but more as if she had received confirmation of some unpleasant facts she had already known, but which she had refused to acknowledge before.

'What shall you do now?' he asked after a lengthy pause, during which Kate continued to stare at the

river, and he to study her profile with concern and
curiosity.

'Go home, I suppose.'

'How did you come here?'

'I bought a ride on a cart from the end of Woodham
Lane as far as Bishopsgate, and walked from there. I
suppose I can go back the same way, as I've enough
money to . . .'

She broke off suddenly, her hand having gone
automatically to her purse, but encountered only the
cut ends of the thongs that had fastened it to her
girdle. 'Oh, no!' she gasped, and wondered desperately
what she could do, with no money for food and
drink, and at least fourteen miles between her and
home.

'I'm about to go back to Woodham myself,' Master
Hartwell remarked, his quick eyes observing the cut
thongs and the look on Kate's face, but making no
reference to either. 'I only came up to query a
boundary-line at the Augmentations office, and that's
done. I mean to have a bite to eat, then ride home, if
you'd care for company on the road.'

'I've no horse,' Kate said, but her eyes and her
voice betrayed how much she wanted to accept the
offer.

'Oh, that's no problem! I can borrow a horse and
gear for you easily enough. Will you join me for a
meal? There's a little tavern just along the road
which does excellent pies, and has decent ale, and
you might feel better with something hot inside you.'

'I've lost my purse,' Kate said. 'I've no money.'

'When I invite a lady to dine,' Master Hartwell
said, sounding a mite huffy, 'I don't expect her to
pay!'

Kate thanked him with unusual meekness, which
made him glance suspiciously at her, and she found

herself wondering about him once more, as he took her through a maze of courts, galleries and even rooms, almost from one end of the palace to the other. Over and over again he had behaved in a manner which was kind and helpful, yet, with Amyas's betrayal so fresh in her mind, she still found it difficult to accept that any member of the King's Court, and particularly of the Court of Augmentations, could act out of genuine disinterest for someone else's good.

'Here we are,' he said at last, as they emerged from the palace, crossed a street and approached a small tavern almost in the shadow of Westminster Hall, which Kate recognised from a drawing she had once seen.

'Is that great building over there the Abbey?' she asked.

'Yes.'

'And is that dissolved, too?'

'Er—well—converted to a cathedral, as we hoped Woodham might have been.'

'We?' she queried, studying his face.

'I certainly hoped so, and I thought you did as well.' There was nothing in his eyes or expression to suggest that he did not speak the truth, so Kate replied with a nod, and allowed herself to believe him.

For a person who might be thought to have suffered a broken heart, she found a remarkably good appetite for the beefsteak pie that was set before her, and ate it all, and the worts which accompanied it, although she thought they had not been very fresh before they were cooked—but then, it must be difficult to get fresh cabbage in a city.

While she was eating, Master Hartwell wrote a brief letter, and sent a boy to deliver it before starting on his own food. As they were drinking the tavern's good ale afterwards, the lad returned with the reply, and collected his penny reward from Master Hartwell.

'The horses will be waiting by the Cockpit Gate,' the latter said. 'Is there anything more you would like before we go?'

'I should like very much to wash my face and tidy myself,' Kate replied. 'If it's possible, that is.'

It was possible. A maid took her upstairs to a small bedroom with a mirror—a scratched and stained one, and only polished metal, but good enough—and brought a bowl of warm water scented with rosewater, and a clean linen towel. Kate inspected her face, and found that there were dirty streaks on her cheeks, where her tears had smudged sooty specks, and her eyes were a little red and sore-looking.

A good wash improved matters considerably. She retied her capstrings, shook her skirts and rubbed some of the dried mud off the hems, and rejoined Master Hartwell, feeling much better. The numbness caused by Amyas's reaction to her visit had begun to wear off, and she found, to her surprise, that she was not as upset as she had expected to be. In fact, she felt something like a mixture of pity and contempt for him, and certainly there was no conviction that her life was in any way over, or no longer worth living, for she was already thinking about Master Hartwell's suggestion that she ask her aunt for refuge.

The Cockpit Gate proved to be the great ornate affair by which she had first entered the palace, and there, in a narrow court running along the inside of the wall, a groom waited with Master Hartwell's black horse, and a sorrel for Kate with a side-saddle and footboard. Master Hartwell helped her to mount, made some arrangement with the groom for the return of the sorrel, involving the handing over of some clinking coins, and they set off back the way Kate had come earlier that day.

At first Master Hartwell pointed out various things of interest as they went along, but by the time they reached the Temple and he had told her that both he and Sir William had eaten their dinners there, he realised that she was not really listening, and fell silent. Presently he took her bridle and led her horse from then on, for she was lost in her own thoughts, and was hardly aware of where she was or where she was going.

She was, in fact, thinking deeply about the whole history of her relationship with Amyas, and wondering if any of it had ever been more than an idle flirtation on his part, magnified out of all proportion by the dreams and longings of a girl with too many romantic notions. The self-examination involved was painful, but salutary, and she concluded that she had been more in love with an idea than with a real person, and, certainly, her idea of Amyas, at least until recently, had borne little relation to the reality.

'I've been a fool,' she thought eventually. 'Because he was handsome, and young, and from the Court, I let him dazzle me, and I was flattered by his interest, fascinated by his charm, excited by his kisses and caresses . . . Surely, if I'd really been in love with him, I'd not have been able to think so calmly about him now, when it's only a few hours since he said all those hard, unkind things to me! I shan't bother to think any more about him!'

At this point her attention returned to the present, and she found, looking about her, that she had not the faintest idea where she was. There was no City around her, no crowded streets, only a long, straight road with a few clusters of houses and clumps of trees at intervals along its course, and an area of tenting-grounds spread with new-woven cloth to her right, with a church tower rising above them about half a mile away. She turned round, twisting in the saddle, amazed at the unexpectedness of the sight, and there was the City behind her, its crowded spires, towers and roofs rising above the patched and shabby walls, and the great spire of St Paul's soaring over all, like a finger pointing the sinful City to heaven.

'Where are we?' she asked.

'Well, now—I don't know where you've been this last half-hour, but we're now at Mile End, going towards Bow Bridge,' Master Hartwell replied lightly, handing her bridle back to her, and, sure enough, just in front of them was the bar marking the end of the City Liberties.

'I didn't come this way,' Kate said dubiously.

'I thought that, as we're riding, it would be better to go up the east side of the River Lea. The road is quieter and less dusty. Fewer wagons use it.'

Remembering the clouds of dust her own convey-ance had stirred up, Kate could not but be grateful for his thoughtfulness, and said so in a slightly abrupt manner. She caught a gleam of surprise in those bright, inquisitive eyes, and said, 'What is it? Why are you looking at me like that?'

'A cat may look at a King,' he replied evasively, then, more seriously, 'I was just thinking that this is the first time that you've managed to say something kindly to me!' His smile managed to look both amused and rueful.

Kate thought about that for a few minutes, and then said, 'I suppose it's because, when you came to Woodham, you were the Augmentations man, and I—we all—expected you to be like the others we'd known, or heard about . . .'

'The greedy, grasping, sticky-fingered crew of

irreligious robbers; the hangers, drawers and quarter-ers of innocent, saintly old abbots; the destroyers of beautiful, ancient, sacred treasures; the pullers-down of the pious gifts of past generations,' he enlarged for her, without any particular expression in his voice. 'And you thought I'd be the same?'

'Yes.'

'There are some honest men among us—or were, perhaps I should say, for we were few to start with, and I think I was the last of us to resign,' he said reflectively.

'How did you come to—to join them?' Kate asked, feeling that she would like to know more about him.

'When it started—the Court of Augmentations, I mean—it was a matter of sorting out the small monasteries—those with too few members or insufficient income to be viable—of transferring their inmates elsewhere, or releasing them to secular life, if they preferred, and administering their property until the King decided what to do with it. It was interesting work, and one tried to be fair to the poor monks and nuns who were being dispossessed. I was in Bishop Gardiner's service when the Court was set up, and he asked me to join it as he was doubtful about its constitution . . . Something set up by Master Crumwell and supervised by Diccon Rich! You can, perhaps, understand his concern!' He gave Kate a significant look, and one eyelid flickered in a slight wink.

He was silent for a few moments then, unusually grave, staring between his horse's ears.

'And then?' Kate prompted.

'And then . . . There were so many small houses, and by the time we'd dealt with them, somehow the whole attitude had changed. We were no longer expected to consider their viability but simply to close them, and by then, too, the greater houses were beginning to surrender. It started with Lewes Priory, I remember, and there was much discussion among us—most of us were lawyers, you understand—about the legality of it—whether a priory or an abbey could legally be surrendered by its members, who did not own the property but only had the use of it, the actual owner being God . . . Master Crumwell dealt with that, of course, by Act of Parliament, and since then . . .' He gave Kate a searching look, and said seriously, 'Can I trust you?'

Kate's immediate reaction was one of resentment, that he should imply that he might not be able to trust her, and then, with some shame, she realised that she had mentally asked the same question about him many times in the past few months. She was moved by the serious tone of his voice, and replied soberly, 'Only if you think it will be safe to do so.'

'Very well. Since then, there has been more beauty and good work destroyed, and more saintly men and women turned from their chosen way of life in these past three years than at any time in the whole history of the Christian Faith!'

Kate considered that in silence, and eventually said, 'It's difficult for me, who see only my own small part of it, to realise how much greater the whole picture must be, and how much some people have had to suffer. My own losses seem bad enough to me, but they're nothing compared with . . .'

'The Carthusians, for instance?' he cut in harshly. 'At least I can thank God that I had no part in that, or Glaston, or Reading, or St John's at Colchester!'

Kate understood him, recalling that, in each of those places, there had been resistance to surrender, and men had died horribly as a result. She looked at him, wide-eyed and troubled, for what he had said in the last few minutes had amounted to treason, or could be made to appear so if it came to the wrong ears. 'I hope you don't go about saying things like that to your old colleagues!'

'No, I only put my life where my heart is!' he said abstrusely, with a crooked little smile. 'Shall we discuss lighter matters? I've no wish to depress you more than the day's events have already done!'

They passed the rest of the journey pleasantly enough, talking of this and that, or riding in companionable silence, passing over Bow Bridge and on to Stratford, past the already half-ruined abbey of Stratford Langthorne, and then turned up Angel Lane and rode northwards, following the road which ran just above the edge of the Lea water-meadows, through the little villages in the valley until the dark bulk of the Forest appeared on their right, poised on the slopes of its ridge like an army about to pour down into the valley.

'Does anyone in Woodham know where you've gone?' he asked.

'No. I crept out of the house very early this morning, telling no one.'

'And they'll not have worried? Surely they'll be anxious, wondering where you are, when you've not appeared all day?'

'I doubt it! Mistress Golding will think I'm gathering herbs somewhere, or tending a patient, and my father takes no notice of anything I do.'

'Is that since . . .?' He seemed unable to finish the sentence, as if at a loss to know how to express his meaning.

'Since I refused to do as he ordered.'

'That was a disastrous day! I'd planned it so carefully, but he wouldn't allow me to speak to you, and that wrecked everything.'

'What else was there to be said? Father told me

what you'd offered, and what he required me to do about it, and I refused. I—I'm sorry if I was rude to you.'

'No, you were not rude—very courteous, all things considered. There were several more things I would have said, or, rather, different things, but, by the time he'd finished laying down the law, it was too late. Perhaps . . .' He hesitated, giving Kate one of his alert, searching looks. 'Perhaps, one day, you'll let me tell you what I would have said.'

'Yes, perhaps—one day . . .'

Kate replied a trifle absently, for she was thinking that she might have been wrong that day. Maybe she should have obeyed her father and married this man, who could be trusted, whereas . . .

Trusted? Good Heavens! How had that change in her attitude come about? It seemed only a few days since she had been wondering whether or not he was honest, and now, quite suddenly, she thought him more to be trusted than the man she had loved—had thought she loved . . . It was all very confusing!

It was evening by the time they approached Woodham, and in the gathering dusk, Kate reined in her horse a half-mile short of the edge of town, and said, 'I think I should walk from here. It will cause talk and speculation if I come riding into town with you.'

Master Hartwell circled back to her, for he had ridden on a little, and said, 'As you wish.' He dismounted, looping his reins over his arm, and helped her down, his hands firm on her waist, but, instead of releasing her as he set her down, he drew her close to him and said, 'Will you be all right? Is there anything I can do for you?'

'I'm not nearly as upset about Amyas as you would expect me to be,' Kate said forthrightly, grateful for his concern and anxious to relieve him of any worry about her. 'I suppose that, in my heart, I knew . . .' She gave a little sigh. 'One does so long to be loved by a gallant, handsome, dashing young knight! I think I let my dreams run away with me. Well, that's over, and I must become used to a drab, everyday world, where Court gallants don't fall in love with simple country maids! If there should be anything you could do for me, I think that now I shall not be too proud to ask, for you've been so kind, and I'm truly grateful to you.'

'Is this really my prickly Kate?' he asked. It was already too dark for her to read his expression, but she thought he was smiling. 'I'm always at your service, my lady. Can you find your way safely home from here?'

'Of course.'

'Then I'll bid you goodnight.' He bent his head, and a feather-light kiss landed on her brow before she could draw back, and then he released her, gathered the reins of her horse, mounted his own, and rode on, leading the sorrel behind him.

Kate watched him go with a strange mixture of feelings within her, then limped off along the road and turned into the town. As she walked, she tried to examine those feelings, but could only be sure that they did not include any particular sorrow or regret for the loss of Amyas, which was very strange.

Mistress Golding came out of the kitchen as she entered the yard, and greeted her return with a surly, 'Well, I hope whoever you've been wasting your time with at least had the grace to be grateful! Hours of time spent on some wretch, and not a penny to show for it, I'll be bound! Now where are you off to?' For Kate had turned about, and was going back towards the street.

'To see my Aunt Cressy,' she replied coldly.

Lady Cressy was at home, sewing by one side of the fire in the parlour, while Sir William dozed on the other. She greeted Kate with a kiss, and said, 'Why, you look quite fagged, my dear! Where have you been? Your skirts are all muddy, and your cap covered with smuts!'

'I've had a tiring day,' Kate admitted, sinking on to the stool which her uncle drew up for her, and stretching her hands to the fire, for the evening had grown chill after the fine, sunny day. 'Aunt, I should like to ask a favour of you . . .'

'Then ask away!' Lady Cressy said, smiling encouragingly as she resumed her seat and picked up her sewing.

'Things are not easy at home—at the Three Tuns, I mean,' Kate began. 'I expect you know that Father doesn't speak to me, and Mistress Golding speaks a deal too much! Aunt, would you let me come and live here?'

'Oh, my dearest Kate! I've been longing to ask you, but didn't like to, thinking you'd not wish to leave your father. I've wanted you here ever since my dear Cecy went away! I do miss her so much, and I need someone to talk to, and to help me with my little problems about the house, and you're so sensible and practical. Why, you shall have Cecy's room! It's stood empty ever since she was married, and I know she'd like you to have it. When can you come?'

'Tomorrow?' Kate suggested.

Her aunt clapped her hands with delight, and Sir William bore the proposal with fortitude—indeed, he went so far as to say it was the best news he'd heard since he got the bells back!

Relieved to find that at least there was someone in the world who loved and wanted her, Kate went back to the Three Tuns for the night, and climbed wearily up to her garret. She undressed quickly, yawning and longing to stretch out in her bed and sleep, but, on taking off her corset, she found the brooch still pinned there, and sat down on the bed with it in her hand, staring at it.

If Amyas didn't send you to me,' she asked it, 'who on earth did?' But the pretty thing lay in her hand, gleaming in the dim rushlight, and gave no clue to its sender, or its meaning.

CHAPTER THIRTEEN

MISTRESS GOLDING was taken aback by Kate's announcement that she intended to move out of the Three Tuns, and Master Cressy almost spoke to her when she told him, but remembered just in time and stood with his face a picture of mixed emotions, in which Kate thought, or at least hoped, she saw signs of regret.

She was soon ensconced in her uncle's house, with Cecy's old room for her own, Lady Cressy's fine large still-room to house her coffer of remedies, and adequate room to work at preparing her mixtures, for her uncle and aunt encouraged her to continue her work with the sick and injured. Her place in the household was that of an adopted daughter from the first, and there was plenty of opportunity for her to show her appreciation of that place by helping her aunt, who was not the most efficient of housekeepers.

Her new position was a great relief to Kate, for Mistress Golding's continual nagging and her father's silent hostility had fretted her nerves even more than she had realised, and it was only now that she comprehended how wretched and unhappy she had been at the Three Tuns.

For a short time, she had depressing and regretful moments, remembering Amyas, but, after a wakeful night spent thinking very thoroughly about him, she came to the conclusion that she had been right in her

first estimation of the matter, made on the way home
from her disastrous visit to Whitehall, that, like a green
girl, she had been more in love with the idea of love
than with the actual man. Soon she hardly thought of
him at all, but, instead, often found herself thinking of
Matthew Hartwell.

At first, it was no more than a tendency to look
towards the Grange house when she walked in the
meadows, collecting her herbs, but presently she realised
that, each time she saw him, even if only a fleeting
glimpse in the distance, she felt a lift of her spirits and
a pleasant, breathless, fluttering sensation in her breast.
When she actually encountered him, she could not help
but smile at him, yet was so afraid that he might guess
her feelings that she was, if anything, even more sharply
spoken to him than ever. He seemed to find this a little
amusing, for she often detected a twinkle in those dark,
observant eyes, and was chagrined to think that perhaps
in trying to avoid betraying her interest in him in one
way, she had only succeeded in revealing it in another,
and so given him grounds to laugh at her.

Despite her uncertainties concerning the gentleman,
she was now much happier and more settled than she
had been for a long time, but most of the townsfolk
were very far from happy or free from apprehension,
for the future of Woodham was still very unsettled. The
Abbey lands and property, apart from Master Hartwell's
small, oddly-rented estate, remained in the hands of the
Court of Augmentations, which seemed to be in no
hurry to transfer it to Lord Dallance. Meanwhile, only
essential work was done to keep the farm animals fed
and tended and the arable land in production. The
domestic buildings, and even the church, apart from
the parish nave, began to fall into dilapidation, for the
Augmentations men had removed all the lead from the
roofs and sent it to the Tower—to be made into bullets,

according to rumour. Any stone in the walls which looked the least little bit loose was encouraged by interested parties to become more so, and then mysteriously disappeared as houses acquired new doorsteps, stone linings to their cellars, well-repaired walls, and carved embellishments to their gardens and gateposts.

Without pilgrims or the employment engendered by a large and flourishing monastery, trade in the town declined, and the market dwindled to half its previous size. There seemed no hope of another visit from the King to bring a little additional income, for he did not make his customary Lent visit to the Abbey. Few people expected that he would ever come to his house in the cattle-market again, but, with only a few days' warning, he arrived in June.

'But why did he not come in the spring?' asked Lady Cressy when she heard the news. 'Why in June? He's never come in June before!'

'In the spring, he was too busy seeking a way to rid himself of his new wife without offending the Protestant states,' Sir William explained (not for the first time). 'But now, the Lady Anne has agreed to a divorce—on her own terms!—and he's to marry the Duke of Norfolk's niece as soon as he's free. They say it's taken twenty years off his age, and he's as fit and active as a young man again, apart from his ulcerated leg. I don't doubt he'll be out hunting and hawking all the time he's here.'

Kate took little notice of the coming visit, for she was busy as she had embarked on an overhaul of her aunt's store of linen, and had half a dozen patients about the town. One of these had a nail embedded in the ball of his heel, and although she had managed to get it out, the wound was a nasty one, and she had been obliged to send to Master Hartwell to beg some

mistletoe from an oak in his grounds, as she knew
nowhere else where it grew.

He brought a bunch of it himself, and she was so
grateful that she spoke quite kindly to him, and he was
emboldened to spend a harmonious half-hour with her
in the stillroom while she compounded some of the
mistletoe leaves with agrimony for a poultice.

'You know that the King is coming tomorrow?' he
asked, watching her work.

'Oh, yes. My Uncle Cressy said that he was coming,
and that he's full of energy and good spirits again!
Have you seen him lately?'

'No. What with the sheep-shearing and the haymaking,
I've not been to Whitehall since . . .' He broke off, and
Kate looked up from her pestle and mortar, met his
eyes, and saw a question in them.

'I never thanked you properly,' she said. 'You must
think me an ungrateful wretch, after all you did for me
that day! I was, and am, truly grateful.'

He made a little gesture with one hand, as if brushing
the matter aside. 'I don't know if Calton will be coming
with the King. I've tried to find out—discreetly, of
course—but without result.'

'It doesn't matter,' Kate replied, looking him straight
in the eyes again. 'I think I really knew all the time
that it was only an idle dream, and I'd imagined some
sort of an ideal man who was not Amyas at all. After
all, I saw him only a few times. Does it sound very
foolish?'

'Not at all. We all dream when we're young, and
imagine how things will be, and often we confuse
reality with the dreams. When the thing really happens,
there's no mistaking it, and the dreams seem insipid by
comparison. You'd not be able to speak as you just did
if you had really loved him.'

Kate felt her cheeks flush unaccountably, and returned

her attention to the green mixture in her mortar, pounding furiously to hide her confusion. She thought about his words later on, when she was alone, and realised that he had spoken as one who had experienced what he had described—'when the thing really happens'—so he must feel for someone. A faint, delicate gossamer-glimmer of hope dawned in her, and was immediately shut away, unexamined, out of fear that it was unlikely—too soon—impossible . . .

Sir Amyas Calton was not in attendance on the King when His Grace arrived in Woodham, but Sir Richard Rich was, and Kate, encountering him unexpectedly in the cattle-market, received a look which gave her quite a jolt, leaving an uneasy feeling and a memory of Master Hartwell's warning about the man's unforgiving, vindictive nature.

For two or three days the King was happy to hawk in the meadows, where the hay had just been cut and carted in time, or along the Forest edge, but, returning tired and content at the end of the day to eat his supper and indulge his liking for serious discussion with his courtiers, he found that, with Master Crumwell out of favour and in hourly expectation of arrest and impeachment, and the Abbot gone, there was no mind among those with him of sufficient acuity or breadth of knowledge, save for that of Stephen Gardiner. The Bishop, however, had spent too much of his life engaged in very tricky feats of diplomacy to retain any facility in the plain-spoken variety of argument which the King enjoyed. His Grace demolished those who essayed debate with him in short order, became bored, and invited himself to supper with the Cressys to fill an evening with a change of company.

Lady Cressy was thrown into a panic, and it took

Kate at her most downright and capable to calm her enough to plan the evening's entertainment.

'It's the food which must concern us,' she said firmly. 'Let my uncle undertake to find guests who can sustain an interesting conversation, for the hall is too small for mummers or dancing. Now, what shall we give him to eat?'

Her use of 'we' rather than 'you' seemed to give her aunt great comfort, and they spent some time discussing what might best be offered for supper, deciding, after some rather fanciful and impractical ideas from Lady Cressy, on simple, fresh, well-cooked dishes rather than anything elaborate and liable to be easily spoiled.

There was no shortage of choice at this time of year, with the seven streams of the river teeming with fish, new green peas in all the gardens, the last of the asparagus still soft enough to be acceptable, radishes, beets, lettuce and dandelion all young and tender, and strawberries and gooseberries in abundance. The royal huntsmen had already brought venison and a swan as the King's contribution, and Harry Warrener had sent word that he could supply as many coneys as they liked at short notice. Kate thought fleetingly that his ferrets must have overheard the King decide to honour the Cressys and reported to him, for he had sent his message within a quarter-hour of Lady Cressy receiving the news herself!

'The thing that really worries me most,' said Lady Cressy at last, when a detailed and satisfactory menu had been drawn up, 'is the hippocras. The King likes it served to him at the end of the feast, according to the old custom, but the last time he came he only sipped a little and left the rest, so I fear it was not to his liking! I don't know how best to make it, Kate. Do you think you could undertake it?'

Kate said that she could and would, and took the

first opportunity she could find to visit the kitchens of the house next door for a word with the King's head cook about His Grace's preferences in the matter, for the hot white wine could be flavoured with a variety of herbs and spices, and it was important to use the right mixture in the right proportions.

'Plenty of cinnamon,' was the answer. 'Whatever else you choose, but *plenty* of cinnamon!' The cook was a self-important person, who approved of the appreciative (and attractive) young woman who had the good sense to consult the oracle concerning a matter so vital to the well-being of the nation.

Both Lady Cressy and Kate worked hard on the day of the supper, but everything in the hall and the kitchen went well, and they were finished in good time for them both to dress in a reasonably leisurely manner. Kate had a grand murrey-coloured brocade gown to wear, one left behind by Cecy, who had not liked the colour, and Sir William gave her a thin gold chain for her neck, on which she hung her elfstone. She had no other jewellery, but, at the last moment, after looking at herself critically in the venetian mirror, she took out the briar rose brooch and pinned it to her bodice, where it looked, she thought, as good as a real gold jewel.

The evening went excellently well. There were no disasters in the kitchen, but every dish arrived looking well and tasting even better.

The King called for second helpings of several dishes, and complimented Lady Cressy on her cook and her choice of menu. Sir William had invited a few friends with both pleasing wives and a sufficiency of wit and knowledge to keep up a good flow of conversation, and Kate enjoyed the talk so much that her normally serious, tight-lipped expression relaxed, and she smiled far more than usual. Sir William noticed, and thought to himself that she would be quite a beauty if she always looked like that, and he wondered how his brother could be so blind to what he had done to his daughter by his lifelong attitude towards her. Master Hartwell also noticed, from his seat on the opposite side of the hall, and he seemed to find the picture of Kate enjoying herself more interesting than the talk of his neighbours or the food set before him.

There were, however, two flies in the ointment for Kate. One was the presence of Sir Richard Rich, who looked in her direction from time to time in a deliberate fashion which made her uneasy, his eyes coldly observant and his customary sneer much in evidence. The other was the matter of the King's hippocras, which must be prepared and served at the end of the meal.

The time came eventually, and, at an unobtrusive signal from Sir William, Kate left her place and went to a small table at the side of the hall, where a servant brought her a tray loaded with a jug of hot wine, and a selection of spices and herbs that Kate had chosen earlier after much tasting and considering. There was also a small dish of ready-crushed loaf-sugar, two or three long-handled spoons and Sir William's best covered cup, a fine golden goblet with a steeple cover set with gemstones.

The mixing had to be done quickly, before the wine became cold, but Kate had practised until she had the quantities calculated to give a flavour to please the King. Swiftly she spooned and stirred, murmuring her list of ingredients over to herself, unaware that her lips were moving, and that Sir Richard was watching with great concentration.

Suddenly, beautifully timed to fall into a lull in the conversation, his voice rang out across the hall, clear and carrying, although he did not appear to raise it.

'What is that woman doing?'

Everyone looked at him, then their eyes followed his outflung arm and pointing finger to Kate, who had been arrested by his question in the middle of transferring a few more grains of sugar from bowl to jug. She stared in surprise, which turned to consternation as all eyes were turned on her in the sudden silence.

'My niece is preparing hippocras for the King's Grace,' Sir William said, sounding and looking puzzled.

'I question what she may be putting into it!' Sir Richard said, and, turning to the King, went on, quickly and smoothly, while he still had everyone's attention, 'Sire, I have observed this woman for several months, both through my agents and with my own eyes, and I suspect that she may mean Your Grace some harm!'

'In what way, Sir Richard?' asked the King, frowning and shifting in his great chair. It was the biggest chair Sir William owned, but it was not over-large for a man of such bulk.

'With your permission, Sire, I would ask her some questions. It may be that she can answer them satisfactorily, or it may appear that she should be further questioned elsewhere.'

The King nodded, and Sir Richard continued, 'Why is it, Mistress Cressy, that, when the chattels of the late Abbey here were sold, you were so insistent on purchasing a certain coffer filled with poisonous substances, which was kept in a locked room in the infirmary?'

Kate put down the spoon she was holding and spread a napkin over the jug as she replied, 'The coffer contained the store of remedies used by the late Infirmarian. They are of great value to me in treating sick and injured people.' She felt quite calm, for she had nothing on her conscience, but she was puzzled, wondering what the man was after.

'They included poisons?'

'Some of the herbs are of great benefit in small quantities, but could be dangerous if too much were used,' Kate replied precisely, keeping her gaze on Sir Richard, but conscious that the King's little shrewd eyes were darting from one to the other as he listened and weighed each word and expression, and that Matthew Hartwell had pushed his stool back from the table, and was attending with such concentration that she could sense the tension in his body, even across the hall.

'And what of the small glass phial which you were willing to pay so much to possess?'

Before Kate could reply, a shrill, wobbly voice cut in indignantly, 'That a did not! The man gave it her for nothing, along with some oddseys, in cause she telt him how to treat his wife's kybes!' It was the serving-boy who had accompanied Kate to the sale in the Abbey, emboldened by indignation.

'How do you know?' asked the King in a kindly, interested tone.

'In cause of I was there, with a barrow to carry what Mistress Kate brought home!' the boy said boldly. 'And she paid but a shilling for the coffer, in cause of the man said that Father Humphrey said she should have it, and fourpence for a mortar and a table, and a penny for the oddseys, which were bandagings and pieces of wood, and the man threw in the little bottle without she asked, and never said a word about it, and anyone who says different is a liar!' At this point, he realised that he was speaking to the King, and his indignation and courage evaporated together.

'And what was in the little bottle?' the King asked, looking at Kate.

'A tincture of poppy-juice, Your Grace,' Kate replied. 'I do not know if it's a poison, but I do know that Father Humphrey used very small amounts, but that may have been because it is costly. The bottle is still sealed, for I've had no need to use any.'

The King nodded once, then looked at Sir Richard, who resumed, unruffled, 'Why do you wear a witch-charm about your neck?'

Kate looked blankly at him for a moment, then, realising what he meant, said, 'Oh, you mean my elfstone! I believe some folk regard them as charms against lightning, but that's only superstition! The Lord Abbot once told me that they're really arrowheads from times long past.'

'Why do you wear an arrowhead, then?' Sir Richard asked sneeringly.

'It's a very pretty thing, like a new beech-leaf, and it was a gift.'

'From whom?'

'From a collier. I treated his infected finger, and he gave it me out of gratitude.'

'You claim to heal ignorant folk by your potions and spells, I believe?'

'By my compounds and simples. I use no potions or spells, for that would be witchcraft, and I'll have nothing to do with that!' Kate sounded as indignant as she felt, and her voice carried conviction, but she was beginning to feel a little afraid, sensing which way his questions were tending.

'It is doubtful,' the Bishop of Winchester interposed impersonally, his eyes on the furthest corner of the hall ceiling, and his pulpit-trained diction reaching every ear, 'if so-called witchcraft is any more than the delusions of old and crazy women, fostered by the superstitions of the ignorant. There is a vast difference between the medicinal use of herbs and the brewing of potions.' His beautiful, sonorous voice spoke with all the majesty and authority of the Church, and there was a brief, respectful silence after he had finished. Kate felt comforted, and assured that she had at least one important supporter.

'You associate with the minions of the Devil, and the known enemies of the peace and well-being of the King and of this realm,' Sir Richard resumed, changing his tack.

Kate made no reply, wondering what he meant, and her mystified expression forced him to enlarge on the accusation. 'You were seen in secret converse with a friar, out in the fields where none could overhear!'

She stared blankly at him for a moment, then gave a gasp of laughter. 'A friar! Your informant must have poor sight! That was my brother John. He was a Benedictine, a monk of St Alban's. He came to see me before he went away, and we were walking across the fields to visit our old home.'

'Away where?'

'To Flanders, I believe. You would know better than I, for it was your Court of Augmentations that gave him permission to leave England!' she replied tartly, and then regretted her tone, for there was no sense in antagonising the man still more.

'Where are you leading us, Sir Richard?' the King asked with a touch of impatience.

Sir Richard turned his most charming smile on the King, and said urbanely, 'I beg Your Grace's pardon if I am tedious in my questioning. It is my belief, Sire, that this woman may have become involved in a plot by Your Grace's enemies to harm Your Grace. The woman is known as a wise-woman. I expect that this friar, whom she claims to be her brother, has suborned her from her natural loyalty. If he was indeed her brother, why did her father not know of his visit?'

Kate opened her mouth to reply, but Sir Richard went on, ignoring her, 'You may observe that she wears a curious brooch of goldsmith's work, yet her father is but a poor pensioner of the late Abbey, and she lives in this house through the charity of Sir William. How, then, does she come to own such a costly piece of jewellery? What is the significance of its design?'

Kate's hand went to her breast and closed on the briar rose brooch, and she shook her head a little in bewilderment.

'Let the brooch be brought to me!' the King commanded, gesturing to one of his attendants, who hurried over to Kate. She unpinned the brooch with fingers made clumsy by sudden real fear, for there were questions coming whose answers were going to sound very strange and unconvincing.

When the brooch reached the King, he examined it closely, tilting it back and forth to catch the light of the candles near him on the table, and looking at the back as much as the front.

'It bears the assay mark of Goldsmiths' Hall in London,' he pronounced, 'and is of fine workmanship. The enamelling is particularly well done, as is the modelling of the briars. It represents a wild rose, an eglantine, with a wreath of briars about it. There is a posy—*SPINAS TRANSIREM UT ROSAM CARPEREM*. How do you read that, Sir Richard?'

'Your Grace is a finer Latinist than I,' Sir Richard replied with a graceful bow, and a smile which reminded Kate very much of a weasel.

'*One must pass the thorns to pluck the rose*, I would say,' the King pronounced after a moment's thought. 'Would that seem a fair translation to you, My Lord Bishop?'

Bishop Gardiner, who was sitting next to the King,

leaned over to look at the posy, considered for a moment, and then replied gravely, 'A very fair rendering, Sire.'

'And what is its significance?' the King asked, looking at Sir Richard.

'In my opinion,' he replied, 'and bearing in mind that I had not before viewed the article closely enough to read the posy, I would suggest that it means that the rose may be plucked—killed—if the would-be assassin has the courage and skill to penetrate its defences. The rose is well known to be a symbol of the House of Tudor, is it not? I believe that this rose represents Your Grace, and the thorns the safeguards which protect Your person.'

'And how do you consider that Mistress Cressy is expected to—er—pluck the rose?' the King enquired.

'Why, by means of the hippocras which she was preparing! The woman has a supply of poison to hand, by her own admission, and she has been standing there, spooning and stirring at a cup intended for Your Grace's lips alone, and muttering incantations as she works her evil!'

'Incantations!' murmured Bishop Gardiner, raising his eyes to Heaven.

The murmur carried remarkably clearly round the hall, and its tone destroyed much of the effect of Rich's words, but he flung out his arm again, the accusing finger once more levelled at Kate. Her reaction was one of indignation rather than fear, for her pride, both as a herbalist and a cook, had been offended. She picked up the jug of hippocras, tossing aside the napkin that covered it, and took a long drink, then set the jug down and glared belligerently at Sir Richard. He looked disconcerted.

'Well, Mistress Cressy? How say you?' the King

asked. He sounded quite neutral, but not as if he expected her to drop dead from poison.

'It needs more cinnamon,' Kate replied, automatically giving a professional opinion, for her thoughts were more concerned with trying to work out whether Sir Richard's accusations were intended seriously, or merely to frighten her. The suggestion that she had poisoned the hippocras was obviously not serious, for it was so easily disproved, and, in any case, everything offered to the King to eat or drink was first tasted by one of his attendants as a precaution against poison. It was the brooch which was likely to prove a real trouble to her, for she could not account for it at all, and the news that it was really gold, and costly, had been a considerable shock to her.

'How do you explain this pretty little thing?' the King asked, holding the brooch up between massive finger and thumb.

'It was sent to me,' Kate said, feeling her way carefully. 'A messenger brought it. He was in a great hurry, for he was on his way to someone else, and he said nothing about who had sent it, or why. I assumed it was a love-token. I didn't know it was gold—I thought it was a fairing, a pretty thing of no great value.'

'And whom did you believe to be the sender?'

Kate stood in helpless silence. She was sure now that Amyas had not sent it, and her pride would not allow her to compromise his marriage by mentioning him in connection with it. 'I don't know,' she said eventually, in a low, trembling voice, her courage evaporating rapidly now that she was on such uncertain ground.

There was silence for a moment, and then a new voice spoke out. 'If Your Grace will allow, I can clarify this matter!' It was Matthew Hartwell.

'Master Hartwell?' the King said, half questioning, half granting permission.

'It hardly seems just,' Master Hartwell said, moving across to stand a little before and to one side of Kate, facing her accuser across the hall, 'that Mistress Cressy should be questioned by the Solicitor-General of England without anyone to advise or support her!'

'This is not a court of law!' Sir Richard snapped, obviously put out by the intervention.

'Nevertheless, accusations have been made,' Master Hartwell replied pleasantly enough, but with a hint of steel in his voice. 'You have made several allegations against the lady, all but two of which have been answered satisfactorily. I can confirm that your so-called friar was, as Mistress Cressy has said, her brother John, a former Benedictine of St Alban's. That leaves the mystery of the brooch, and the answer to that is simple. I sent it to her myself!'

'You!' exclaimed Sir Richard and Kate in unison, and it would have been difficult to say which of them was the more surprised.

'It was, as Mistress Cressy surmised, a love-token. It was made to my own design by Thomas Webb in Cheapside, and delivered by his messenger on his way with a piece of plate for another customer in Ware.'

'Yet Mistress Cressy says that she does not know who sent it,' put in the King.

'There is no reason why she should, as she was not told by anyone, but I hoped she would eventually have guessed.'

'And what is its significance?' the King asked, looking at it again.

Master Hartwell smiled, and said a trifle slily. 'Your Grace is fortunate in loving a rose without a thorn! I fear that mine is—er—otherwise!'

The King looked startled at having his own description

of the Lady Katherine Howard quoted at him, but then he laughed heartily, taking Master Hartwell's meaning, and, of course, everyone else joined in his merriment. 'Sharp, is she?' he asked. 'Given to scratching?'

'Shall we say a little sharp-tongued to me!' Master Hartwell replied ruefully. 'Our relationship began on a misunderstanding, but I hope eventually to win my way past its thorny results, and gain my rose.'

The King laughed even more heartily, and Kate, her cheeks crimson, stood rigid with surprise, too much startled by the implications of what Matthew had said to feel anything but a tremulous and unexpected joy amid her surprise as she stared at him, hardly hearing the uproar of merriment, some sycophantic, some genuine, which shook the hall. Even the Bishop was smiling broadly.

When the noise died down, Master Hartwell looked at Sir Richard, and said quietly but clearly, 'Are you satisfied, Diccon?' His voice had an oddly edged tone, and the byname sounded strange in the circumstances.

'Quite satisfied, thank you, Matt,' Sir Richard replied, smiling in a singularly honeyed fashion. 'I am content to consider the matter ended.'

'Well, Sir Richard,' boomed the King, looking curiously from one man to the other, and obviously, with his quick intelligence, sensing an underlying current of feeling. 'We thank you for your diligence concerning our safety, and we thank you, Matthew, for preventing a possible injustice—and we wish you good fortune in your wooing!' he added with a wink, holding up the brooch. Ambitious courtiers noted the 'Matthew' and began to calculate Master Hartwell's value to them in terms of quails, hawks and hunting-dogs.

Master Hartwell went to fetch the brooch, and returned it to Kate, standing in front of her to shield her from curious eyes. She looked up at him uncertainly,

catching her lower lip between her teeth, half overjoyed
by what he had said, half fearful that she had
misunderstood.

'May we talk tomorrow?' he asked softly, those alert
eyes studying her face.

She nodded, and then he was gone, and the King
was inviting her to prepare his hippocras, so she had to
send for more hot wine and start again, pinning her
brooch on awry in her haste. The King drained every
last drop of the resulting mixture, and presently Kate
and her aunt were able to retire, Lady Cressy insisting
that her niece take a posset before she went to bed.
She must have put something in it, for Kate slept very
well, and awoke in the morning wondering if she had
dreamed the whole thing.

As soon as she could slip away, she set out for the
Grange house, torn between a wild, extraordinary
feeling of elation and hope and a fear that she had
misunderstood everything that had been said the
previous evening.

'He was so right!' she thought as she walked along
the river-bank in the morning sunshine. 'There's no
mistaking it when it happens! How could I ever have
thought that what I felt for Amyas was love? How
could I ever have believed that I disliked Matthew?'

She found Master Hartwell near the house, inspecting
his northern boundary hedge in the company of a
squirrel, but whether the same one as before or another,
she could not be sure. The little creature ran up a tree
as she approached, and watched what followed from a
safe distance.

Master Hartwell looked at her with a wary smile,
and said, 'I meant to visit you later. I thought you'd
sleep late, after last night's events. How are you?'

'Well, thank you,' she replied, suddenly nervous and

shy. 'What was it all about? What was he trying to do? Did he really think I'd been plotting against the King?'

'Good Heavens, no! He saw you mixing the hippocras, and decided on the spur of the moment to take his revenge for you pushing him in the river. His case was too poorly presented to have been properly planned. It was opportunism, that's all!'

'All!' exclaimed Kate. 'Why, I might have been condemned for treason!'

'No, for nothing he said could be proved. Any competent lawyer would have demolished the whole string of accusations! Do you think your uncle would have let it go on if he'd thought you were in any real danger? You were conducting your own defence most admirably until he brought the brooch into it, and then I had to intervene, for I knew you couldn't answer him. He was only trying to frighten you! That's the end of it now. You heard him say he was satisfied.'

'Why did you call him "Diccon"? I didn't think you were friends.'

'We're not. It was an oblique reference to someone else, who always calls him "Diccon" and could put a noose about his neck if he chose! I was just reminding him that I knew about it, too. But never mind Rich! Are you angry with me?'

'Angry? Why?'

'For putting you to the blush before the King.'

'Oh, that . . . Did you really send me the brooch?'

'Of course. I thought you'd guess as soon as you read the posy.'

'I haven't enough Latin. And was it you, singing in the Forest?'

He nodded, and there was a pause while each studied the other's face, and then he said, 'I loved you from the first time I met you, and that was why I asked you to marry me, but your father insisted on speaking first, and I had no chance after that! The whole thing was bungled. I'm sorry.'

'I didn't love you then,' Kate said, her eyes shining.

'And now?'

She took a hesitant step forward. 'Perhaps you could teach me to read Latin, and maybe you could ask me again now,' she breathed. 'If you still want to, that is . . .'

He smiled and opened his arms to receive her as she took another step forward and was gathered into his embrace, her head tilting back and her lips parting as he sought them in a kiss which lit every fibre of her body with radiance, and made her feel that she had never been fully alive until this moment. He kissed her again and again, as if he had been starving for want of her, and her own hunger for those kisses increased with every one, like a flame which grows with feeding to a conflagration.

The squirrel chattered and threw a few oak-galls at them, then lost interest and wandered off about its own business, leaving them alone together in the summer sunshine. The sweet scent of the briar roses in the hedgerow drifted about them in their private paradise, so that, for the rest of her life, Kate had only to smell the scent of eglantine to recapture the deep happiness of that moment of discovery and fulfilment.

Happy Mother's Day.

This Mother's Day, instead of the usual breakfast in bed, why not ask your family to treat you to the Mills & Boon Mother's Day pack. Four captivating romances to enthral you.

THE EMERALD SEA by Emily Spenser

A marine biologist finds herself out of her depth on an Italian film set — and with the director.

THE MARRIAGE BED by Catherine George

A holiday in the Algarve becomes a nightmare when the heroine is kidnapped in revenge for an injustice she knows nothing about.

AN IDEAL MATCH by Sandra Field

Despite two broken engagements, a young woman still believes in marriage — she comes to love a widower left with three children but finds he had lost his faith in love.

ROUGH DIAMOND by Kate Walker

Can a successful businesswoman and a garage mechanic really bridge the gap between two such different backgrounds?

FOUR UNIQUE LOVE STORIES IN A SPECIAL MOTHER'S DAY PACK AVAILABLE FROM FEBRUARY 1987.

PRICE £4.80.

MASQUERADE

YOU'RE INVITED TO ACCEPT

2 MASQUERADE ROMANCES
AND A DIAMOND ZIRCONIA NECKLACE
FREE!

Acceptance card

| NO STAMP NEEDED | Post to: **Reader Service, FREEPOST, P.O. Box 236, Croydon, Surrey. CR9 9EL** |

Please note readers in Southern Africa write to:
Independant Book Services P.T.Y., Postbag X3010, Randburg 2125, S. Africa

YES! Please send me 2 free Masquerade Romances
and my free diamond zirconia necklace – and reserve a Reader Service Subscription for me. If I decide to subscribe I shall receive 4 new Masquerade Romances every other month as soon as they come off the presses for £6.00 together with a FREE newsletter including information on top authors and special offers, exclusively for Reader Service subscribers. There are no postage and packing charges, and I understand I may cancel or suspend my subscription at any time. If I decide not to subscribe I shall write to you within 10 days. Even If I decide not to subscribe the 2 free novels and the necklace are mine to keep forever.
I am over 18 years of age   EP22M

NAME _____

                                                    (CAPITALS PLEASE)

ADDRESS _____

_____

_____ POSTCODE _____

The right is reserved to refuse an application and change the terms of this offer. You may be mailed with other offers as a result of this application. Offer expires March 31st 1987 and is limited to one per household. Silhouette is an imprint of Mills & Boon Ltd. Offer applies in UK and Eire only. Overseas send for details.

Bewitched in her dreams she awoke to discover the face of reality

The same dark hair, the same mocking eyes. The Regency rake in the portrait, the seducer of Jenna's dreams had a living double.

But James Allingham was no dream, he was a direct descendant of the black sheep of the Deveril family.

They would fight for the possession of the ancestral home. They would fight against desire to be together.

Unravel the mysteries in
STRONGER THAN YEARNING,
a new longer romance from
Penny Jordan.